Music In The Blood

Margaret Duffy

PIATKUS

First published in Great Britain in 1997 by
Judy Piatkus (Publishers) Ltd of
5 Windmill Street, London W1

**The moral right of the author
has been asserted**

*A catalogue record for this book is available
from the British Library*

ISBN 0-7499-0382-1

Set in 11/12 pt Times by
RefineCatch Limited, Bungay, Suffolk
Printed and bound in Great Britain by
Biddles Ltd, Guildford & King's Lynn

Prologue

The woman had been buried, lightly and shallowly, beneath the massive, spreading branches of a beech tree. It grew on a bank that had at one time been a wall marking the boundary of a long-abandoned hill farm. The house and bothy, built at a time when the tree was no more than a slender sapling, were now tumbled ruins in the rough grass and heather. The tree, sheltered from the cruel winds of winter by the configuration of the hills – it stood several hundred feet above sea level – held the stones of the wall in implacable embrace beneath three feet of leaf mould.

The site of the grave on this gentle west-facing slope was peaceful, the calls of curlews and bleating of sheep the only intrusive sounds. After a hot summer's day the soft medium in which the woman lay was warm and, as there had been no rain for a month, dry. A heavy piece of broken branch had been placed across her legs; her upper torso was untrammelled but for the peaty mould and, over her face, a layer of dry crisp leaves. Through them she breathed easily, unknowing.

It was a thunderstorm that roused her, the rain soaking down to where she lay, the thunder and lightning perceived dimly. *Through a glass darkly*, she thought vaguely. Only there was no glass, just a sort of scratchiness on her face. And the smell of wet earth and gardens.

After a while, beginning to shiver, she moved a hand in the pressing softness and felt the moistness of the loam between her fingers. Perhaps if she went back to sleep, she reasoned, everything would be normal when she awoke.

Yet the growing pain made sleep impossible. Fretful, she

tried to move. She raised one arm as high as it would go and encountered what felt like twigs and thin branches. Bending her arm at the elbow and pushing her hand up vertically proved to be far more successful and it burst into fresh air.

Was there anyone to wave to?

Chapter One

'Perhaps you ought to get a set and keep them in your desk drawer,' said Joanna Mackenzie to her male companion.

James Carrick had been regarding the medieval thumb-screws with detached curiosity. 'I'm sure the factory went out of production several centuries ago. Anyway, these days we're only allowed to torture them with canteen coffee,' he said with mock regret.

She smiled and took his arm. 'Are we progressing to Song Dynasty jars, English stained glass, armorial tapestries or lunch?'

'In other words, you're hungry.'

'I can see why they made you up to DCI. Yes, I'm starving.'

He changed course and went in the direction of the restaurant. 'I can renew my acquaintance with the Tang horse on the way.'

It was late morning but the galleries of the modern building that houses the Burrell Collection in Glasgow were practically empty of visitors: fitting surroundings, Joanna thought, for a very private attempt to salvage a relationship.

The windows of the restaurant overlooked the wide green spaces and tree-lined paths of Pollock Park. Recent hot, dry weather had caused the maples to colour early and a few bronze and crimson leaves had already fallen, swept down overnight by a heavy thunderstorm.

They both decided on corn chowder and fresh salmon salad and had to be content with a table right in the centre of the bright airy room. Clearly all the art lovers who had been

3

absent from the galleries were, like Carrick and Joanna, having an early lunch.

'Glad to be on home territory?' Joanna asked lightly before she began to eat.

'I left Scotland when I was ten,' Carrick reminded her.

'I know. But you've been back quite a few times since. Revisiting your roots.'

'Despite my name, and the fact that it stems from Burns country, I do regard myself as a sort of Highlander.'

'So?'

He smiled. 'So I won't feel at home until we reach Perth. Where I was born.'

'Your father was drowned in a fishing boat accident before you were born, wasn't he?'

He looked up from his soup in surprise. 'He was drowned at sea. Nothing to do with fishing boats. Where did you get that from?'

'Haine.'

Haine had been DCI towards the end of the time when Carrick and Joanna had worked together, but had recently been posted to HQ in Bristol to help implement the Sheehy report recommendations. Carrick now had his job.

'It was a yacht,' Carrick said. 'He was knocked overboard by the boom when it was hit by a sudden squall. His body was never found.'

'Was he alone?'

'No. It was a big racing yacht that belonged to some friends of his.'

'It must have been dreadful for your mother, with you on the way.'

'Yes. Especially as they weren't married,' he said wryly.

'Is that why your grandfather was so cruel to you?'

'It had a lot to do with it. He was an Elder of the Kirk and was convinced that the Devil would get me if I wasn't thrashed at every opportunity. "A brat begotten in sin!" he used to shout at my mother – I can hear him now. She managed to get us away after a while and we went to live with an understanding aunt in Crieff.'

'I find it hard to believe that those attitudes survived until so recently.'

4

'What made it even worse was that my father was a married man. By all accounts he was very good-looking, a swash-buckling figure who swept impressionable young girls off their feet. He didn't mention them to his wife, though.'

'Am I allowed to know who he was?'

'It wouldn't mean anything to you if I told you. Carrick wasn't his surname but he was a distant cousin of the then Earl. I think my mother changed her name to Carrick out of pure bloodymindedness.'

'Do you look like him?'

'No idea.'

'And she was from Orkney? That makes you a blue-blooded Viking.'

Carrick gave a derisive snort. 'Hardly.'

She refrained from saying that with his fair hair, blue eyes and bleak features, a blue-blooded Viking was precisely what he looked like: behaved like, even. He was fond of good living and beautiful things, yet ruthless in the pursuit of criminals, especially the violent ones. He was quite prepared to work himself and his staff to the point of exhaustion until the quarry was safely captured – and if there was danger he would be right out in front, more than ready to shed a little of his own blood in the name of law and order. Any excess energy was expended on the rugby field, which was perhaps just as well as far as the lawbreakers of Bath were concerned.

Joanna was uncomfortably conscious that, interesting and diverting as Carrick's background might be, they were skirting the problem. *Her* problem. In the days when she had been a CID sergeant – his assistant – life had been hectic but fulfilling. She had been a member of his team for about eighteen months. Although he had not spoken of it, everyone knew that his wife Kathleen was dying from a rare form of bone cancer. They had only been married for four years and every day he had had to watch her getting weaker. As Kathleen became worse, confined first to a wheelchair and then to bed with a hired nurse in attendance, Joanna gradually realised that Carrick found her own close physical presence a hindrance to his concentration on the job in hand. All too aware of the reason for it, she made an effort to distance herself from him: did not stand at his elbow during briefings, refrained from so

5

much as brushing past him. In the end it merely became a question of when the strain would cause him to snap.

Oddly, the moment had come after a particularly exhausting day culminating in a series of arrests. The Territorial Support Group had provided assistance when the situation deteriorated into a running battle at a housing estate near Weston. Afterwards Carrick had piled his battered team into his own car and driven everyone home. He himself had had grazed knuckles and a sprained wrist, while the rest sported a motley collection of bloody noses, split lips, cuts and bruises. And because Joanna lived nearest to him, Carrick had taken her home last.

It had been a strange feeling, saying goodnight and then walking towards the entrance to the flats where she lived, half hoping that he would follow and at the same time praying that he wouldn't. When she had heard the quick, light footsteps behind her she had not looked round but had hurried up the stairs, fumbled for her front-door key and let herself in. Short of shutting the door in his face, there had been nothing she could have done to stop him. She had not *wanted* to stop him, had rejoiced in being undressed and made love to with breathless urgency right there on the hall carpet.

They had been discreet about the affair that had followed but somehow someone found out and reported them to the Chief Superintendent. And that had been the end of it. The end of her career too; she had been too proud to accept the dead-end posting she was offered. Carrick had received a severe reprimand: that was all. But they were still lovers. He still discussed his cases with her and eagerly sought her ideas. She was still his assistant – but unpaid, unsung and off the job. The fact that he had asked her to live with him, to marry him one day, did not compensate.

Kathleen – the woman must have been a saint, Joanna now realised unhappily – had died shortly after the affair with his sergeant had got Carrick into trouble. He had made a full confession to his wife. Kathleen had said to him several months previously that she would not blame him if it was all too much for him to bear and he sought solace elsewhere.

'She patted my head like I was a child,' James had whispered on the sole occasion he had mentioned it. 'She said she loved me all the more because it showed I was suffering as much as she was.' He had broken down then, and wept.

'Is business any better?' he asked now.

Joanna had started up a small private detective agency with a colleague from Bristol, Lance Tyler, but Lance had been killed in a road accident a few months previously. She had taken on an assistant, Greg Perivale; his presence had made her holiday possible.

'No. I'm going to have to lay Greg off.'

'Can't you sell it as a going concern?'

'It isn't,' she answered shortly, and there was another silence.

'Joanna . . .'

'Yes, I know. It's crunch time, isn't it? We didn't have to come all the way to Scotland to decide that.'

He finished his chowder, laid down the spoon and gazed at her.

'I shall just have to accept the situation or get out of your life. There's no middle course,' Joanna said.

'You could rejoin.'

'And how many years would it take to regain what I've lost?'

'I seem to remember a mutual friend offering you a job in London. MI5.'

'I remember how he worded it too. "Come and work for me and you'll be too busy to have time to feel sorry for yourself." Thanks, but no thanks.' She stared at him angrily. 'Would you have taken up an offer like that?'

'No, but—'

'I'm forgetting. You don't have to – you have a brilliant career in front of you.'

Uncharacteristically, he swore. A few heads turned in their direction. 'This isn't the time or place to discuss it,' he said.

Ten minutes elapsed, during which neither of them spoke. Carrick broke the silence. 'I promised that I'd call in and see an old friend this afternoon. I can drop you in the city centre if you fancy looking at the shops, or pick you up later here. Whichever you prefer.'

'A maid from the isles with limpid green eyes?' Joanna snapped, knowing that she was being downright childish.

'No, a bloke by the name of Neil Macpherson whose eyes

7

are usually bloodshot from lack of sleep,' Carrick replied calmly. 'We met on a course at Hendon police college and now he's come home to be DI at the Brig Street nick.'

'And is the Brig Street nick in the city centre?'

'Close.'

'I think I'll stay here.' She patted the catalogue on the seat beside her. 'I might go and admire the Demon roof tiles.'

It was all her fault of course. If she'd played her cards right she could have gone with him. Listened to them talking shop. That would at least have given her some vicarious pleasure.

Margie Gillespie had been taking her dog for walks on the moors near her cottage ever since she had moved back to Scotland. A succession of different dogs, unfortunately; they seemed to have such a short lifespan compared with human beings. She felt her age herself on that particular morning, struggling to pull on her boots, her back protesting at the previous afternoon's gardening.

'Patience!' she scolded Gumps, her mongrel, a black and white blur of movement as he tore round the kitchen, his lead in his mouth. Like all dogs, Gumps was quite useless at hiding his emotions.

'And if you think you're going to paddle in the river and roll in the mud and not get the hose turned on you when we get back, you've another thought coming,' Margie said, stumping out of the small utility room near the back door and into the open air. 'Give me that lead, you stupid animal, before you hang yourself.'

He raced up to her, dumped the lead at her feet, then leapt the garden hedge and bounced off across the heather. It was the same every morning: their little game. She smiled as she watched him. He was good company – together with the old tom cat who had wandered in one evening and made it very clear that he intended to stay. She had called him Glooms because of his grim way of dealing with a world that, up until now, had not been kind to him.

Anyone seeing Margie in her boots, faded trousers and old cardigan would be surprised to learn that she was a rear-admiral's widow. Her husband, Calum, was now – as Margie herself put it – sailing celestial seas. After spending half a lifetime travelling the world with him she had returned alone to their native Scotland. He had died, very suddenly, five years before he was due to retire. Friends had warned her that returning to Scotland was a mistake after all the years spent away and told her she would be lonely. But for years, privately, Margie had yearned for her heathery mountains and moors.

Her home, Brae Head Cottage – her *last* home, as she insisted upon calling it – was situated at the entrance of Mosslaw Country Park. At one time, when the park had been a private estate, it had been the gatekeeper's lodge. The 'big hoose', as the local people called it, had been demolished many years previously and a visitors' centre built in its place. During the summer months the road by Margie's cottage was choked with cars bringing walkers or sightseers who wished to picnic by the waterfall, where the river Muir plunged into a ravine. The winters were far quieter, with the road frequently blocked by snow. Margie didn't care. She came from farming stock and relished living in her very own winter wonderland.

Now it was late summer and the air, unusually for that part of the world, was heavy and oppressive. An overnight thunderstorm had not freshened things up and more heavy rain seemed promised, the distant hills obscured by murky clouds. It was very warm; Margie soon unbuttoned her cardigan.

Gumps was barking. He barked at everything: rabbit holes, birds, beetles, anything that moved or might move given half a chance. The sound was coming from the direction of a row of pine trees and she did not really want to go that way. She called Gumps to her, but he ignored her. She felt in her pocket for the whistle that she usually carried with her but encountered only a hole in the material. She had been meaning to mend that for ages.

'I shall put you in a pie,' she promised him darkly, setting off in the direction of the pines. 'For my supper. With onion sauce and tatties.'

She passed by the ruined farmstead and, as always, felt a tiny shiver run up her spine. What was it about old ruined houses that was so eerie? She paused to call the dog again but still he took no notice. Margie hurried; he never normally barked like this, so frantically and persistently. Perhaps he was hurt.

9

Then she saw him. He was a short distance on from the pines, right by a magnificent beech tree, its splendour in marked contrast to the gnarled pines which took the full force of the wind. And he was caught, his collar ensnared in something that was sticking up out of the ground.

'Poor old Gumpy,' Margie puffed, out of breath. 'Just keep still and I'll soon get you free.'

He was trying to lick whatever he was entangled in. 'Gumps, that doesn't help matters—'

Margie froze.

It was a hand.

The fingers were tightly locked into the dog's leather collar. Margie, kneeling, trembling and dry-mouthed, fumbled to unbuckle it. The fingers came alive then, groping the air, dropping the collar.

'Dear God, I'm going mad,' Margie moaned. Tentatively, she touched the thing from the dead. The fingers clasped hers with an iron grip.

Desperately, with her free hand, Margie began to dig.

Chapter Two

Brig Street was just round the corner from the Broomielaw, the old city harbour on the river Clyde. It had all the hallmarks of a thoroughfare that once took pride of place in the history of a city but which in modern times had been rendered redundant. One end of it had been demolished entirely, the desolate site surrounded by hoardings promising future redevelopment. The remaining buildings – for the most part warehouses either boarded up or used to house a variety of ramshackle small businesses – were grey with centuries of grime.

The police station, at the end of the street farthest from the river, had the unusual distinction in that area of being listed. There was a large modern extension at the rear but the original structure, built of suitably dour granite with a 'corbie step' gabled roof, was still very much in everyday use. Part of it now constituted the main entrance and lobby area. Carrick had been inside the building before and knew that several small grim cells were now used as locker rooms and that a 'rest room', presumably a forerunner of the contemporary canteen and complete with iron range, was now being utilised as a stationery store.

The entrance was rather grand, with a pair of wrought-iron lamps in the shape of dolphins, their upturned tails supporting opaque glass globes. Carrick spared a glance for the two grotesque faces carved in stone on each side of the portal. No one he had spoken to on previous visits knew the history of these carvings but they were universally referred to as Bonnie and Clyde.

He went past the display cases that housed a collection of

11

Victorian handcuffs and truncheons and the medals awarded to several police officers at the turn of the century following a local riot. Times did not seem to have changed very much.

'And which case would this be in connection with?' was the somewhat wary response from the duty sergeant when Carrick asked to see DI Neil Macpherson.

'It's a private visit. He's an old friend. We met at Hendon during a course run by the Drug Squad,' Carrick explained.

There was an almost imperceptible straightening of the man's back. 'I'll see if he's free, sir.'

There was a brief telephone conversation.

'He has to go out immediately, sir, but wonders if you'd like to accompany him.'

'That's fine by me.'

An arm in a crisply ironed shirt pointed towards the rear of the lobby. 'If you go through that door, down the corridor, turn left at the end and then right through the swing doors, he'll meet you there.'

The first door was, in effect, the boundary between a museum and the other, more familiar, world of scuffed vinyl flooring, faded posters with curling edges and the all-pervading smell of frying chips. There were glimpses through doorways of desks loaded with the customary clutter; files piled high in wire trays, half-eaten bacon rolls sitting forlornly alongside polystyrene cups with half an inch of cold coffee in the bottom. In one room a uniformed constable stabbed dejectedly with two fingers at the keyboard of an old-fashioned typewriter. It was a real home from home.

Carrick went through the swing doors. Macpherson was coming down the corridor towards him.

'You don't change,' Macpherson sighed.

Neil had. He had gained at least a stone in weight and his face was now a little puffy, especially beneath the eyes. His complexion had coarsened: small broken veins were evident in his cheeks and he looked older than his forty-five years. The mid-brown hair was less thick than it used to be. But his smile was as wide and welcoming as ever.

They shook hands. Then unexpectedly, Macpherson grabbed his old friend in a bearhug.

'You don't change,' he repeated delightedly. 'Life must be

suiting you down south. How are things with the Avon and Somerset? Tell me as we go – I've an urgent call to attend to.'

'Busy,' Carrick replied as they walked. 'Fairly heavy organised crime is trying to get a toe-hold in the West Country. Not all that long ago we were having to cope with nothing much more serious than joy-riding and small-time pushers. Now we're getting tooled up with all the latest in computers and communications technology to fight the big stuff.'

'Drugs,' Macpherson said disgustedly. 'If only the pushers killed themselves instead of the poor stupid kids who get hooked on the filthy muck.' He paused in his stride. 'I'm forgetting my manners. How are you? Coping? I mean, I've only seen you the once since Kathleen died.'

'Coping,' Carrick answered hesitantly. 'Yes, it's getting better. I still think of her a lot. I only have to walk into the kitchen to see her there, giving me a roguish grin while she concocted one of her incredible risottos with everything you could think of in it.'

'Och, it was a terrible tragedy,' Macpherson murmured, aware that Carrick did not speak of his late wife to many people.

'So where are we off to?' Carrick asked when they were seated in an unmarked car, driving at some speed towards the west of the city.

'Some lassie's been found in a shallow grave in Mosslaw Country Park. It looks as though she was hit by a car and then the driver tidied away the evidence.'

Carrick whistled. 'That takes hit and run to a new low. Who was she?'

'Perhaps I shouldn't have said grave. She isn't dead.'

Carrick stared at him in amazement. 'How in God's name did she survive?'

'It seems there was only a thin covering of leaves over her face. A woman walking her dog found her – actually it was the dog that did the finding. When we left they were checking on the registration number of a blue Astra that'd been left in the car park. Chivvy them up, Rob, would you?' he asked the driver.

But just then the information came over the radio. The car was registered in the name of Kimberley Anne Devlin, of

Merryburn Terrace, University Road, Glasgow. Macpherson immediately ordered that enquiries be made at that address. 'Which hospital's she been taken to? St Mungo's, in Paisley, is it? Make sure there's an officer stationed by her bed. And I'd like a report on her injuries as soon as the hospital have carried out a full examination.'

'Kimberley Devlin is an opera singer. A soprano,' Carrick said.

Macpherson's eyebrows rose in surprise. 'Might not be one and the same girl.'

'It's not a common name.'

'Do you know what she looks like?'

'I've been to a couple of Scottish Opera productions she was in. She's about five feet five, around thirty. Her hair's light brown, long when I saw her. I'd say her eyes are probably the same colour.'

'You remember well. I ken you're a fan of hers,' the inspector said blandly. 'Do we have a description yet, Rob?'

They were on the city link road now, heading towards Paisley.

'No, sir. I spoke to one of the crew who answered the nine-nine-nine call. Young Hughie. He said she was too covered in earth and muck for anyone to be able to tell what she looked like.'

Ten minutes later they had left the heavily built-up suburbs of Glasgow behind and were near Johnstone, weaving through traffic slowed by vehicles turning into the entrance to a school. Macpherson fumed; he was a bad driver himself and recognised it, preferring to be driven. But this did not ease his impatience.

Carrick, still in holiday mood, was enjoying the occasional glimpses of rolling green hills, the high ground between the Garnock valley and the Forth of Clyde. Soon they were driving along country lanes that climbed, slowly at first and then steeply. They passed through a village with a long, straight high street, the fruit and flowers outside a greengrocer's shop the only colour amidst the stone cottages. A noticeboard at the side of the road informed them that Mosslaw Country Park was one mile down the next turning left.

This did the heart good, Carrick thought, twisting round to

gaze up the narrow valley as they emerged through a stand of beech trees. The road, little more than a cart track now, followed the contours of the hillside. On the far side of the valley water fell from the tops of the hills in narrow silvery ribbons. It was a pity that violence had brought them to such a peaceful place.

They bounced over a cattle grid set between stone pillars and rolled down a slight slope into a car park containing a single police van, a blue Vauxhall Astra and a Land Rover belonging to the Parks Department. Standing by the side of it were a uniformed sergeant and another man whom Carrick guessed, correctly, to be the warden.

'SOCO seem to have got lost,' Macpherson muttered, getting out of the car. It occurred to Carrick that professional pride might be at stake here.

'How far is it?' Macpherson demanded.

'About two hundred yards up behind those trees, sir,' said the sergeant. 'Mr Logan here, he's the warden, he doesn't live inside the park. And he isn't aware of anything untoward happening last night.'

The inspector eyed the warden who smiled in apologetic fashion. 'Then Mr Logan's not a lot of use, is he?' Macpherson said dismissively. 'Is someone already up there?'

'Meikle, sir. He's cordoned the area off.'

'Didn't bring any damned boots,' Macpherson grumbled, setting off. He glowered at the black clouds massing on the hills. 'Didn't bring a coat either.'

'Was this Astra here last night when you went off duty?' Carrick asked the warden.

The man shook his head. 'No. Definitely not. At that time of night the car park's always empty.'

'What time was that?'

'I was here until just after six.'

'What about when you arrived this morning?'

'It was here. But I didn't think anything of it. We sometimes get a few ornithologists and suchlike early in the morning. Even when the weather's bad – it was raining like hell up here when I arrived at eight thirty.'

'You didn't see any other vehicles around, either last night or this morning?'

15

'No. Oh, a local farmer drove through in a pick-up, on his way up Moss Loan to look at his sheep, about half an hour after I got here. I was over by the visitors' centre repairing a path. I didn't even know that someone had been found until the police arrived.'

'Have you been anywhere near the area the police are interested in during the last twenty-four hours?'

'No.'

Carrick clapped him on the shoulder. 'Thanks!'

'James? Are you coming or not?' Macpherson bellowed.

It was so quiet that the noise of their shoes tramping through the heather seemed very loud. Some ten yards from the road the undergrowth became much taller – and much wetter, following the rain. Soon Carrick's trousers were soaked to the knees. He paused for a few moments; the tranquillity of the hills flowed over him. Small sounds broke the silence; the flow of the river, the distant croak of a raven, sheep bleating. The air was like wine, heady with the scents of damp peat, pine trees, the sun on moss and wet rock.

'It's half a mile at least,' Macpherson called over his shoulder, breaking the spell.

Borne on the faint breeze came the sound of a vehicle labouring up the hill.

'About time,' the inspector said grimly when the white van came into view, black smoke issuing from its exhaust. 'We're not always the shambles that we appear,' he added, swinging round to Carrick who was surprised to see the anger in his face.

'I know that,' Carrick said quietly. 'Only last month one of our rapid response vehicles skidded and ended up in Bristol docks, alongside the *Great Britain*.'

Macpherson carried on stumping up the hill. He tripped over a thick heather stem and swore under his breath. 'Bit dull in Bath, isn't it? I know you said things were changing, but on an everyday basis you can't be dealing with anything worse than tourists losing their passports.'

Carrick smiled reflectively. 'Let me see – what have I been up to recently? Well, I got involved with a drugs baron in the north of England, after a film producer was murdered on my patch. There was a cosy little plot involving the local DI up there – he was in on it too – had me done over and arrested for

16

being drunk and disorderly. After that, when the police had let me go, the drugs bunch grabbed me and shut me up inside an old boiler, not to be opened until Doomsday.'

Macpherson had stopped dead in his tracks. 'How the devil did you get out of that one?'

'I was found by a friend of mine. He works for MI5 and if you met him you'd know why. His mind doesn't function like yours and mine. He knew there wasn't time for anything careful and painstaking so he found the worst pub in the town and looked for yobs with bloody noses – the reasoning being that I wouldn't have gone down without a fight. And when he found a few he put a lot of money on the table.'

They made their way through the pine trees and soon saw Constable Meikle. The patch of ground he had cordoned off with tape looked very small and insignificant beneath the branches of the beech.

'Two hundred yards!' Macpherson scoffed, out of breath. 'I'll give him two hundred yards. It was a man who did this, you know. A youngish, strong man at that. No woman could have carried her this far.'

Carrick tried to picture the person who had regarded the still figure in the road and then coldly decided to get rid of it. Had they fetched a torch from the car to examine their victim more closely? Had they felt for a pulse? Tried to check if Kimberley Devlin was still breathing?

'Half a mile *easily*,' Macpherson said. He gazed down into the shallow depression under the tree. 'It's really soft, easy to dig isn't it? You could make a sizeable hole with just your hands. I mean, if chummie had had a shovel with him we're talking about a premeditated crime. Perhaps he's banned from driving, and that's the reason for it. There has to be a damned good reason to do such a thing.'

'She might have driven out here to meet someone,' Carrick said. 'If they had an argument—'

'Yes, of course,' Macpherson interrupted. 'Naturally, I shall try to trace all Miss Devlin's friends and acquaintances.' He stared back the way they had come. 'Where the hell *are* SOCO? Are their legs only firing on one cylinder too?'

As if on cue three figures lugging equipment came toiling over the slight rise.

17

'They'll be here for ages to no avail,' Macpherson said, looking at his watch. 'And I've a lot on. I could do with interviewing this Devlin woman but I've a feeling she'll be out of bounds until tomorrow at the earliest – you know what they're like at hospitals. I vote we go back to base, grab a cup of tea and have a yarn before you pick up your ladyfriend. I shall have to work late, so planning anything for tonight's out, I'm afraid.'

It was with a faint shock that Carrick heard these words. *It wasn't his case . . .*

'Okay?'

'Absolutely,' Carrick hastened to say.

When they reached the car a call came over the radio. Carrick left Macpherson to deal with it, strolling the short distance to where the sergeant was examining the road.

'I reckon this is where it happened,' said the man, pointing to clearly discernible skid marks. 'There's a fifteen-mile-an-hour speed limit just near the car park, so no one's normally going to be racing along.'

'No young hot heads? Trying to impress their mates?' Carrick suggested.

'It could have been that.'

'How do we know she *was* knocked down by a car before someone shoved her in that hole? Couldn't someone have hit her over the head?'

'You'll have to ask Inspector Macpherson, sir. He's handling it – we were called up from Kilbirnie and I don't have the full details.'

Carrick looked round to see his friend gesturing urgently to him.

'I've got to go,' he pronounced as Carrick approached. 'The new head of the Regional Crime Squad's going to honour us with a visit and the chief's threatened me with a fate worse than death if I'm not there.' He struck his forehead with an open fist. 'Damn! I forgot to ask someone to talk to the woman who found her, get her to come in and make a statement.' Agitated, he looked at his watch again. 'She only lives just over there, by the entrance to the park. Perhaps if I—'

'I'll do it,' Carrick offered.

18

'But—'

'It's obvious that you're tied up for the rest of the day. I'll do it. It'll be a pleasure. I'll make a note of what she says, get her to make a statement at the local nick and give you a ring tomorrow. Joanna and I are going to be touring in the Highlands for about a week – I could call in and see you on the way back.'

'You're a good lad,' Macpherson said with real feeling. 'And when you return remind me that I owe you a round.' He moved to get in the car and then froze. 'But, man, how will you get back to your motor? And your girl?'

'Don't you have trains in Renfrewshire?' Carrick asked with a grin.

Macpherson laughed with obvious relief and got in the car. As it moved off he wound down the window. 'Mrs Gillespie. That's her name.'

A dog began to bark from within as Carrick approached the cottage. He opened the narrow wooden gate and the hinges squeaked, causing the animal to redouble its efforts. Then a woman's voice called out, bidding it be quiet.

This was a very sheltered spot; a high beech hedge, neatly clipped, kept the worst of the weather off a pretty garden that had an English quaintness about it. Brightly coloured annuals bordered the path that led to the front door and as Carrick reached it the door was promptly opened.

'You don't look like a reporter so you must be a policeman,' said the occupant of the house, flinging the door wide.

'You've just made my day, Mrs Gillespie,' Carrick said with a smile. 'Actually, I'm standing in for the genuine investigating officer, an old friend, as he's grossly overworked.' He introduced himself.

'So where would you be normally?' she wanted to know. 'Do sit down – and please forgive the muddle. I don't seem to be able to get going today.' She sat down heavily in an armchair.

'The West Country.'

'We lived in Plymouth for a while,' Margie Gillespie said reflectively. 'It's probably the only city in Britain that looks better since the Germans bombed it flat. They made a good job of rebuilding it.'

19

The front door opened directly into the living room; not usual in Scotland, it suggested to Carrick that the building had been altered over the years. Decorated in shades of deep pink, the walls virtually covered with pictures in dark wooden frames, the room might have been gloomy had it not been for the small lamps, on occasional tables and each side of the stone fireplace, creating a warm and very cosy atmosphere.

Practically all the pictures were nautical in tone: large oils of sailing ships, watercolours of Thames barges, photographs of Royal Navy destroyers and frigates. There were a couple of model ships in glass cases in the room, one of them a schooner in full sail.

'Take a look,' Mrs Gillespie encouraged. 'There's a photo of your namesake somewhere – the *Carrick* – that my husband took on a trip to Glasgow once. But I believe it sank when they tried to tow it away for repairs.'

'Yes, it was moored on the Clyde for a while,' Carrick said. 'But I think you'll find it was raised and is now at the Scottish Maritime Museum awaiting restoration.'

The remains of a light breakfast were still on a table, a cardigan thrown untidily over a chair. A dog's lead lay on the floor by the hearth.

'Would you like me to make you some tea?' Carrick enquired gently.

Her lips quivered; she quickly placed a hand over her mouth. 'Yes, please. Lunch didn't quite happen. I'm afraid I . . .' And she burst into tears.

Carrick found a box of tissues in the kitchen and placed them discreetly at her elbow. There was a kettle on the Rayburn but the fire was almost out; after throwing a couple of logs on to the fire from a large wicker basket he poured the water from the kettle into an electric one standing on the worktop. That done, and the kettle singing – the water had been quite warm – he rinsed out an earthenware teapot he found on the draining board, discovered mugs, sugar, milk and teabags and made the tea. It was the work of a moment to clear the small table in the living room of crockery and put it into a fresh bowlful of hot soapy water in the sink: the work of a moment more to wash the dishes and leave them to drain.

'You're a useful sort of bloke to have around,' Mrs Gillespie commented dryly. She had recovered a little and was mopping her eyes. 'There's a box of home-made shortbread in the larder. And let Gumps out, would you? He's in the utility room by the back door – I had to put him in there as he was so muddy.'

Most of the mud now seemed to be on the cotton rugs on the floor of the utility room; a little more was transferred to Carrick's trousers.

'I can understand why people don't like dogs,' Margie said, eyeing her pet severely. 'Those who expect others to love their dogs as they do are frightful bores. I mean, you go to their house for dinner and this dreadful evil-smelling little beast like a long-haired rat jumps up on your best dress. And there they are, *drooling* over the animal, telling you that its father was a champion, when all you want to do is go and flush it down the nearest lavatory. Gumps! Leave the nice policeman in peace and lie down!'

'He's the hero of the hour,' Carrick pointed out, fondling the dog's ears. 'Milk and sugar?'

'Please. Two spoonfuls of sugar. I think I need it sweet. Good for shock. Sorry to make such an idiot of myself.'

'Tell me about it.'

'I think I shall have nightmares for ever,' the woman said. 'It was like something out of a horror film. Her hand was sticking up out of the ground – like a corpse coming back from the dead.' She gave Carrick a strange, fierce look. 'She isn't, is she? Dead, I mean.'

'Not so far as I know,' he answered carefully. 'Inspector Macpherson had asked for the latest information about her condition but it hadn't arrived when I left him. Did her injuries seem very bad?'

'It was impossible to tell. She was covered in soil and leaves – I didn't notice any blood, I must admit. I was really concentrating on her mental state, I'm afraid. All I could think of was that she might lose control when she realised what had happened to her. So I just talked to her – any nonsense that came into my head.'

'Drink your tea while it's hot.'

She seemed to notice it, on the table next to her, for the first time. 'Oh, yes. Thank you. I had to come back here to phone.

21

That was the worst part – having to leave her. I'd had to brush most of the stuff off her face one-handed – she was gripping hold of the other and wouldn't let go. In the end I had to prise her fingers off and just run. I had explained to her that I had to get an ambulance, but I wasn't sure if she'd heard. And Gumps wouldn't stay with her. He was too scared.'

'What did she say when you – unearthed her?'

'She screamed when she first saw me. I think that was when she first knew she'd actually been buried alive. Then she started crying. The only thing I can remember her saying was, "Please don't leave me." Over and over again.'

'She didn't mention any names?'

'If she did I don't remember. I was talking to her all the time. Just like you do to a child that's frightened and in pain.'

'So you telephoned and went straight back to her?'

'Of course.'

'Did you think of alerting the warden?'

'I'd have alerted all sorts of people if they'd been in sight. But I wasn't about to go on a man-hunt – the warden can be miles away when he's working. I can't see the car park from here, either, so it was anyone's guess as to whether his Land Rover was there.'

'And at no time did this woman volunteer any information as to what had happened to her?'

'If she did, I didn't take it in.'

'How was she when you returned?'

'Calmer. But still crying. I think she was in a lot of pain. It was the longest fifteen minutes of my life until the ambulance and police arrived. I just sat and held her hand. Goodness knows what I said! I think I told her about Gumps, how I'd got him from a rescue centre. He was found wandering around with a piece of frayed rope round his neck. He just wanted to sit on my lap when I got him home. I cuddled him for two solid hours. Perhaps she reminded me of how he was then.'

'Do you take the dog up there for a walk every day?'

'No. Hardly at all. We usually go in the other direction, towards the river. You can't take dogs very far in any direction because of the sheep and game birds. Gumps must have smelt her.'

'Had you ever seen her before?'

22

'Hard to say, when her face was all brown and dirty. But I doubt it. Not if she was just visiting the park. I'm a private person, I don't want hordes of backpackers peering in. That's why I let the hedge grow.'

'And you heard nothing strange last night? No cars going past at odd hours?'

'No. And the thunderstorm started at about two thirty this morning. I heard nothing at all before that – except for the owls.' Mrs Gillespie paused, then resumed, 'The mind really does play tricks when something like this happens. All the time I was clearing away the leaves and earth I just *knew* I was going to find a dead body. I was convinced that I was in some hideous kind of waking dream and that the hand gripping mine was an illusion. And when I found her, I still thought I was staring at a corpse. It was the way she was looking at me.'

'Remember, you saved her life.'

'Yes. I shall keep on telling myself that.'

'If you visit her in hospital it might help banish your own bad memories.'

She looked surprised. 'Do you think so? Would she want to see me?'

'I'm quite sure it would help her get over the experience too,' Carrick replied, offering up a quick prayer that the woman was both in a fit state and willing to see her rescuer.

After asking Mrs Gillespie to make a statement as soon as possible at her nearest police station, Kilbirnie, and borrowing her phone to let them know she was coming, Carrick left. It was still only 3.45 when he left the cottage and he paused, wondering if he had time to pay another call on the way back to Glasgow. When he returned to the car park it was to discover that the decision had been made for him: Macpherson had radioed to say that Carrick was to be driven wherever he wanted to go.

Had Kimberley Devlin been going for an innocent stroll when she was struck down? Why had she not heard the vehicle's approach? And why go to such a deserted place? Whatever Kimberley Devlin was, she clearly had her fair share of spirit. Or was she merely foolhardy?

But there was no point in further conjecture, not until

Kimberley Devlin could be interviewed. Carrick was not expecting for a moment to be permitted to see her. He had planned only to ask after her, request that Mrs Gillespie could call in, and then take himself back to Brig Street where he had left his car. He was quite unprepared, then, upon arrival at a side ward on the third floor of St Mungo's Hospital, to be met by a staff nurse in an uncharacteristic flap.

'You want to see Kimberley Devlin? You aren't family, I suppose?' There was a note of desperation in her voice.

'No,' Carrick said.

'Only we've tried to contact people on all the phone numbers she can remember and no one seems to be around. Her agent's in the south of France, so I can't ask him to talk some sense into her.' She realised that she had been indiscreet. 'You're not from the press, I hope. I've strict orders to—'

'No, the police,' Carrick said, more firmly this time. 'What's the problem?'

'She wants to discharge herself. And that's most unwise. She's suffering from shock, apart from her other injuries. She sent the policewoman who'd been sent to interview her away after only answering a few questions and—'

'Shall I try talking to her?' Carrick interrupted.

'Nothing ventured, nothing gained,' said the woman, leading the way. 'You must excuse me, but it's been a most difficult day.'

'You mentioned her injuries.'

'Actually, she's been very lucky. There's general bruising, contusions, a cut on her head. We don't *think* there's any concussion, but it's too early to say. She *must* stay in overnight for observation.'

Kimberley Devlin was sitting up in bed, hands clasped around her knees.

'I don't know him either!' she shouted at the staff nurse.

Carrick was utterly unprepared for both her fury and the wonderful golden-brunette hair, flawless complexion and magical hazel eyes, lit with green and gold tints, like sunlit pools in Highland rivers. Right then, he wanted to drown himself in them.

'Yes, you do,' he said quietly. 'You once blew me a kiss at the end of *The Magic Flute*.'

24

'I blow hundreds of men kisses,' she pointed out impatiently.

'I'm devastated,' he whispered, sitting on the edge of the bed. 'I've just come from Mrs Gillespie. She's devastated too – she thought you were dead.'

'Who—'

'The woman who found you.'

Searchingly, she gazed at him. 'You must be a policeman. Who the hell else can you be? I don't want the fuzz – I want my *friends*.'

'So the world isn't answering the phone. You've sung enough opera to know that life's tough sometimes.'

'In other words I've got to make do with a copper?' she enquired angrily.

'Yup,' Carrick answered cheerfully.

Suddenly, she was blinded by tears. Shakily, she held out a hand. 'I'm being really horrible to you. Please, hold me.'

Carrick took the hand and then found that he had both arms around her. What had Mrs Gillespie said? Yes – 'I cuddled him for two solid hours'. He thought it worth a try.

Chapter Three

'James, you don't have to keep on apologising,' Joanna said.

Standing waiting in the rain she had wished him in hell. When he had swept up in a cloud of spray half an hour after the Burrell Collection had closed and pecked her cheek distractedly, contrite but oddly excited, she had forgiven him. But here he was, uncharacteristically intent on grovelling.

'Neil's still working too hard,' he said, threading the car neatly through rush-hour traffic.

Comprehension dawned. 'So you undertook a little detecting for him!'

'I went to see a woman in hospital. Someone might have tried to kill her.'

She brushed his cheek with the back of her hand. 'That was kind of you.' She looked hard at him, but there was no clue in the impassive profile. 'James—'

'I said I'd go and see her again in the morning,' he interrupted, the strange tension still in his voice.

'I thought you said we were travelling on to Fort William in the morning.'

'That was the plan,' he agreed.

The lights were red; they were at a standstill. As they changed, Joanna said, 'So you seem to be on the case.'

He engaged first gear and the car moved off. 'No, not really. It's Neil's case. It's just that . . . well, she's Kimberley Devlin. The singer.'

'The opera singer?'

'Yes.'

'I still don't understand.'

Carrick was clearly exasperated. 'It's just that none of her family and friends can be contacted at the moment, so she needed someone to talk to. I promised, that's all. We can hit the road directly afterwards.'

'I'm still not quite sure why you have to see her again.'

'It looks as though someone knocked her down with a car. They buried her alive – somehow, she didn't suffocate. She's all alone now and—'

He broke off abruptly.

Joanna wanted to say that she failed to see how a couple of visits from a complete stranger could help the woman, but she bit back the remark. Neither spoke again until they reached their hotel and then only to decide what time they should dine.

It was hardly a good start to the rest of their holiday.

Philip Graham sat hunched, staring sightlessly at the keys of his grand piano. He had a headache; thunderstorms always gave him headaches and when he had a headache he could not compose. After a few fruitless minutes he banged out 'Chopsticks' as fast as possible, then slammed the lid down over the keys.

'Sulking, Philip?' asked his wife Sarah, putting her head around the door.

'I didn't know you were in,' he replied. *Damn you*, he thought. *Damn you from the top of your tinted head to the tips of your high-heeled shoes.*

'Surely it doesn't take *that* much effort to write jingles for frozen peas,' she said snidely and went away before he exploded.

'One of these days, Sarah, I'm going to wring your bloody neck!' he yelled after her. 'They pay me, don't they? You were the one who insisted we live in the most expensive part of Glasgow and this house has got to be paid for. Do you think I *enjoy* writing songs about frozen peas?' In an impotent fury he hurled the blank sheets of music manuscript paper at the open doorway but was thwarted even in this, the paper fluttering gently down, each sheet like a white bird in curving flight, to land softly on the carpet and sofa.

'Don't crowd me,' she said when he had followed her into the kitchen.

27

'I want some coffee,' he said, refusing, for once, to rise to the bait. 'Anyway, why are you home?'

'There's a power cut at the office so I thought I'd come home to lunch.'

He glanced at his watch. 'God, is it lunchtime? I'll have whatever you're having.'

Sarah sighed. It had got to the point where she found it hard to be in the same room as this man who was her husband.

Everything had started to go wrong for Philip Graham on the day, a couple of years previously, when he had boarded a light plane at Prestwick airport with a few friends to fly to Edinburgh for the Festival. The plane had developed engine trouble over Stirling and had made a forced landing in a ploughed field. Everyone but Philip had escaped with cuts and bruises. He had suffered serious injuries from which he had convinced himself that he would never recover. Those injuries were now more mental than physical. The crash had destroyed his music and music was his life.

There was no doubt that he had been talented: he'd written the music for a critically acclaimed six-part crime series for Channel Four, incidental music for a number of TV dramas and – his one big success – the theme tune to a film called *The Devil's Agenda*, a story about a fictitious British spy taken from the novel with the same title. There had been good royalties from sales of compact discs and cassette tapes; awards were beginning to collect on the mantelpiece.

Then – though Philip had always hated flying – he had been persuaded into taking the air taxi to Edinburgh. And it seemed that all his premonitions of disaster had been correct.

It went through Sarah's mind, as she covertly watched him, that he had chiselled and polished the Martyr to his Art image to perfection. He was almost contemptible.

They had come a long way from the heady, carefree days when they were first married; Philip with his aristocratic connections, fair good looks and a smile for everyone, Sarah with style, high intelligence and classical beauty. Magazines had gushed over the society wedding, referring to Philip as 'a flower of English chivalry'. Sarah snorted with derision as she beheld him now: more like a weed these days.

Yes, I was beautiful, she thought, catching sight of herself in a mirror. She had kept most of her good looks and, thanks to rigorous dieting and exercise, her figure. Her business – an interior design consultancy – was pretty successful, which was just as well with Philip moping around the house all day.

'Harry wants us to go to stay with them soon,' Philip said, fixing his own coffee. 'Someone's bought that huge barn of a house next door and mentioned that they're going to get an interior designer in. He thought you might be interested.'

'What's this person's name?'

'Harry did say – it's slipped my mind.'

'It would help, you know, if you could be a bit more positive when your brother tosses us the occasional bone.'

It was a constant point of contention between them. Sarah resented Harry's patronage, knew he was only being charitable when he introduced her to possible clients at his country house in Fife. His wife was an enormous snob and Sarah had to endure her supercilious coldness when they accepted the invitations. In Sarah's view it was people like herself, hard-working and self-motivated, who enabled women like Francesca Torran-Genemeade, to give her her full maiden name, to sit on her backside all day long. Sarah failed to see why she should be treated like the poor relation.

She dropped a couple of slices of bread into the toaster. Her business would have to stay buoyant for them to remain in this house. Frozen pea commercials were lucrative, but they were few and far between. Moving up to Scotland had been a good idea as far as she was concerned; there were lots of wealthy people living in the Forth and Clyde valleys who were pre-pared to spend money on their homes. She had never been quite sure why someone like Harry had decided to live in Fife; but then again you could buy a whole estate in Scotland for the price of a flat in Chelsea.

She broke three eggs into a bowl and beat them with a fork, allowing her resentment full rein. Lofty rooms meant that the heating bills were enormous. Not only that, she had to employ a cleaning woman as Philip didn't know one end of a vacuum cleaner from the other and refused to learn. There was a big garden, too, that they had to have help with. God, if only the bloody man would interest himself in *that* it would leave more money to pay the bills, never mind the mortgage. They had a

29

car each, which was quite unnecessary; Philip insisted that country drives helped his inspiration. But all he had managed lately was the frozen peas jingle. What was he working on now? Spaghetti hoops? How the mighty had fallen.

Sarah scrambled the eggs, shared them between the two slices of toast, slapped them on to two plates and headed towards the living room with hers on a tray. She studiously avoided the crueller reflection given by the large mirror in the hall: she didn't want to see the beginnings of bitter lines around her mouth, her chin and neck less firm than she liked to think they were, her hair grey at the roots.

'What time did you come in last night?' she called. 'I didn't hear you.'

'About ten. I shouted out that it was me but you didn't reply.'

'I was in bed,' Sarah answered shortly. They had had separate rooms for years – on account of his snoring, she always said.

The front door banged; it was Jeremy, their son. 'College is closed,' he reported. 'Floods in the basement or something. Oh, good, I'm just in time for grub.'

Sarah smiled at him fondly and handed him her lunch.

'No, that's yours,' he protested. 'I'll fix myself some baked beans.'

'It won't take me a minute to rustle up something else,' she told him briskly. 'Not another word,' she added when he opened his mouth to argue.

Jeremy never won arguments with his mother so he sat down to eat. He was always hungry. Tall, thin and dark-haired, his enthusiasm for square meals extended to life in general. Sarah found it slightly unnerving, the way in which her only offspring hoovered up facts and figures of every kind, not just those connected with his chosen subject, music. And whereas his father would play the piano by ear, extemporising, banging out bastardised versions of popular tunes, Jeremy preferred to explore the mathematical perfection of Bach fugues, analysing them on his computer, trying to understand how and why music worked.

Philip's nightmare, Sarah knew, was that Jeremy would soon outshine him. Already he had attracted the attention of

30

various musical luminaries for a short piece of chamber music called *Landscape with Clouds*, which he had written as part of his degree course. 'Thin,' Philip had commented upon hearing it.

'Must be,' Jeremy had said. 'Someone wants to buy the rights and turn it into a love song.'

'You only have to start worrying when it gets turned into a hymn,' his father had said, grinning wolfishly.

'Oh, I don't know,' Jeremy had murmured. 'That didn't do much harm to Sibelius and Mozart.'

With a face like thunder, Philip had left the room.

That was the trouble, Sarah mused, staring dully into the fridge, looking for something to eat. Of the actual structure of music, Philip knew very little. He had no academic knowledge or textbook skill to fall back on. He had always relied on perfect pitch and what amounted to a headful of tunes.

'In the old days, anyway,' she said to a loaf and some weary-looking lettuce. 'He's got a headful of nothing now. I'm living with a has-been.'

'And I'm living with a bloody liar!' he shouted right in her ear, making her start violently. 'You *weren't* at home in bed last night when I came in. I know, because when you didn't reply I went into you room and looked. So where the hell were you?'

Sarah was furious. 'You were probably so drunk you wouldn't have noticed if I'd been in bed with an entire football team.'

Philip smiled thinly. 'Wishful thinking. And you know damn well I never drink when I'm going for a drive.'

'No, the famous composer could hardly be found drunk behind the wheel,' Sarah countered sarcastically.

Jeremy, on his own in the living room, shovelled the last of his lunch into his mouth, laid the plate aside and left the living room via the other door which led into the dining room. Quietly he went into the hall and up the stairs to the sanctuary of his room. Quickly, he put on a CD – one of his favourites, Beethoven's 'Choral Symphony' – and flopped on to the bed with a sigh of relief, closing his eyes.

He had heard all the rows before. It was like a play his parents rehearsed almost every day: the same bitterness, the same acid words. They seemed to be wasting their lives trying to destroy one another.

And it was all because of that Devlin woman.

Carrick was angry on several counts – mostly with himself. He felt horribly guilty about the way he was behaving towards Joanna; it was her holiday as well. He was sure that he had somehow cheated her further in buying flowers for Kimberley Devlin: he rarely bought flowers for Joanna. And somehow he suspected he was behaving with less than his usual level-headedness.

The curtains were drawn around Kimberley's bed and a nurse asked him to wait. He sat on a chair in a corridor feeling awkward and foolish: new sensations entirely. Anxious to keep everything above board, he had phoned Neil early that morning to relate what Mrs Gillespie had said – not that it had been of much use – and had gone on to inform Macpherson of his intentions. Macpherson had been delighted, adding that he would interview Kimberley Devlin as soon as he was able but had to attend a monthly meeting scheduled to finish just before lunch.

'I think I persuaded her to stay in hospital for a couple of days,' Carrick had ended by saying.

'You have a way with women,' Macpherson had said with a chuckle before ringing off.

'Ah, the fuzz,' said Kimberley Devlin with a wan smile when Carrick was eventually ushered into her presence. 'How did you know I like white freesias?'

'I'm a mind reader,' Carrick told her. 'And I once saw a magazine article about you in which you were photographed surrounded by them.'

The bruising was much in evidence now. 'Do I look as bloody awful as I feel?' she asked plaintively.

'No,' he lied.

'They've just given me a jab so I don't keep hitting B flat every time someone knocks against the bed.'

He drew up a chair and sat down, careful not to do that very thing. 'That bad, eh?'

'You didn't tell me your name yesterday, Mr Policeman.'

'Names weren't important yesterday. It's James Carrick.'

'Just that? No middle names?'

'Robert.'

'The Bruce!' she declared, resoundingly rolling the R.

The bedside cabinet was crammed with floral arrangements, as was a nearby windowsill. One enormous basket of fruit and flowers resembled in its perfection a still life painting.

'From Tony Capelli, my agent,' Kimberley said, following his gaze. 'He's always one for the flamboyant gesture. He rang me this morning from where he's staying – some unpronounceable and no doubt overpriced place in the south of France. He swore on his mother's grave that he can't come back until after the weekend. Sometimes I hate him.'

'He's on holiday?'

'Business. So he says.'

The ever-present copper in Carrick came to the fore. 'Don't you trust him?'

'He's Italian,' she replied, as though that explained everything. Then she added, more tactfully, 'He's one of those people who would rather tell a little lie than offend you.' She beamed at him; obviously the painkiller was taking effect. 'Now I suppose you're going to whip out your little notebook and grill me about what happened.'

'No, a friend of mine will do that later. Strictly speaking, I'm on holiday.'

'Not on your own, surely!'

'With my girlfriend, Joanna Mackenzie.'

He had not imagined it; she looked disappointed. Then she said, 'There's nothing to tell, anyway. I don't remember what happened. I went to the park to look at the hills and then – nothing.'

'Was it getting dark?'

'Yes. It was about nine thirty. I love the dusk and sunsets. But there was nothing to see that night, the sky was murky, like a fog. I knew a storm was on the way so I didn't walk far, just to the gate. I think there was another car but . . .' She shook her head. 'Maybe, maybe not.'

'Can you remember the colour of the car?'

'I told a policewoman who was here that I thought it was light-coloured. White, perhaps. Silvery or cream? I'm not at all sure – I might have imagined it.'

'And you hadn't agreed to meet someone there?'

Her eyes flashed. 'Like some little housewife deceiving her husband? No.'

'Has anyone made threats against you?'

'I thought you said you weren't investigating this.'

'Sorry. Nature seems to have programmed me to ask questions.' He got to his feet. 'I ought to go and meet Joanna.'

There was a long silence and then, as she had done the previous day, she held out a hand. He took it, but this time she had herself under control.

'You know, don't you?' she said under her breath. 'How I can't stop thinking about the pressing earth, and the insects on my face, the worms . . . To start with I couldn't make sense of what had happened to me but then . . .' She gripped his hand convulsively. 'How do you know? Do you have a particularly vivid imagination?'

'No,' Carrick said. 'Earlier this year someone shoved me inside an old boiler and left me there to die. I know what it's like to be put in a coffin alive.'

'Is that why you came?'

'One of the reasons.'

'How has it affected you – or mustn't I ask?'

'I try to live each day a little more fully.'

After another silence Kimberley Devlin turned her face away and spoke. 'There is someone who might have good reason to want me dead. I once had an affair with her husband. It was a very fleeting thing – I think I felt sorry for him more than anything. His wife found out. She sent me a dead bird through the post. There was a little note attached, saying if I saw Philip again I'd end up the same. It was a thrush – a *song* bird. I love birds.'

'Do you think she'd killed it?'

'I doubt it. I expect she found it and it gave her the idea. It had been dead quite a while.' She gave his hand a little squeeze. 'I suppose I ought to tell all this to your friend when he arrives.'

'Yes.'

'If the police go to question her, she'll take it out on Phil.'

34

'If she's arrested and in custody she won't be able to,' Carrick pointed out. 'Are you still seeing him?'

'No. At least – we did have lunch together about ten days ago. Phil's a composer and he's been in the doldrums since he was hurt in a plane crash a while back. I've commissioned him to write a song for me, to help get him going again. Surely Sarah can't object to that!'

'She's the bread-winner?'

'Yes. To be fair to her, Phil isn't the sort of man who would go and get any old job to help her pay the bills. He has very clear ideas of what a composer should be expected to do. Apart from compose, that is.'

'Not a lot?'

She sighed. 'No.'

'And has he? Composed anything, I mean?'

'He's had a couple of small jobs. Tunes for television commercials, that kind of thing. Sarah's had a field day. She despised him anyway and now she can really look down on him.'

'Is she capable of knocking someone down deliberately, do you think?'

'She's a very strong-willed woman.'

'How did you meet Phil?'

'At a recording session several years ago. We just bumped into each other over coffee in the studio canteen and got talking. He was quite up and coming then. Good-looking too – the crash aged him a lot.' She lay back on her pillows and closed her eyes.

'You're tired,' Carrick said. 'I'll go now.'

'You could ask your policeman friend about Jimmy Barr. I don't *think* he'd do anything like that but . . . .'

'Jimmy Barr?'

'He's one of those strange men who develop fixations about people in the public eye. A stalker. You know, like that man who follows Princess Diana around. He's an ardent fan, and I have no right to complain, but when he started sending flowers and phoning me at all hours of the day and night, and then began hanging around outside my flat, I'm afraid I had to call the police.'

'Did he threaten you?'

35

'No! He wanted to marry me.'

'Has he threatened you since you made a complaint about him?'

'I did get another letter in which he said I'd be sorry. But I didn't really regard that as a threat. He's rather a pathetic little man – apparently he was brought up in care. The usual sad story.'

'Do you know if he has a car?'

'Yes, one of those three-wheelers. A Reliant Robin. He parked it outside my flat once.' She frowned. 'I think it was grey. Or maybe it was just very dirty.'

'Inspector Macpherson will give you police protection for a while if you ask,' Carrick said soberly. 'He might do it even if you don't.'

Self-consciously, they realised they were still holding hands. Kimberley Devlin gently withdrew hers. 'Well, James Carrick, I want you to know that I appreciate what you've done. I hope we meet again.'

'Just promise me one thing,' Carrick said.

She smiled broadly. 'I'll try.'

'Don't stop singing.'

The smile faded.

He leaned over, kissed her cheek quickly and then left. He didn't look back.

'Yes,' said the doctor Carrick button-holed at the entrance to the ward, 'her injuries are consistent with being hit by a car. It must have been travelling fairly slowly or she would have been more seriously hurt. As it is, she's been very lucky – normally I would have expected several broken bones. The poor girl will be black and blue for a fortnight, though. But she got off lightly.'

Chapter Four

Sarah Graham was a little late for work but this did not prevent her from carefully folding the morning paper so that the headlines on the front page – OPERA STAR LEFT FOR DEAD – were uppermost. She placed it on the breakfast bar, where Philip normally ate his bowl of cereal, and went back to her room, ostensibly to apply her make-up. She did not have to wait long.

'Have you seen this?' he called from the kitchen. Moments later he made an appearance; not for the first time she could barely disguise her contempt. He did not look as though he had washed that morning, let alone shaved, and his shirt was so creased he might have slept in it. The once aristocratic nose, now pinched and beaky, was only a matter of inches from the newspaper. *He's almost an old man*, Sarah thought.

'The bastard buried her in a shallow grave. God! I can't believe it.' He flung himself from the room. 'Where the hell are my bloody glasses? Sarah, have you seen my glasses?'

'*That* won't help her pre-performance nerves,' Sarah said in an undertone to her reflection in the mirror. With a steady stroke, she applied a little more eyeshadow; she smiled as she admired the effect.

There was a cry of triumph as Philip found what he was searching for.

'On the piano, where they nearly always are,' Sarah murmured. She chose her perfume, dabbed it on wrists, throat and behind the lobes of her ears and then gathered up her bag. She met her husband in the doorway.

'I can't believe it,' Philip lamented.

'I'm late,' Sarah said, manoeuvring herself past him.

37

'Have you been listening?' he asked furiously. 'But then, I expect you're crowing over this, aren't you?'

'If people go blundering about the countryside in the dark they must anticipate that passing drivers might not see them,' she observed coolly, taking her car keys from the hook in the hall. 'I shall be late tonight. A client's taking me out to dinner.'

'It says here that the police think it might have been a white or possibly light grey car.'

'That's hardly evidence – that could describe half the cars in the UK. They'll have to do better than that.'

He yelled after her as she closed the door. 'Your car's white. Isn't it?'

She opened the door again and put her head through. 'Indeed it is. And I seem to remember that it was you who used it, "to go for a drive" that night.' With this parting shot, she finally exited.

Alone, Philip savagely pounded the newspaper into a ball with both hands and sank to sit on the bottom stair. He caught sight of himself in the full length hall mirror and stared at his reflection, appalled. Was this the person he had become; a hunched, withered old man? Surely it was a trick of the light that caused his eyes to look so weak and watery, his complexion so grey.

'I'm drinking too much,' he muttered.

It was rather alarming, this stranger staring back at him from the mirror. When had he last looked in a mirror? He tried to avoid it when he used his electric razor in the mornings; a small triangle of stubble on his chin confirmed that fact. Since the accident it seemed to take all his energy to become mobile when he got out of bed; an aching and stiff body now ruled what had once been a lively mind.

It was mostly Sarah's fault.

'Damn the woman!' he declared. 'I shall have to do something about it.'

But what?

And perhaps it was already too late.

Neil Macpherson sat in the canteen at Brig Street police station consuming a vast plateful of sausages, beans, egg, chips and peas. 'I know, I know,' he fretted when Carrick joined him at his table. 'I'm overweight already. Don't tell the wife, for pity's sake – I'm supposed to be on a diet. "You'll be one of those statistics", she keeps telling me. "The Scots are the unhealthiest people in Europe and you're going to drop dead on me at fifty-four like all the rest." But what can I do when I'm starving hungry?'

Carrick fetched himself some coffee and a large sticky bun to help alleviate his friend's guilt as well as his own mid-morning hunger pangs. 'Tony Capelli,' he said, prior to taking a large bite out of his bun.

'Can't say that I've heard of him,' Macpherson admitted.

'He's Kimberley Devlin's agent.'

'I'm off to the hospital when I've had this. What about him?'

'He's a crook. *Mafioso*, even.'

Macpherson dissected a leathery fried egg. 'You seem very sure.'

'I am. He's on our files. I first heard of him when I was in the Met at West End Central. He runs a theatrical and musicians' agency based near Leicester Square. The reason I'm interested is that his brother-in-law has recently moved into Bristol with the idea of setting himself up as a drugs baron. I assure you that Capelli knows some highly dubious people. The agency's genuine as far as it goes but I suspect it's also a front for other activities.'

'You think there's a link between that and what's happened to the Devlin girl? It doesn't necessarily follow that— '

Carrick interrupted. 'Look, Neil, I'm not interfering but I'd really appreciate it if you'd ask her what she knows about him.'

'It's all the same to me if *you* ask her.'

Carrick tasted his coffee, grimaced and stirred some sugar into it. 'No. Right now there's a limit to the amount of questioning that can be done – she's not well enough to be interrogated by all and sundry.'

'And that young lady of yours won't be too happy if . . .' He grinned and left the rest unsaid.

'She isn't,' Carrick said shortly.

Macpherson laid down his knife and fork to take something from his pocket. 'Almost forgot. Take a look at this. The wife got it for her cousin in the States but she didn't bother posting it when she saw how expensive it was.'

What Carrick had been given was a small booklet, glossy and expensively produced. The cover depicted a Highland landscape – Lochaber, he thought – in winter, the snow on the mountain peaks perfectly reflected in the mirror-calm loch. Crimson lettering read: LIVE LIKE A SCOTTISH LORD; printed beneath this, DISCOVER YOUR SCOTTISH ROOTS ON A DREAM TRIP TO THE OLD COUNTRY.

'Weekends at a castle in the Highlands,' Carrick murmured as he read. 'It's aimed almost exclusively at Americans, by the look of it.'

'Kimberley Devlin's one of the attractions,' Macpherson said. 'Read on.'

Carrick skipped the pages about trips to whisky distilleries, shopping in Inverness, visits to sheepskin warehouses and kilt and bagpipe makers and went on to Evening Entertainments.

'"Listen to some of the world's most beautiful songs and arias",' he quoted. '"Opera star Kimberley Devlin will enchant you with Wagner, Rossini and Purcell. And (upon request) she will sing popular numbers from American musicals and Scottish ballads".'

'Look at the cost, man!'

Carrick turned over. 'I see what you mean. Prices start at five thousand dollars for a double room. Goes up to six if you have what's referred to as the "Duke's Suite". Champagne and a four-poster bed. But the price is all-inclusive of a special train from London, three nights at the castle and all meals, including a banquet with "minstrels" on the Saturday. You get to meet a "real Scottish nobleman" and there are also what's referred to as "local celebrities". There's clay-pigeon shooting, fishing and a free boat trip on the Moray Firth. Not bad value. All the booze is thrown in too.'

Macpherson grunted. 'And they get dressed up in kilts and all that tosh. Yanks in kilts!'

'Some of them have clan connections,' Carrick told him. 'They have their own clan societies and chiefs.'

'It just doesn't seem right,' his friend grumbled. 'Call me a patriotic fool if you will.'

'These trips are run by Capelli Enterprises, see?'

40

Macpherson pointed his fork at him. 'And you, laddie, have always been one to get a bee in your bonnet. It's been known for you to get yourself stung.'

'May I keep this?' Carrick enquired, holding up the booklet.

'Aye,' the other sighed. 'And you've got that thrawn look on your face. Did the Devlin woman say anything really interesting?'

'She'll tell you about Sarah someone or other whose husband, Phil, she had an affair with. I'm more interested in a man called Jimmy Barr.'

'I've already arranged for him to be brought in. He has form for making obscene phone calls and peering through women's windows. Nasty piece of work.'

'Kimberley Devlin didn't seem to know about any of that – or if she did she didn't say anything. She thinks he's rather pathetic.'

'No, he's a bad lot,' Macpherson stressed. 'Jimmy gives the impression that he's sad but harmless. But he's not harmless, you can take my word for it. We'll see him up on a rape charge one day.'

'She thought he had a grey Reliant Robin.'

'It's all in the records,' Macpherson said lightly. 'I've had the file sent over from Johnstone, which was where she first made a complaint. There are others too. She's not the first woman unfortunate enough to be the subject of one of his fixations.'

'Did any of the others come to harm?'

'Only insofar as he indecently exposed himself to one of them. But that's bad enough in my book.'

Macpherson had nearly finished his meal so there was nothing Carrick could do but shake hands with his friend and leave. *It wasn't his case . . .*

He had arranged to meet Joanna for lunch in Prince's Square and, as this was an enclosed area with no adjacent parking, he left his car in a multi-storey car park near Central Station and walked. It wasn't far and he was hoping that he would arrive first to give him valuable thinking time. This wish seemed to have been granted – he had suggested that they should wait for one another outside the cookshop on the lower terrace – and he strolled over the mosaic floor in the vicinity.

The square was on four levels covered with a glass roof with a large open area in the centre, each level with shops and small stalls bright with craftwork and paintings by local artists. Escalators and lifts, the latter clear glass with brass metalwork, carried shoppers smoothly to each floor and the balustrades and ornamental lamps showed the influence of Charles Rennie Mackintosh. It was an extremely civilised place to have lunch.

Suddenly Carrick noticed Joanna standing close by, watching him.

'I hope I haven't kept you waiting,' he said.

'No. I bought a pair of shoes.'

Still she gazed at him.

'Are you hungry?' he asked. 'Shall we eat?'

'You don't want to go north, do you?'

'I've just filled up the car with petrol. We can set off as soon as we've eaten.'

'You haven't answered my question.'

'I think I have. I've been looking forward to this holiday with you for a long time.'

Slowly, she came towards him. 'I was in an electrical shop just now when the local news came on television. They were interviewing Kimberley Devlin from her hospital bed.'

Carrick made no comment. The expression on her face gave him stark warning.

'She said she's been talking to a really delightful policeman who's helped her get over the trauma. She wouldn't name names, but it's you, isn't it?'

'I have no control over what she says to any reporter who gets through the blockade they've surrounded her with,' Carrick said. Even to his own ears he sounded pompous.

'She also said that she thought she'd fallen in love with you. She seemed quite besotted with you.'

'She's an opera singer, she's an expert in the art of exaggeration. It's just her way of showing her – gratitude.'

'Is that why you went back this morning? To lap up her gratitude?'

'I went back because I promised I would.'

'I think I'll take the train home,' she said, turning to walk away.

'Tell me how you'd behave if you'd been buried alive!' he was stung into saying.

42

She paused. 'I will. When it happens.'

Carrick was desperate. 'She mentioned the name of her agent, Capelli. I know from my time in the Met that he has criminal connections.'

'Then perhaps you'd better go and talk to your little opera singer about them.'

He stared after her as she disappeared from sight among the shoppers. He began to realise that they had had an audience; neither had been shouting but their words, judging by the number of people leaning on the wrought-iron balustrades, had carried to at least the second level. He had the distinct feeling that no one thought the play was over.

But it was.

Jimmy Barr was of short stature with mouse-coloured hair, protruberant brown eyes and a moist, thin mouth. His hands, nervously making wringing movements in his lap, looked clammy. Detective Inspector Neil Macpherson found him utterly repellent.

'You drive a pale grey Reliant Robin? Correct?' he said curtly.

'Yes,' Barr said miserably.

'Miss Devlin thinks that the car that knocked her down was pale in colour. I think it was yours.'

'No,' Barr said in a whisper.

'Speak up! Neither I nor the tape can hear you,' Macpherson bellowed.

'No,' Barr repeated, a little louder.

'You have, despite several warnings, persisted in pestering the woman,' Macpherson continued. 'You've followed her to rehearsals, hung about by stage doors and outside her home. You've telephoned her, written to her and quite recently threw a stone through one of her windows.'

'I deliberately waited until she was out in case I hurt her,' Barr said quickly. 'There was a letter wrapped around it – damage was not my objective.'

'And did you think Miss Devlin would be sympathetically inclined towards someone who showered her home with broken glass?' Macpherson enquired. He drew the man's file towards him. 'So. You were born in Nottingham fifty-one years ago and when you were thirteen your parents moved to Glasgow where your father got a job in a shipyard until he was laid off due to ill health. They were both killed in a fire at your home one day while you were at school. You were regarded as being unsuitable for fostering – too old – so were placed in care. Is that right?'

'It was called an orphanage in those days,' Barr said.

Macpherson stared him down. Although Barr had lived in Scotland for most of his life he did not possess a Scottish accent and was, despite his lack of education, surprisingly articulate. He evidently had hidden depths, but Macpherson did not want to dredge them. He continued. 'When you left school you also got a job in the shipyard and stayed there until it closed in 1963. Since then you've had a variety of jobs: stores clerk, electrician, currently fork-lift truck driver. You're unmarried.'

Blinking, Barr nodded. Then, with a worried glance in the direction of the tape recorder, said, 'That's right.'

'I don't suppose for one minute that you intended to hurt her,' Macpherson went on. 'But it all went wrong, didn't it? You meant to try to talk to her so you followed her car to the country park. Before you knew what was going on you had knocked her down. The light was bad, a thunderstorm was brewing. You panicked. You thought she was dead so you dragged her away from the road and out of sight. You found a spot where it was easy to hide her under the fallen leaves.'

'No!' Barr said. He sounded vehement. 'I didn't. I wasn't anywhere near Mosslaw that night.'

'Yes, I know you said you were in a pub, but we've asked and no one remembers seeing you. You'll need a better alibi than that.'

'But it's the truth,' Barr protested with a rare show of spirit.

'Shall we go through it again?' said the policeman with Macpherson, DS Kerr. 'What time did you get home from work?'

'The usual time. About five thirty,' Barr answered sullenly.

'Did you go straight out to the pub?'

'No. I tidied the place up and then got changed and fetched myself a carry-out from the Chinese. I usually do that on Mondays.'

44

Macpherson could not imagine Barr doing housework. He had been to the flat and the overall impression had been the grubbiness of the place, a veneer of the accumulated dust and dirt of years.

'And when you'd eaten you went to the pub?'

'After I'd watched the seven o'clock news on Channel Four.'

'Funny how no one remembers seeing you that evening.'

Privately, Neil Macpherson was admitting to himself that Barr was the most instantly forgettable person he had ever clapped eyes on.

'No, well, they mightn't, might they? The place was full to bursting because of the football match. The pub's got one of those big screens.'

'Which match?'

'I couldn't tell you, I'm not interested in football. All I know is that it was Scotland playing some European team.'

'You'd rather be peering through people's bedroom windows than watching sport, eh?'

Before Barr could make any reply to this there was a knock on the door of the interview room. The preliminary forensic reports on Barr's clothes and car had arrived.

'Right,' said Macpherson after quickly reading them through, 'first of all I'd like you to explain how your car came to be dented on the near-side wing.'

'I clouted a lamp post when I was parking last month.'

'Forensic seem to think it was done very recently.'

'Well, perhaps it was a couple of weeks ago. Less, maybe. I can't really remember.'

Macpherson folded his arms and leaned them on the table. 'Most people remember it all too well when they've damaged their vehicle.'

Barr shrugged. 'Mine was already battered when I bought it. I don't worry about the odd scrape.'

'What about the mud and fragments of heather on the soles of your shoes? And ground into the mat under the pedals?'

Barr shook his head, eyes downcast. 'I don't know. I could have picked them up anywhere.'

'Let's go back to this lamp post.'

'It was a week or so ago but I can't remember exactly when. I was parking outside my flat and there wasn't as much room

45

as usual because the bloke in the next block had hired a trailer and it was hitched to his car.'

'And – don't tell me – you'd been wearing the shoes to do some gardening,' Sergeant Kerr said sarcastically.

Barr refused to rise to the bait. 'I live on the first floor. I don't have a garden.'

'You were really angry when Miss Devlin made a complaint about you,' Macpherson said. 'You've brooded about it ever since. You wrote her a threatening letter saying she'd be sorry.'

'I could do with a pee,' Barr muttered.

'I'll think about it. Answer the question.'

Barr took a deep breath. 'I felt she'd acted unnecessarily harshly. I only wanted to ask her—'

'To marry you?' Kerr jeered.

'No, actually—'

'You've been making her life a misery for almost a year,' Macpherson interrupted. 'You have form for making women's lives hell.'

'That's all in the past,' Barr said. 'You can admire, can't you? From a distance? I'm entitled to admire her talent. Since I got a steady job I've been able to save up and go to concerts and the opera sometimes. I buy music tapes. I can't afford a CD player of course, but—'

Kerr butted in. 'From a distance? You've been hanging around her flat for weeks. She said she thought the car that hit her was pale in colour and yours is grey. It has a dented wing and mud and heather are all over your shoes and the mats in your car. I don't think you realise how much trouble you're in.'

Kimberley Devlin stared at her reflection in the hand-held mirror and then tossed it on the coverlet of the bed. She looked dreadful, like something out of a nightmare; her face seemed to be one large bruise with eyes and a mouth. She hurt all over; even breathing was agony. If she asked the nursing staff they gave her pills or painkilling injections but these tended to make her feel tired and woozy. And she didn't want to go to sleep.

An Inspector Macpherson had appeared shortly after lunch

46

and interviewed her at length, mostly about Jimmy Barr. He had not seemed too interested in Sarah Graham but had taken down all the details carefully in his notebook. Lightly, as he was leaving, she had asked him about his friend James Carrick and he had chuckled and shut his notebook with a snap.

'I ken he's a real fan of yours.'

'I didn't get round to asking him about himself. Where does he live?'

'Bath. And he's done very well for himself, has James. They've just made him up to chief inspector. Mind you, he deserves it. He works like the very Devil.'

'He doesn't look old enough to be a chief inspector,' she had protested.

Macpherson had done some mental arithmetic. 'He'll be thirty-one, I think,' he had concluded. 'He's got an old head on his shoulders.'

'But he's not involved with your investigation?' she had asked earnestly. 'I mean, he really is on holiday?'

'Not involved,' Macpherson had assured her, looking puzzled. 'He's heading up into the Highlands with that lassie of his.'

'I hope so,' Kimberley had said fervently, after which her visitor had given her an odd look. Well, at least she couldn't be prosecuted for trying to break up the romance of a chief inspector. But it had been a silly impulse to say what she had said – lights and cameras always went to her head. And those damned pills didn't help . . .

Up until now life had been good to her. Brought up in a loving home, the only child of happy, musical parents who had carefully nourished her budding talent, nothing had threatened what the whole family regarded as a bright future.

'It seems I might have been a naive little fool,' she said to herself.

She had spoken to her parents on the phone – they had emigrated to New Zealand two years previously to be near her brother, Charles, who was married with twin boys – and had sought to play down her fear. But when she was alone she found it hard to conceal her terror. Somehow the real world, a dark, ugly place newly discovered, had eclipsed all her sunny

47

memories of the past. Even now it was darkening a present inhabited by someone who had buried her alive.

There was nothing but darkness.

And worms.

Chapter Five

The venue for the 'Live like a Lord' weekends – Castle Stalker – intrigued Carrick. He knew the country of his birth well enough and had actually seen a castle of that name when on holiday several years previously. But that had been on a tiny rocky island off the Isle of Lismore in Loch Linnhe and to all appearances had been uninhabited: little more than a ruin. The booklet, however, described Castle Stalker as being 'sited near Inverness overlooking the Moray Firth on a south-east facing promontory.' This was some fifty miles away as the corbies flew up the Great Glen. With the aid of an Ordnance Survey map Carrick pin-pointed the only building that fitted the description: the home of the head of an ancient and illustrious Highland clan. But that castle had another name. This could only mean that the correct name was not being used, for reasons known only to the owner and organisers. Perhaps, Carrick thought, there was the suspicion – at least as far as the owner was concerned – that the whole enterprise was more than a tiny bit naff.

He had parked at the side of a minor road – one of many built in order to pacify the Highlands after Culloden – overlooking the Firth, the castle directly below him. Originally a massive tower-house, it had been much enlarged and embellished during the eighteenth century when a new wing had been built, complete with grandiose turrets and a banqueting hall. This much Carrick had gleaned from a local guide book.

The booklet that Neil had given him the previous day was still in his pocket and he drew it out and leafed through it again. The trips were principally aimed at Americans on holiday in Britain; presumably they could be pre-booked in the States. Three had already taken place that summer and there were two more to go, one the coming weekend and another early in the next month, September.

He had not examined too closely his motives for driving north to seek out Castle Stalker. There had been no point in chasing after Joanna; it would only have meant postponing, yet again, the crossing of that threshold of no hope.

He was unsure of Kimberley Devlin's motives for her all-too-public remarks, though there was no reason to disbelieve what Joanna said she had heard. He supposed he ought to feel flattered, but he didn't. Kimberley had diminished what he had set out to do. Perhaps she had misinterpreted his sympathy. On the other hand, he might be blinded by his own apparent misanthropy and the truth might be . . .

'I'm a real fan of hers,' Carrick groaned under his breath. 'And I went rushing off—' But he wasn't in love with an opera star.

Was he?

'I shall stay away from her,' he solemnly promised a hundred square miles or so of Scottish scenery.

He took a deep breath and gazed across the Firth. Water, mountains, sunshine and heather beguiled him and he felt the tension ebb from his neck and shoulders. High above a skein of geese flew, a quivering arrowhead against the blue sky, their calls faintly heard in the vast silence. As always, when in Scotland, he asked himself why he chose to live five hundred miles away in the traffic-blighted south. He clambered down the steep slope below the road for a short distance and picked a sprig of heather. The tiny bell-shaped flowers were just coming into bloom and as he looked at them his vision blurred.

'Damn everything,' he said and sat down suddenly on a lichen-covered boulder.

Nothing moved in the precincts of the castle. A lone flag hung limply on a pole. Then, as he watched, a Land Rover drove through an archway that presumably led into the inner courtyard and stopped outside the main entrance of the building. A man wearing overalls got out and went indoors. Moments later, another man, dressed in a kilt and jacket, came out, got into the vehicle and drove away down the drive, to vanish behind the trees.

It was a surprise to Carrick – beginning to doze in the afternoon sun – when a few minutes later, the car came into view on the road above him. It slowed as it approached and Carrick turned to discover that he was being subjected to a searching scrutiny. Almost immediately the driver accelerated away, only to brake and reverse back to the same place.

'My apologies for staring,' called the middle-aged man through the open driver's window. 'I thought for a moment – you could be my new gillie's younger brother.'

Carrick went up to the road. 'I thought you looked a bit fierce. I hope he's not in trouble.'

The hard features softened slightly. 'Probably not. No doubt he's at work *somewhere*. Bit of a dreamer – likes to stop and admire the scenery.'

'One can't blame him, really.'

'You haven't broken down, I hope?'

Carrick shook his head. 'No. I'm on holiday. Admiring the scenery.'

The other man waved his hand expansively. 'Go anywhere you like – take a look around inside the park if you're interested. Just say *I* said you could if anyone stops you.' He gave Carrick another searching look. 'You speak like an Englishman, but you're not, are you?'

'Not many Englishmen would know that you're a clan chief from the three silver feathers on your bonnet crest badge. I presume I'm talking to Lord Muirshire.'

'You are,' said the Marquess. 'I'm sorry to disturb you. Do enjoy your holiday.' And with that he drove away.

The opportunity was too good to miss; the grounds of the castle were not normally open to the public. Not many minutes later Carrick was cruising slowly down the long drive, the building looking much more imposing from ground level. The afternoon sun glinted in the windows; Carrick, not usually possessed of a fanciful imagination, could visualise the gleam of light reflected on the weapons of a watchful guard shortly after the fortified house had been erected.

Not wishing to impose his presence too close to what was, after all, a private residence, he turned on to an unmade track and parked on the edge of a clearing where mature spruce had been felled. Then he donned the walking boots he had brought with him, zipped up his Barbour jacket – the breeze was chilly – and headed for where he had spied water shimmering through the trees. A quarter of a mile later he discovered a fair-sized loch in an almost secret glen, the sides steep and thickly wooded. At a landing stage a couple of dinghies bobbed at their moorings.

He was accosted almost straight away. But the man who called to him, thick-set and dark-haired, striding from a birch copse with a Gordon setter at heel, did not address him as Carrick might have expected.

'You wouldn't have the right time? My watch has stopped.'

'Four forty,' Carrick told him.

'Thanks,' said the man, removing the offending timepiece and making adjustments. Like the marquess he was attired in a kilt. This was topped by a green army-style sweater with leather patches on the elbows and a sleeveless gilet. On his feet he had walking boots like Carrick's, worn over heavyweight long socks. A businesslike skene-dhu was tucked into the top of one of these.

'You're the estate manager?' Carrick hazarded.

There was a broad smile. 'Which, translated, means general dogsbody.'

'And your name's probably Kennedy.'

This time there was surprise. 'You a detective or something?'

Carrick laughed. 'Yes, as a matter of fact, but the clue's in your kilt. I wear the same tartan.' He went forward and held out his hand. 'James Carrick.'

It was grasped in a strong grip. 'Andrew Kennedy. You're serious? You're really a detective?'

'I'm on leave from the police.'

'And you're staying here?' He gestured in the direction of the castle.

'Oh, no. I met Lord Muirshire up the road and he invited me to have a look round.'

'He would. I think he sometimes feels a bit guilty, having all this to himself. That's why I wouldn't have been surprised if you'd been a guest. All sorts of friends of friends come for

52

weekends and so forth. He gets lonely, rattling around in the place on his own most of the time. His wife died about eighteen months ago and there are no children.'

'What about the succession?'

'A cousin in Nova Scotia. They can't stand one another.'

'So the weekends, when the castle gets filled up with Americans . . .'

Kennedy looked pained. 'Don't remind me. There's another one this weekend. That's when I put on yet another hat and act as master of ceremonies – and *maître d'hôtel*, come to think of it. But the food's all done by outside caterers – except for breakfast. Aggie would never manage. Want an invitation? I could wangle it for you.'

'I'm short of the several thousand bucks.'

Kennedy shook his head, laughing. 'No, no. I'd just put you on the list of helpers and you could sing for your supper. Quite a few local people get roped in on Banquet Night. Can you dance?'

'Highland dancing?'

'Yes. I know some of them.'

'Only we have demonstrations and then everyone has a go. How about the pipes?'

''Fraid not.'

'Make a bit of a show with a claymore?'

'Did a bit of fencing years ago in London.'

'Nothing so complicated. We just get a couple of the lads to put on the gear and prowl around taking safe swings at one another. The Yanks love it.'

'Look, I'm not even planning to be here at the weekend.'

'That's a real shame.'

'I understand that Kimberley Devlin sings at these gatherings.'

'Aye, she does. Usually on the Friday and on the Sunday evenings when the dinners are formal with no roistering. There's a lassie who plays the Irish harp too, and a display of local crafts in the armoury.'

Of course, Carrick thought; *you don't have loud fun and games on the Sabbath in Scotland.* 'But Miss Devlin won't be coming this weekend.'

'Why not?' asked Kennedy blankly.

53

'She was knocked down by a car on Monday night. She was out for a walk, by herself, and got in someone's way. I thought you would have heard.'

Kennedy looked appalled. 'Good God, no! Why the hell didn't someone tell me before?'

'She's all right,' Carrick said calmly. 'She only has minor injuries. But it was reported in the papers and on TV. You might have been one of the people she tried to contact.'

'I've been working all hours and then just falling into bed. You seem to know a lot about this. Were you there?'

'I have a friend in the CID at a nick in Glasgow. I called in to see him just as the call came through and went with him.'

'And how come the CID are involved?'

'Whoever knocked her down tried to hide the evidence by putting her under a pile of leaves and earth while she was unconscious.'

'*Buried* her? That's bloody awful.' He regarded Carrick in less than friendly fashion. 'Let's get this straight. You *are* on holiday?'

'Everyone keeps asking me that. Yes, I am.'

'There's a big "but" in there that you're not going to tell me about.'

Carrick smiled, non-committal.

'If you think there's a connection with what's going on here you'll need my help to get to the bottom of it.'

'Why should there be a connection? And if there was, and it goes official, CID will put their own people in – with the help of the Marquess.'

'Is this anything to do with Capelli?' Kennedy said quietly.

'*Capelli*?' Carrick said, his ears pricking up.

'Tony Capelli. He runs the show. "Live like a Lord", I mean. And he's Miss Devlin's agent.'

'What makes you think he might be involved?'

Kennedy sought inspiration in the sky and then burst out, 'He looks the sort of heathen who would have his granny boiled down for glue! That's what.'

Carrick found this a perfect description of some of the men with whom he knew Capelli consorted. 'You've met him?' he enquired.

54

'Several times. Quite often he turns up on the last evening, sometimes he's here beforehand. No one seems to know when he's going to arrive. Now, are you going to forget you're a policeman for five minutes and come back to my place for a dram?'

The estate manager lived in the grounds in what could only be described as an enormous cottage. It had been built in the early nineteenth century as a dower house, Kennedy explained. What had originally been stables and a coach house had been incorporated into the ground-floor living space to create a large, luxurious living room with picture windows overlooking the sweep of parkland to the east of the drive. It was to this room that Kennedy took Carrick, fetching glasses and a bottle of single malt from a cabinet.

'Are you married, Mr Kennedy?' Carrick asked, admiring the view.

'Andrew, please. I was. My wife couldn't decide which was worse here: the boredom, the midges or me. And there was no way I was going to get a job in a city just to please her. But the break-up was fairly friendly. What's the point of bad feeling? You make a mistake in life, you have to muddle through as best you can.'

'Your health,' Carrick said, on receipt of his dram.

'Aye, health, wealth and happiness to us both,' Kennedy said, sighing. 'I can't help but think of Miss Devlin,' he went on, having taken a generous swallow of his whisky. 'But I'm sure she'll get over it. She's not the sort of woman you could describe as a nervous wee lassie.'

'Presumably you know her quite well. Has she been coming here long?'

'The trips only started last year but I suppose she's been up about half a dozen times.'

'Do you know a couple whose first names are Philip and Sarah?'

'Would that be Philip Graham?'

'I've no idea. All I know is that he's a composer.'

'Yes, that'll be him. I've never met the man, mind. Miss Devlin mentioned to me that she's commissioned him to write her a song. Have you heard her sing?'

'Yes.'

A dreamy look came over Kennedy's face. 'Emotion is the word. People are moved to tears as they listen.'

'The whole experience is probably pretty emotional for most of your guests.'

'Aye, it is that. One chap came face to face with a portrait of his great-grandfather in a museum in Inverness. He was really put out when the curator wouldn't sell it to him. Personally I'd have let him have it – he offered a hundred thousand dollars and the painting was dreadful.'

'You sound as though you appreciate the arts.'

Kennedy gave him a twisted grin. 'It's the long winter evenings. You try to turn yourself back into a civilised human being after puttering through the freezing cold mud in a Land Rover all day.'

'And you're more than a little in love with Kimberley Devlin.'

'You're not going to do your Sherlock Holmes stuff in here,' Kennedy countered, only half-joking.

'So where were you last Monday night?' Carrick persevered.

'Well, I wasn't in the middle of some God-forsaken country park in Renfrewshire.'

'I didn't say where she was found. The exact location is being withheld.'

Kennedy dropped his gaze and stared into his drink. After a pause he said, 'Well, she and I know each other quite well. She mentioned that she often goes up there to unwind.'

'What colour is your car?'

'Red.'

'What about the Land Rover you mentioned?'

'It belongs to the estate.' Carrick carried on looking at him. 'It's a dirty sort of cream. I think it's been hand-painted at some stage of its life.'

'So where were you on Monday night?'

'Here.'

'Can you prove it?'

'No. But look, you said— '

'Yes, I'm on holiday.'

'You're giving nothing away,' said Kennedy stiffly. 'I ken

you're a fine policeman, but something tells me that you've taken a shine to the lady yourself.'

Carrick finished off his dram and carefully replaced the cut-glass tumbler on a side table.

'If it came to it, I'd fight you for her,' Kennedy blurted out.

'That sort of talk belongs to the age of claymores,' Carrick remarked.

'Aye, it does,' Kennedy agreed with a grim smile.

Walking away, Joanna had felt wildly relieved. Vindicated. Almost happy. These sensations had lasted until she reached the hotel room and started to pack her clothes. By the time she reached Central Station there was only sorrow, guilt and downright misery. That had *not* been the best way to do it.

'Is there a right way?' she asked herself as she boarded a train for London.

Well, at least she intended to take James's advice.

The following morning, having made an important phone call, she left her hotel in the Strand, took the tube to Westminster and walked up Whitehall. She was still not at all sure that she was doing the right thing. Had Patrick Gillard been serious when he offered her a job in MI5?

Both she and James were pleased that they could count Patrick and his wife Ingrid among their friends but he was not the sort of person one could be 'chummy' with. Gillard wasn't chummy with anyone. Joanna was well aware that in calling to see him now she would be encountering one of the facets of his complex persona with which she was not familiar: that of a keeper of Her Majesty's national security. And in that capacity, although he had sounded perfectly friendly on the phone, he might just freeze her right off his doorstep.

However, she discovered that the man on the reception desk knew all about her and that a visitor's pass had been prepared. What was more than slightly unnerving was that it had her photograph on it.

In the company of a uniformed usher she travelled up seven floors in a lift. There was then a long walk down a carpeted corridor: panelled walls with a few gloomy oil paintings. She was hoping that she would be able to find her way out again.

The usher knocked discreetly at one of the doors and went

straight in without waiting for a response. The room was empty.

'He won't keep you waiting a moment, Miss Mackenzie,' said the usher, and withdrew.

There was a superb view across St James's Park, Joanna discovered, wandering across to the window, not feeling able to seat herself uninvited. She turned and gazed around the room. There was not a single clue to the character of the man who must spend at least part of his working day within the four walls – not even photographs of his wife and children. The desk held a computer terminal, a pen tray and blotter and a telephone. No personal clutter. There was not so much as a jacket hanging on the old-fashioned coat stand.

This must be just the front parlour, as it were. His real office would be somewhere else. Next door, perhaps.

Gillard did eventually appear from next door, so this guess could have been correct. But Joanna had not expected him to be in his lieutenant-colonel's uniform.

'Joanna. How nice to see you,' he said as they shook hands. 'You didn't give me much notice,' he continued ruefully when they had seated themselves in two of the room's three armchairs. 'I'm all done up like a dog's dinner – I've been roped in to help at an Investiture at the Palace. So I'm afraid I've only a few minutes. What can I do for you?'

This was the stuff of her worst dreams. Here she was, about to tell someone who looked like the Chief of Defence Staff, that she had left her boyfriend. She decided to come straight to the point.

'You once offered me a job. My circumstances have changed now, so does the offer still hold?'

There was a silence that seemed to go on for ever. His unholy grey eyes bored into hers. She held the gaze.

'Yes,' he said at last. He looked at his watch. 'I'm free at about four. Can you come back then?'

'Yes,' Joanna said.

He rose to his feet; she had no choice but to make for the door. 'I'm really sorry, but duty calls. How's James?'

'I left him in Glasgow,' she replied tersely.

He did not miss the emphasis on the second word. 'I'm sorry.'

'Don't be. He appears to have moved on to pastures new. He's fallen for an opera singer who got knocked down by a car.'

Gillard paused in opening the door, his arm falling back to his side. 'Joanna, I find that rather hard to believe.'

She shrugged. 'That's the way it looked to me. He did mention someone by the name of Capelli but I wasn't really listening at the time.'

Swiftly, he went to the computer terminal and punched keys. 'First name?' he asked.

'James didn't say.'

Gillard read what was on the screen. 'Leave it with me. I'll get someone to look into it and give you an update when you return.' He regarded her soberly. 'It was Kimberley Devlin, wasn't it? Someone buried her alive.'

'Apparently.'

'James knows what that's like – being shut in somewhere and left to die.'

'I'm aware of that,' Joanna said stiffly.

He smiled bleakly and opened the door. 'See you later then.'

Left on his own, Gillard grabbed his hat from a desk drawer, gave himself a cursory glance in a mirror and left the room the way he had come. He had a car waiting.

Joanna did not come off the boil until she was outside the building on the pavement, the lifts and corridors having been negotiated apparently on auto-pilot. She was not at all sure that she would go back at four; she actually went into a phone box to call Gillard's office, to say that she had changed her mind. For reasons which she could not really explain she called Directory Enquiries instead and a few minutes later was talking to Detective Inspector Macpherson. After quite a lengthy conversation Macpherson promised to call her back but Joanna said she would call him as she was speaking from a phone box. When she did speak to him again, from a different phone in a restaurant, Macpherson was distinctly annoyed.

More important right now was what Gillard thought of her. That carelessly uttered question, 'How's James?' had gone right to the heart of the matter with the finesse of a brain surgeon's scalpel. She was not convinced that she wanted to work for a man who could read what was written on her very soul.

One thing puzzled her: why would his presence be required at an Investiture? Surely there were plenty of semi-retired army officers and courtiers only too willing to assist. At least he would look the part: tall, slim and imbued with a certain gravity.

It did not occur to her – at this time she did not know Gillard very well – that he might have been commanded to present himself by the monarch herself. She found him – how should she put it? – amusing.

When Joanna returned at four Gillard was waiting for her in the lobby. He had changed into a grey suit and white shirt with regimental tie.

'I thought you might like some tea,' were his first words.

The restaurant was darkly panelled with heavy red velvet curtains at the windows. The waitresses wore dated black dresses with frilly aprons and caps. It was all very traditional.

'I thought you'd be in the new MI5 building,' Joanna said when he had ordered tea and cakes for them both.

'I am. That wasn't my office. But I had to come over here for a couple of meetings, as well as doing my stint at the Palace.' He shot her a glance that, surprisingly, looked worried. 'Still mad?'

'It's complicated,' she replied. 'Probably not quite as mad as I was this morning.'

'I thought I saw a friendly gleam in your eye.'

'I shot down a detective inspector's case in flames – well, sort of.'

He smiled. 'Go on.'

'It's quite simple. I rang a friend of James's, Neil Macpherson, to find out what was happening with this business of Kimberley Devlin. He said they'd made an arrest, a man by the name of Jimmy Barr who, to cut a very long story short, has a history of making a nuisance of himself. Kimberley had already reported him to the police. He wrote her what amounts to a threatening letter. His car has a dented wing and there was heather and mud and stuff all over his shoes and on the interior of his car. He utterly denies knocking her down.'

'And?'

'I asked Macpherson what variety of heather it was. He laughed at me at first, but when I pointed out that his whole case might hinge on it he went away to look at the report. The report didn't specify, so I suggested he get on to an expert. When I spoke to him later, after one of his team had tracked down a professor of botany, he said that the plant had been identified as *Erica darleyensis*. I know enough about plants – my dad's a bit of a boffin – to be able to tell him that that isn't a heather that grows wild in Scotland. It's a garden hybrid. But he'd already been told by that time, by the professor. That heather's not enough to place Barr at the scene of the crime. I imagine he picked it up blundering through someone's garden. Macpherson still thinks that Barr's his man – he's getting his team to try to trace men in a pub where Barr said he was that night.'

'We'll ignore Barr for the moment and concentrate on persons unknown. And Capelli. He *is* bad news. He has associates in the Mafia. Worse, he dabbles in dodgy arms dealing and that's why we've got him on our computer.'

'His agency's a front, then.'

'Actually, it seems perfectly genuine. He has quite a few famous names on his books. But that gives him a valid reason for world travel, doesn't it? I've an idea that his commission pays the air fares to meetings for all sorts of illegal deals. One assumes that his musical clients are in total ignorance of his other interests.'

'Are you out to get him?'

He laughed outright. 'Good Lord, you make me sound like James Bond! He's innocent till proven guilty, but if he's selling weapons to lunatics who might use them on the British mainland, I want to know about it.'

'He runs holiday trips for Americans to the Highlands. All very innocuous. Apparently.'

'I'd be *very* interested in hearing about those.'

'At a place called Castle Stalker. I've never heard of it, but Macpherson said that that's where James might have gone.'

'What else did the good inspector say before you singed his beard?'

'Not a lot. But Kimberley Devlin gives song recitals for the guests.'

'Joanna, I simply can't believe that James has shot off to some Scottish castle because he's fallen madly in love. He just isn't like that. It's far more likely that he wants to keep an eye on Capelli. Our records show that his brother-in-law has set up his own little outfit in Bristol. James must be aware of that.'

'Time will tell,' Joanna said. 'Macpherson finished by saying that Kimberley Devlin has discharged herself from hospital and left for destinations unknown. She might be determined to fulfil her engagement to sing at the castle this weekend.'

'*This* weekend?'

'According to Macpherson.'

Their tea arrived. When the waitress had gone Joanna discovered that her prospective employer was smiling upon her gently.

'For your first assignment . . .' he began. He broke off, the smile becoming a grin.

'Don't you dare,' Joanna protested.

'Call it – an assessment mission,' he responded, calmly pouring tea.

'But I don't even know where it is. And neither does Macpherson.'

'You used to be a detective sergeant,' he pointed out cruelly.

'And how come you had a photo of me to put on this?' she enquired, tapping the pass pinned to her jacket.

'Like a boy scout, I'm always prepared,' he said, beaming in seraphic fashion. 'Do you know, I've always yearned to hail from the American mid-West. Shelvoke Dempster the Third. How about that?'

'It's a dustcart,' Joanna remarked.

'So it is. What a shame. But look, if you find out where this castle is pretty smartly, I might . . .'

'It's Thursday today. I think the visitors arrive tomorrow night.'

'Then you'd better get a move on.'

'But you can't just *gatecrash*!'

'Watch me,' he whispered succinctly.

He had just had time to do a little research since he had

seen Joanna that morning and was fully aware of Kimberley Devlin's destination. All in all, there seemed to be plenty of reasons why a man in charge should show personal interest in a case. And Scotland was wonderful at this time of year . . .

Chapter Six

The invitation to dinner – it was more like a summons – was delivered by hand during the early evening to the small hotel where Carrick was staying. He quickly penned an acceptance and went down to reception where the messenger, a young woman clad in bike leathers, was waiting. Without a word she took it from him and exited; moments later there was the roar of a powerful motorbike starting up.

'She's the head gardener's daughter,' said the hotel proprietor, in response to Carrick's questioning look. 'Lord Muirshire's Girl Friday.'

Carrick considered the comfortable cord trousers and matching sweater in which he had decided to spend the evening. Dress informal, the invitation had intimated: that meant his kilt, shirt and tie and his other sweater.

'I'll have a bottle of your best single malt,' he said.

'He actually prefers a blend – Old Lodge,' the hotel keeper said, grinning. 'I'll ask the wife to put a bit of paper round it for you.'

Thus armed, Carrick presented himself at the appointed hour: seven thirty. Several cars were parked near the main door; clearly there were other guests. The girl who had brought the invitation answered Carrick's ring at the door, this time wearing an elegant black dress. With quiet aloof efficiency she conducted him across a vast entrance hall and up a magnificent curving staircase to a room on the first floor.

The room was small and cosy – by castle standards – but Carrick had no time to examine it closely just then, for the Marquess came forward to greet him.

'I know who you are, because Andrew told me, so allow me to introduce you to everyone else,' said his host.

That was all. No explanation as to why the company of a virtual stranger had been requested.

Andrew Kennedy was the first person they came upon; as Carrick knew he had Kennedy to thank for the evening's hospitality he gave him as friendly a smile as he could manage. They were, after all, claymores notwithstanding, almost kinsmen, he reminded himself.

There were two women present: the local minister's wife, Mrs Hilda Smillie, who wrung his hand enthusiastically and explained that her husband, referred to indulgently as 'poor wee Archie', was laid low with a heavy cold; and Flora MacDougal, a tall, angular woman who bore a strong resemblance to the Wicked Queen in Disney's *Snow White*. Apparently, she wrote historical novels. This much only Carrick learned before coming face to face with a man who had been standing on his own near the fireplace.

Tony Capelli.

Carrick's heart missed a beat as he waited with dread to be introduced as 'a policeman on holiday', any chance of future surveillance at the castle blown to the four winds for ever.

'This is James Carrick,' Lord Muirshire was saying. 'I knew his father, so was delighted to find him travelling through the area.'

'My pleasure,' murmured the Italian politely. He was a plumply dapper little man with smooth brown hair, which looked as if it had been painted on. 'Carrick – is that a local name?'

'Ayrshire,' boomed the Marquess before Carrick could muster his wits. 'Burns country. Have you read our exalted national poet?'

'Alas, no,' said a silky-toned Capelli. 'But one day, when I have more time, I intend to acquaint myself with the British classics.'

'Well, I don't know that he's quite *that*,' the Marquess muttered, a firm grip on Carrick's elbow. 'Come, James – let me introduce you to Fergus Weir, who breeds the finest gundogs in the world.' And Carrick, who hoped that the set of his jaw resembled a smile, was abandoned to the dog breeder and

65

found himself discussing the merits of brown labradors, a subject about which he knew very little.

Carrick wondered who would bring up the subject of Kimberley Devlin. Predictably, it was the Marquess who did so as they were going into dinner – a short walk back down the stairs and into a room to the right of the front door. Leading the way, he stopped as he reached the bottom of the stairs and addressed them as a headmaster might his pupils.

'I'm sure you've all heard that Miss Devlin has been knocked down by a car. She should have been with us tonight – she was to have entertained our American visitors this week-end. I understand that she's not badly hurt and can only pray that she makes a quick and complete recovery. Please have her in your thoughts this evening.'

'I have good news,' Capelli said quietly. 'I telephoned the hospital on my way here and was told that she had left and plans to be with us after all. But not,' he continued when the exclamations of relief had subsided, 'to sing, I think. She is much shocked and upset.' Darkly, he added, 'The police do not think it was an accident.'

'Have they made an arrest?' Carrick asked.

'Apparently so, but the doctor I spoke to said that the man was released due to lack of evidence. The policeman in charge of the case did not want her to leave the area but when she said that she would hire a bodyguard he gave his permission. This she has done. He – this bodyguard – will bring her here, tomorrow.'

Carrick hoped fervently that the minder was not all brawn and no brain. Less altruistically, he was glad to see that Capelli had been seated next to the Wicked Queen at dinner and that she was proceeding to tell him all about her latest novel which was set, he gathered, in medieval Kilwinning.

'Don't you thank the good Lord every day that you weren't born into a time before bathrooms were invented?' Carrick's neighbour, a latecomer, said wryly.

'Yes,' Carrick said. 'And in the days of decent roads, unadulterated food and drinkable whisky.'

The man chuckled. 'Talking of food, it'll be venison for sure. Himself always gets a few people in when the herd in the park needs thinning out. The deer are quite tame – he hates having to shoot them. But you can't just leave all the bucks to breed.'

'No doubt they come in handy for the banquets too.'

'Oh, yes. There'll be a haunch or two over the weekend. Personally, the way Agnes cooks it I could eat it every day.'

He was quite right; the meal was a triumph, the huge joint of venison carved at the table by their host and each plate heaped with home-grown vegetables of the diner's choice. As the Marquess said, 'Gets cold if you have everything in dishes spread all over the table – people *will* talk instead of passing them round.' This was followed by an apple pie of similar proportions to the roast and, for those with a few nooks and crannies still to fill, locally made cream cheese with oat biscuits. Coffee was then served next door in the library.

'I understand that you're to assist this weekend as a steward,' Capelli said to Carrick as they sipped their coffee.

'It hasn't actually been confirmed,' Carrick said carefully. He smoothed the hair on the back of his neck to check if it really had stood on end. And hadn't Kimberley said that Capelli was in France?

Capelli nodded briskly. 'It must have slipped the Marquess's mind. He mentioned it to me earlier.'

Carrick did not have long to wait. He was drawn aside as the other guests were making moves to depart.

'Stay,' said Lord Muirshire in an undertone. 'There's going to be a short meeting to discuss arrangements for the weekend.' He gazed at Carrick earnestly. 'I mean, it's what you want, isn't it?'

'Yes,' Carrick said. 'And thanks for not letting the cat out of the bag.'

'I spoke the truth. I did know your father.' He patted Carrick's arm. 'We'll speak later.'

The meeting was a small one, those present being the Marquess, Andrew Kennedy, Capelli, Carrick and his neighbour at dinner, know to everyone as Hutch, who co-ordinated the evening events behind the scenes, though he worked during the week as a landscape designer.

Carrick had established from Kennedy in the twenty minutes after the last guest left and the meeting began that Capelli had a chauffeur, Luigi, a man of surly mien who spoke little

English and had been seen by Agnes cleaning his nails with the point of a flick knife. She had immediately banished him from her spotless kitchen with a shrill broadside of Gaelic and the man was forced to wait for his employer in a rear lobby where overcoats and wet dogs were left to dry. It hadn't improved his temper, by all accounts.

Capelli seemed to be anxious to leave. He was not staying at the castle that night as he had an appointment elsewhere the following morning. He kept glancing at his watch while the Marquess satisfied himself that his guests were happy and had all they wanted.

'All going smoothly, I hope,' Lord Muirshire said to him. 'Have you found someone to replace Miss Devlin this weekend?'

'It is very short notice,' Capelli replied. 'But there is time yet. I might be able to get a young artiste from Glasgow. I have also asked the lady writer here tonight if she would like to attend. She tells me she has enjoyed huge success in the States.'

Kennedy groaned. 'Did she also tell you that she's a huge bore?'

'Culture is what we promise,' Capelli said, his voice edgy. 'And she is a woman of culture. In the circumstances—'

'Absolutely,' the Marquess soothed. 'Beggars can't be choosers.'

Capelli responded to this double-edged comment with a very small smile and continued. 'Even now, the guests are boarding the train at Euston. They will travel overnight and spend a morning in Edinburgh before rejoining the train for Inverness. I have confirmed arrangements with the caterers and they will be here at the usual time. The menu has been agreed. I trust that you have asked for flowers, groceries and sundries to be delivered as usual.'

Carrick had discovered that the castle staff provided breakfasts and packed lunches while the catering firm from Inverness cooked the more elaborate evening meals. Wives, girlfriends, sisters and mothers of estate workers were roped in to help wash up and wait at table as well as acting as chambermaids for the duration.

The Marquess turned to him. 'I've been increasingly worried about security since a passing back-packer wandered in and

68

took a look around. We've never had locks on the bedroom doors. James, I was wondering if you'd organise yourself and the head forester's two boys into some kind of patrol?'

'Excuse me, but has Mr Carrick experience of this kind of thing?' Capelli said. 'Would it not be more sensible to call in a professional security adviser?'

'There probably isn't time to do that as far as this weekend's concerned,' Carrick said smoothly. 'I'm sure it's only a matter of common sense. But I'll need more people to do the job properly.'

'There's young Hamish,' the Marquess offered. 'And Jim Logan's brother. I'll ask them. Give them a tenner and a bite of supper for their trouble.'

'And don't worry,' Capelli said directly to Carrick, 'I intend to test the efficiency of this minder Kimberley has hired. Perhaps Luigi could help me? When people's lives are at stake, one can't be too careful.'

'Quite,' Carrick said.

'And now I must depart,' said Capelli. He gave the Marquess a formal bow. 'Lord Muirshire, many thanks. I shall return tomorrow evening, if I may, to greet Miss Devlin. Until then, business calls.' Fleetingly, he glanced at those present. 'Let us hope there are no more – unfortunate occurrences.'

'That guy gives me the shivers,' Kennedy said as the door closed behind him. 'He's as nice as pie for most of the time, and then he gives you a look that reminds you of a rattlesnake after a rabbit.'

'Have there been any *other* unfortunate occurrences?' Carrick asked innocently.

'Not to my knowledge,' Lord Muirshire answered.

'One of the Americans was taken ill last time,' Hutch said thoughtfully. 'Don't you remember? That bloke who was travelling on his own. Capelli had him carted off to hospital.'

'Suspected appendicitis,' the Marquess said.

'Did you call a doctor?' Carrick enquired.

'God, yes, the man was in agony.'

'Has anything else like that happened?'

The Marquess and Kennedy looked at one another. 'I seem to remember that last year another guest had to leave in a hurry because his mother had died in London,' Kennedy said. 'He'd travelled over here with her and left her with his sister down south.'

'So presumably neither of these men rejoined the tour,' Carrick said.

'Not here,' Lord Muirshire said, shaking his head.

'Any other odd incidents?'

Kennedy smiled broadly. 'Only the couple who left in a huff! This year, from the first party. Nothing was right for them – they never stopped complaining.'

'Capelli said he'd given them their money back,' said the Marquess. 'He reckoned that's all they wanted. Glad to get rid of them, frankly. A most unpleasant pair.'

'Husband and wife?' Carrick wanted to know.

'They *said* they were. Hardly domestic bliss, though. When they weren't complaining they were at each other's throats. In public, too.'

'Why are you asking?' Hutch said. 'Do you think there's any connection between that and what happened to Miss Devlin?'

'Take no notice of me,' Carrick hastened to say. 'I just have an enquiring mind.'

It was now almost midnight and Kennedy and Hutch left, Kennedy reminding Carrick that the following day would be a long one. Carrick, who had left the gift of whisky in his car, also rose to his feet, meaning to fetch it.

'I should have guessed you were Bob's son as soon as I saw you,' Lord Muirshire said. 'You look uncannily like him. Is that what really brought you here – the fact that he used to come here too?'

Carrick was stunned. 'No! I mean – I didn't know he was ever here.'

'We were close friends. I was on the yacht when he went overboard.'

Carrick sat down again. He didn't trust himself to speak.

'We searched for him for two hours but he didn't stand a chance in that water. He'd have been dead in five minutes.'

'He was never found.'

'I'm not surprised. The currents and rip tides in that area are killers. Look, James . . . I want you to know that he wasn't a complete bastard. He was a fool where women were

70

concerned, and that was that. Another thing – he was thinking of leaving his wife for your mother. He said he was really in love with her. And he desperately wanted children – his wife couldn't have any.'

'Thank you,' Carrick said after a long silence had elapsed. 'I must just –' He left the room and walked in a daze through the entrance hall and out of the front door to his car. He felt he needed a few moments alone. He sat in the driver's seat, for a minute or two, his vision dimmed by tears for the father he had never known. Then he retrieved the bottle of Old Lodge and walked back inside, to where the Marquess stood waiting for him.

'I'm extremely grateful to you, Lord Muirshire,' Carrick said. 'For much more than a splendid evening.'

'I would be happy if you'd regard this as your second home,' Lord Muirshire said, as they shook hands. 'Robert Kennedy was a *very* good friend of mine.'

After a sleep as slept by infants – he had gone to bed at peace with the world – Carrick went down to breakfast at the hotel the next morning to discover that another guest had arrived.

'Joanna!'

She glanced up from half a grapefruit. 'Why, James. Fancy meeting you here.'

He sat down abruptly. 'Don't "why, James" me. What the hell are you doing here?'

Unruffled, she carried on with her breakfast. 'This is my first mission for MI5. Don't crowd me, you're almost in the cruet.'

He shoved it out of the way. 'Macpherson didn't know where Castle Stalker was!'

'No, but I'm a t'riffic sleuth.'

Carrick breathed out hard.

'It was easy,' Joanna said. 'Inverness is regarded as the capital of the Highlands, so I flew up from London. It was just like in the song – I asked a policeman.'

'You asked . . .' Words failed him.

'*Everyone* round here knows about the American trips, it seems. I got a taxi out here and as there's just the one hotel nearby . . . Are you going to have your breakfast at this table

71

or the one with your room number on it? If the former, you can't put it on my bill. I'm on expenses and Patrick wouldn't like it.'

'It depends whether you want me to be rude to you from here or shout abuse across the room.' He then outlined, very briefly, what had transpired.

'I hope I haven't screwed it up for you without meaning to,' she said when he had finished speaking.

'How, for God's sake?'

'Patrick's going to gatecrash.'

'What?' he shouted.

'Keep your voice down. Yes, I'm afraid he must be in one of his irresponsible phases. I had quite a chat with Ingrid last time we met and she said he once swopped places with one of his men on a mission to Canada and almost wrecked the whole thing by masquerading as – what as the phrase she used? – "an obscene gnome-like gardener". He got a hell of a carpeting from his boss over it.'

'Just explain to me how a strapping senior army officer over six feet tall can masquerade as an obscene gnome-like anything.'

'You mustn't scoff. Ingrid told me, and she should know. She said he frightened the living daylights out of her. *We've* never seen him in action – he wasn't pretending to be someone else when he rescued you last winter. He's going to gatecrash, all right. As an American, perhaps. He said he'd call himself Shelvoke Dempster the Third until I reminded him that it's a make of dustcart.'

Carrick took several deep breaths. 'I think he was winding you up.'

'I'm sure he meant every word of it.' A faraway look came into Joanna's eyes. 'I can just picture it: gold-plated bagpipes, a kilt made of lurid Hollywood tartan, cigars a foot long – straight out of vaudeville.'

'Now you're trying to wind *me* up.' But Carrick had a terrible feeling she wasn't.

Chapter Seven

It was mid-afternoon on Friday when the woman who lived in the flat beneath Jimmy Barr's visited a friend on the second floor and, in passing noticed that Barr had not taken in his milk that day. Aware that he was a creature of habit and that the milkman normally came very early – around six in the morning, before Barr left for work – she immediately started to worry. Not that she held Barr in any great regard. In fact, she found him repulsive, and if she met him in the communal entrance she tended to hurry past with a muttered greeting. Jean Dunlop worried because she was a worrier by nature. She went out into the street and looked up at the first-floor windows. The curtains were still closed.

Barr had been in trouble with the police in the past, everyone in the neighbourhood knew that. For a while Jean agonised, then went back up the stairs and rang his bell. All was silent within. She rang again: still no reply. It was pointless, she knew, to confer with her friend above; that lady was elderly, nervous and likely to contribute no more than a display of hand-wringing. No, Jean would fetch Wullie.

Wullie lived in the next block and was of sensible and decisive nature. She fetched him and Wullie, ever-practical, tried the door. It was not locked. What Wullie found in Barr's bedroom caused him to phone for the police and for an ambulance, in that order. Then he made Jean a large pot of tea. Afterwards, when he had made a short statement to the police, he went home and was just in time to catch the end of the football on TV.

*

There were three words scrawled in the thick dust on the dressing table in Barr's bedroom: I DID IT. The letters were irregularly formed, as if the person executing them had been drunk or ill, the crossing of the final T a wavering line in the dust that went right off the edge of the dressing table.

'Suicide,' Macpherson said, wrinkling his nose because of the stench. His gaze went to the dressing table. 'I think it got to him, that he'd knocked down the Devlin woman. But I'm sure he never meant to hurt her.'

'If *he* wrote that,' Kerr said quietly.

'You think he was *murdered*?' Macpherson said incredulously. 'Who, in God's name, would want to kill *him*?'

They found themselves staring with something close to pity at the still form on the bed. Barr was fully clothed and lying face-up, eyes wide open, his mouth caked with vomit. On the bedside table was an opened bottle of whisky, half full, and a plastic container that had, according to the label, held sleeping tablets. It was now empty.

'The forensic evidence—' Kerr began.

'I know, I know,' Macpherson interrupted testily. 'Did you notice the wee garden as we came in? Heather plants. I want you to take a few samples and give them to SOCO when they get here. I bet they'll find that that variety of heather is the same as was in Barr's shoes and in the car. No doubt he blundered through them when he was drunk one night. He was up at Mosslaw all right, I'm convinced of it. Come on – we'll talk to the neighbours.'

Jean Dunlop was with her nervous friend from the second floor, just about to make another pot of tea. It seemed the logical thing to do after the short journey up the stairs to tell her friend what had happened. Upon seeing that they had visitors, she put some more water in the kettle.

'No, I heard nothing last night,' she said in response to Macpherson's question. 'He was as quiet as a mouse. Used to give everyone the horrors, the way he crept about.'

'So you didn't hear any visitors go to his door?' Kerr enquired.

She shook her head. 'No, but I have the telly on quite loud. So I can't hear the couple across the way shouting at one another. They're both out at work,' she added, as Kerr made a move to the door. 'And it's no use you asking Morag here, she takes a sleeping pill at nine and goes to bed and it would take a third world war to wake her.'

'Have you any idea what time he came home?' Macpherson asked.

'No. I never heard him and never wanted to. I tried not to think about him at all.'

'The same goes for me,' muttered Morag, making her one and only contribution to the investigation.

There was the sound of tramping feet on the stairs; Macpherson and Kerr departed, turning down the offer of tea. They returned to the flat below to discover that SOCO had arrived together with the pathologist, Cameron McFee. McFee hated having people breathing down his neck so the policemen, on Macpherson's instructions, waited in the living room while he examined the body.

'Been dead for *about* twelve hours,' McFee reported when he emerged. 'Ten to twelve – I'll be able to tell you more when I've done the PM. There's one odd thing, though. He'd vomited small pieces of what could be some of the tablets. I've never come across anyone who *chewed* them before.' And he swept out.

'With Barr I'd believe anything possible,' Macpherson commented sourly. 'Well, what are you waiting for?' he thundered. 'Get on with it!'

It was purely routine. Samples were taken; the flat was a rich source of extraneous matter of all kinds. There were what appeared to be decades of fingerprints, mostly of the deceased; the edges and the frames of doorways were grimy with dirt where Barr had groped his way around his home in an alcoholic haze.

' Probably bloody thousands of people have been in here,' Kerr said with a dispirited shrug. 'Everyone who's been to mend fuses, dripping taps and God alone knows what else ever since he moved in.' He went into the kitchen where Macpherson stood looking depressed. 'Do you think we ought to get a handwriting expert in to look at the so-called confession, sir?' he asked.

'Have you found a sample of Barr's printing?' Macpherson demanded to know.

'No, but I expect—'

'Never expect,' Macpherson said. 'You won't find anything. When did you last print anything out – at school?'

But they did. A pathetic little shopping list: TEA, BREAD and MARGARINE, very neatly printed on a little notepad with roses on the cover. Kerr, gravely, put it into a sample bag.

'What I should do next,' Macpherson said an hour later, after every inch of the flat had been stripped of its secrets, 'is go and see that couple Miss Devlin mentioned. The Grahams. I must say that it slipped my mind. But I'm not attaching too much importance to the fact that Miss Devlin admits to having an affair with the husband.'

'Why's that, sir?' Kerr asked.

'Because it's all over, man, that's why! Over and done with. Why should the wife take it into her head to attack Miss Devlin *now*? No, I'm still sticking to my theory that Barr knocked her down. But I need to tidy up the loose ends.' He glanced at his watch and realised that he had promised to be back at the nick for yet another progress assessment meeting – or was it target assessment? – half an hour ago. 'You know how it goes,' he said as he wearily went back to the car. 'Every lead, no matter how vague and time-wasting, has to be followed up. One other thing – and this is important – I want no word that Barr was a suspect in the Devlin case to get out to the media. Is that clear?'

Kerr gave him an odd look. 'That rather contradicts what you've just said, sir.'

'Sometimes loose ends turn round and bite you,' Macpherson said.

Sarah Graham was out at work but Philip was at home, listlessly picking out a tune on the piano. There was a glass of white wine in front of him but when he heard the doorbell ring he quickly picked it up and hid it in a cupboard in an alcove on one side of the fireplace. Then, first carefully brushing his hair off his face with his hands, he opened the front door. His disappointment upon perceiving his somewhat lumpish visitors was almost tangible.

Macpherson introduced Kerr and himself and requested that they might enter.

'Nothing's happened to my family, I hope,' Philip said quickly.

'No, sir. We'd just like to have a little chat about Miss Devlin,' Macpherson purred. He had immediately changed tactics when it became obvious that the wife was not at home.

'You'd better come in,' Philip said grudgingly. He led the way into the sitting room but did not ask them to be seated and all three stood around awkwardly until Macpherson took the initiative, pulled forward a chair and sat down. Kerr and Philip Graham lowered themselves on to the sofa and there was a short silence.

'You're aware of what happened on Monday night to Miss Devlin,' Macpherson began by saying.

'Of course,' Philip said. 'I read about it in the papers.'

'She didn't contact you?'

'No. That would have been – difficult. She would have worried that Sarah would answer the phone.' He cleared his throat carefully and continued. 'You must understand, the relationship I have with Miss Devlin now is purely a professional one.'

'And for how long was it *un*professional?' the inspector inquired.

Graham's pale cheeks coloured. 'Six months. But I really don't see why—'

'I need to ask such questions?' Macpherson said. 'Well, you see, Mr Graham, policemen always ask questions in cases of serious assault. Where were you on Monday night?'

'Here.'

'All evening?'

'I stayed in until about eight thirty but then went out for some fresh air. It was very humid and I had a headache. I thought of going for a drive in the country, then remembered that my car was almost out of petrol. I had no cash on me and couldn't be bothered to go into the city centre to find a cash machine so I borrowed Sarah's car and went for a bite of supper at the Nolan Hotel.'

His alibi sounded polished, fluent – as if he had rehearsed it in advance, Macpherson decided.

'Why not stick to your original plan and go for the drive?'

'The car had a slow puncture. That's why Sarah hadn't

taken it to work earlier. She'd gone by bus. I had to call in at the local garage to put some air in it.'

'Why not change the wheel?' Kerr asked. He was a practical man.

'The – er – spare was flat too.'

'You could have bought petrol with a credit card,' Macpherson pointed out.

Philip looked sheepish. 'We're trying to keep expenses down,' he said. 'I haven't worked much since I was injured in a plane crash.'

'I'm sorry to hear that,' Macpherson said. 'So have you had the punctures fixed now?'

'Yes.'

'At your local garage?'

Graham nodded. 'There'll be a receipt for the work somewhere.'

Why was he so anxious to justify himself? Macpherson wondered.

'Did your wife stay in that evening?'

'No. She was still out when I got back, at about ten.'

'Do you know where she was?'

'Sarah has her own business and is often out with clients. It's a design consultancy so she visits people's homes quite a lot.'

'But she didn't have any transport that night, did she?' Kerr said triumphantly. 'You had her car.'

'Someone collected her.'

'What colour is the car?' Macpherson asked.

'Mine or hers?'

'Both of them.'

'Sarah's is a white Rover 600. Mine is dark blue – Metro.'

'Let's get this straight. Was your wife in or out when you left at eight thirty?'

'She was out.' He was silent for a moment and then blurted out, '*She* told you all this? Kim, I mean. About us? She thinks *I* did it?'

Macpherson chose his words carefully. 'I asked Miss Devlin if anyone had been threatening her. No doubt you are aware that your wife sent her a dead bird through the post.'

78

Philip Graham registered shock. 'No, of course I didn't know . . . A *dead bird*! Good God!'

'Miss Devlin likes birds,' Macpherson went on. 'That made it worse.'

'When was this?'

'Last year, I believe. When you were still seeing one another. Tell me, Mr Graham, have you been in Miss Devlin's company recently?'

'Yes, we had lunch together about two weeks ago. But it was only to talk about the music I'm writing for – *surely* you don't think that Sarah—' He broke off again: this time because the front door had slammed.

'Would this be her?' Macpherson asked, noting the hunted look that had come into Graham's eyes.

'It might be my son, Jeremy,' Graham mumbled. 'I'll go and see.'

When Graham had gone from the room Kerr whispered, 'Do we *know* that it was Mrs Graham who sent the bird?'

Macpherson got to his feet to examine the framed photographs on the mantelpiece. 'According to Miss Devlin there was a note with it. And she followed up the parcel with a phone call warning that other unpleasantness might follow. So we're reasonably sure, unless of course Miss Devlin is lying and trying to land an old enemy in trouble. But what would be the motive? She doesn't seem to be that kind of woman.'

'He's no great catch, is he? I can't imagine a woman getting so stirred up about losing him that she'd go to such lengths. Mrs Graham'd probably be a lot better off without him.'

'Perhaps she's possessive,' Macpherson said, 'but we'll soon see,' he added as the door opened and both the Grahams entered.

Sarah Graham was furiously angry. 'So,' she said, glaring at Kerr who lumbered to his feet, 'she's got you on to us, has she? I was wondering why I hadn't had a visit from the police yet. I suppose she told you all about how I mowed her down with my car and then lugged her off and threw her in a hole. In the dark, too! But of course I eat plenty of carrots, and I go weight-training, so it's all in a day's work as far as I'm concerned.' She dropped into an armchair and surveyed them scornfully.

79

'Miss Devlin has made no such allegations, Mrs Graham,' Macpherson said gravely.

'I'm pleased to hear it. Why the hell are you here, then?'

'It seems that you once made certain threats to Miss Devlin.'

'I wanted her to leave Philip alone. She has done. End of story.'

'Where were you last Monday night?'

'With a client. At his house, at Drymond.'

The inspector produced a notebook. 'Name?'

'I thought you said the woman hadn't accused me of anything!'

'She hasn't. This is normal procedure.'

'His name's Simon Adams. He's bought a house that the previous owners just about ruined internally and he wants to restore it to what it was when it was built. It's old – around two hundred and fifty years old. Does that answer your question?'

'Address?' Macpherson went on inexorably.

She gave it to him and then said, 'He picked me up, I was at the house for practically all the evening and then he brought me back home. My own car had a puncture and I'm not married to a man who can fix things like that.'

Since mention of the client's name Philip had stared at his wife stonily but he did not say anything, not even when Macpherson asked what time she had got home.

'It was pretty late – I didn't look at the clock.'

'And you went nowhere near Mosslaw Country Park.'

'That's where it happened? No, of course not.'

After slipping his notebook back into his pocket Macpherson said, 'I'd like you to stay in the area. Both of you. I may have more questions to ask.'

'So I'm to post my completed ballad for Miss Devlin as though it's a football pools coupon?' Philip said stiffly.

Macpherson knew where the victim was planning to go and that she had hired herself a protector. 'She won't be at home, Mr Graham.'

'I'm fully aware of where she'll be. The recitals for the American tourists are hardly a secret between professional musicians.'

'So you wish to give it to her personally,' Macpherson said. 'At Castle Stalker.'

'That was what we agreed,' the composer replied, drawing himself up to his modest height. 'How can I convince her of its merits if I'm unable to play it to her?'

Whether it was because the hostile looks Graham was receiving from his spouse engendered in Macpherson some sort of fellow-feeling, or that his normal caution was over-ridden by weariness, the result was the same; he gave his permission. He then departed, aware that he had left a sizeable storm in his wake.

'*Simon Adams*!' Philip spat at his wife when she returned from showing their unwelcome visitors out. 'Correct me if I'm wrong, Sarah, but he didn't pay you for the last project you did for him.' When no reply seemed to be forthcoming he yelled, 'Or *did* he? He pays the bills in bed, is that it?'

'Sometimes, Philip, you think too much,' Sarah said venomously. 'I shouldn't if I were you – it's not good for your health.'

'And there's the matter of his car,' Philip continued triumphantly. 'A silver-coloured Merc? Now there's a coincidence!'

But Sarah had left the room.

Having been receiving a carpeting for non-attendance at the assessment meeting – the full title of which he was still in ignorance – Macpherson was not on hand for the post-mortem on Jimmy Barr. DS Kerr therefore had no choice but to stand in for him. Post-mortems were nobody's favourite way to spend the afternoon and he emerged from the mortuary, took several deep breaths, found that that did not help much and headed for the nearest pub, where he immediately downed a double of The Macallan. More than aware of the rules concerning drinking on duty he resolved to confess his sin to Macpherson and then realised that in fact his day's work had officially ended an hour and a half previously. However, he should convey to his boss the findings which, to say the least, were interesting.

The inspector, who never seemed to go home, was in his office eating sandwiches with the disinterest that stale corned beef and pickle in even staler bread can create. He was endeavouring to liven his mind with *The Herald* but even this did not make life particularly enchanting and he looked up with relief when Kerr entered.

'Ah,' he said. 'I can tell by the look on your face. There have been developments.'

Kerr sat astride a chair, resting his arms on the back. 'He probably didn't top himself.'

'Go on.'

'There was a *lot* of booze inside him. More than was missing from the bottle on the bedside table. In his blood and in his stomach, with the remains of the pills. McFee reckons they were crushed before he ingested them. And there's bruising to his face.'

Although his conclusions were tumbling like a pack of cards, Macpherson felt a surge of excitement. 'Someone bashed him about and then poured drink and drugs down his throat?'

'The findings can be interpreted that way,' Kerr replied carefully.

'That's nasty,' Macpherson said, rubbing his hands over his face.

'Cause of death was inhalation of vomit.'

'Poor wee bastard.'

Chapter Eight

At precisely 18.16 on Friday evening the train bringing the American visitors drew into Inverness station. There was a small audience of train spotters, for the rolling stock was privately owned and preserved and had been luxuriously fitted out in late Edwardian style. The locomotive, a Class 47 hired from Rail Express Systems, was spared hardly a glance.

The train comprised six carriages; dining car, saloon with bar, galley and staff quarters, and the remaining three consisting of sleeping accommodation and baggage stowage space. All were painted in a rich maroon and gold livery, matching the uniforms of the stewards.

Carrick, who had volunteered to meet the train for reasons other than merely a desire to help, went on to the station concourse and arranged the transfer of luggage to the waiting coach. He had to raise his voice; a piper included in the welcoming part was earning his fee with volume rather than accuracy. It mattered little though; very quickly the man was surrounded by camcorders.

A large lady attired in a horrifying pink and yellow plaid suit button-holed Carrick. 'Say, can you tell me how long it will take to get to the castle? I'm real worn out with all the travel.'

'About twenty-five minutes,' he answered.

'Just a round dozen for you this time,' said one of the stewards to him. 'It just *feels* like more,' was his parting shot.

There was enough baggage for fifty, Carrick thought, commandeering Scotrail luggage trolleys. No sign of gatecrashers, though. Walking back down the train he gave the driver and his mate a hard look but didn't recognise them. There was no time to relax; he rounded up all his charges, who were busily recording the station and its environs for posterity, with the promise that there would be time for photography on another occasion. Everyone had to be delivered to the castle by seven to give time for settling in and changing for dinner, which would be served at eight thirty.

Perhaps, he thought flippantly, he ought to be a travel courier instead of endeavouring to uphold the law. But by the time the piper had played all the way back he had changed his mind.

Carrick already knew that there were only twelve tourists on this occasion – he had obtained a guest list from Andrew Kennedy. There were five married couples, including a Mr and Mrs Folkins from Montreal, and two men travelling alone, one of whom was very elderly. Carrick had made a point of not taking any particular notice of the other, a bearded man who preferred to carry his own luggage.

After breakfast Carrick and Joanna had parted. She had not requested any help from him with regard to access to the castle and he had not offered it. Despite her levity there had been a guardedness in her manner and Carrick was firmly of the opinion that Patrick's decision to send her – and there was no doubt that he had, for why should Joanna not tell the truth? – was a mistake. Carrick fervently hoped that any irresponsibility on Gillard's part did not extend to playing ducks and drakes with his friends' relationships.

'Say, isn't that the *prettiest* castle?' sighed the plaid-encased American lady to her husband as the coach crunched to a standstill on the gravel by the building's austere frontage. 'Do you think the Dook will come to greet us?'

'He's the Marquess of Muirshire, actually,' Carrick said.

She swung round towards him eagerly. 'Gee! Is that better or worse than a dook?'

For the next five minutes he picked his way carefully through the minefield of similar questions as he shepherded them off the coach and indoors. Where the hell were Kennedy and Hutch? This was *their* duty.

'Sorry, sorry, sorry,' murmured the pair, arriving all at once. Kennedy said to Carrick, 'Capelli turned up without notice. He demanded to know all about your security arrangements,

84

so I've been telling him as much of what you told me as I could remember. He's in the library with Himself.'

Carrick swallowed his professional pride. But perhaps he had not made as good a job of it as he thought, for when he entered the large, lofty room, Capelli jumped perceptibly. Before Carrick had even closed the door he was grabbed from behind, a hand in his hair yanking his head back. There was the distinct sensation of sharp steel against the skin of his throat.

Capelli bawled a stream of Italian and Carrick was released instantly, turning to come face to face with Luigi's slab-like face.

'Cretin!' Capelli spat at him. 'I tell you to test the *bodyguard*, not everyone who comes into the room! Get out!'

Somehow, Carrick mastered the urge to kick the knife from the man's hand and lay him out neatly on the Persian carpet. But he was not about to advertise that he had any ability in that direction. Inwardly seething, he forced himself to ignore the chauffeur as he left the room.

'Allow me,' said Capelli, coming forward and proffering a silk handkerchief. 'There is a little blood. My apologies – sometimes Luigi is a fool.'

Carrick refused the handkerchief and used his own.

'You look a bit pale,' the Marquess said to him. 'Have a small bracer. I could do with one myself actually – always get a bit nervous when everyone arrives.' He sloshed whisky into two glasses on a drinks trolley. 'You don't take this, Capelli, do you?'

'A little wine with dinner is ample, thank you.'

'I understand that you were asking about security,' Carrick said. He was still holding the handkerchief to his neck; the flow of blood was sufficient to threaten the cleanliness of his collar. 'First of all, I insist that you give me an undertaking that that knife-happy moron will be kept on a lead.'

'He will take no part in what you have arranged,' Capelli replied. 'But you must understand that he protects me – and, if the bodyguard she has hired proves to be unsuitable, Miss Devlin also.'

'This is my home,' Lord Muirshire said quietly but forcefully. 'And if the entire venture turns into some kind of—'

He was interrupted. 'Nothing will spoil it,' Capelli said. 'Please – trust me.'

Carrick, in receipt of his drink and a quizzical look from the Marquess, said, 'This building is far too large to arrange security patrols outside with the small number of people available. So really we're talking about keeping a careful eye on entrances and exits, as well as surveillance in the accommodation areas. Exterior doors not in general use are being locked for the duration of the weekend and at all times a member of staff will be stationed at those which are until they are locked for the night. Our visitors have already been issued with tour passes which they have been requested to wear at all times attached to a lapel with the pin provided. With Andrew Kennedy's help I've made passes of a different colour and these will be given to the outside catering staff and all *bona fide* helpers. It's a little rough and ready – as you really need to have photographs of the person concerned on each pass – but in the time available it was the best I could do. Anyone without such a pass will be asked for credentials. When the guests are not in their rooms there will be patrols. Discreetly done – there's no point in worrying people.'

'Thank you,' said Lord Muirshire. 'That puts my mind at rest. Should have done something about it before now.'

'I am content,' Capelli said, and took his leave.

'Damned if I am,' said Lord Muirshire. 'It makes me want to call the whole thing off. There was no excuse at all for that thug to attack you.'

Carrick's neck had stopped bleeding and he put away his handkerchief. 'He must have been ordered to – to see how I reacted.'

The other was still looking extremely uneasy. 'Look, James, Andrew has been feeling rather unhappy about Capelli for some time and I must admit he's not to my liking either. Do you know of anything against him?'

'He has some – unpleasant associates. But there's nothing to show that his musicians' agency isn't above board and that's the side of him we're dealing with at the moment.'

'Capelli Promotions is what I deal with. I get ten thousand pounds a time for the use of the castle and for shaking a few hands. Money's been tight for a while and it's the only reason I put up with him.'

'It's generous.' *Very* generous, Carrick thought.

'*Do* you think there's something going on? In an unguarded moment Kimberley once said that she was scared of the man – but she wouldn't say why.'

'I'm fairly sure there is, but what, is anyone's guess. It looks as though this is going to be a busman's holiday after all.'

'Can't you call in some of your colleagues from Inverness?'

'Not without blowing the whole thing wide open. We need evidence first.'

'But suppose Miss Devlin got wind of something and Capelli tried to silence her? She's arriving any time now.'

'Just put your hope in a bloody good bodyguard and—'

'James, he's ordered that baboon of his to "try the man out"—'

Carrick, standing near the window, looked out when he heard tyres on the gravel. And Lord Muirshire, watching him, saw his lips move in an inaudible exclamation. Looking out himself he perceived nothing that might have brought this about until Kimberley Devlin was helped from the car.

'She's here,' he said anxiously.

But Carrick wasn't looking at the woman. He had eyes only for the man assisting her. He found himself wondering where, if they had Luigi stuffed and mounted, he could be displayed to best advantage.

'I beg your pardon?' said Lord Muirshire.

'I'm sorry, I hadn't realised I'd spoken aloud,' Carrick said, and swiftly excused himself.

'Fairly representative,' Hutch commented. 'The sort of people we usually get.'

He and Carrick were standing at the bottom of the grand staircase waiting to usher the guests in to dinner. Carrick had had to make a lightning dash into Inverness earlier in the day to hire a Prince Charlie coatee and bow tie as he had not brought evening wear with him. He had packed his best kilt, however, and the rest passed muster.

'You've got yourself rail-roaded into helping by being around,' Hutch continued. 'Just like I did, last year. Ah, there she is – the light of my life. Poochie MacTavish. I reckon that if we'd fielded her in that dress and left Wallace at home the British parliament would be in Edinburgh instead of London.'

'And I'm a fan of Kimberley Devlin,' Carrick said, beholding the large lady of the pink and yellow plaid suit, who was now wearing a similarly colourful purple gown sporting emerald-green polka dots at least two inches in diameter.

'Ah, so *that*'s it. You realise you'll run into trouble with Andy in that direction?'

'I reckon we'll all keep our distance with her minder around.'

'*Minder*? James, *that* is an escort. Have you seen him? He looks like a one-time Guards officer who's never wielded anything more dangerous than a cricket bat.'

Mrs MacTavish was sweeping down the stairs towards them, her husband bringing up the rear. 'Am I first?' she called. 'I'd rather not be.'

'A tenner on the minder being what he's supposed to be,' Carrick said softly.

'Fifty!'

'Done.'

'Madam, you are first and foremost,' Hutch said in ringing tones. 'A beacon for your compatriots, if not your nation.'

'My, I do like the way you Scots talk!' she said, all smiles and dimples.

They all came down then: Lucy and Gene Cameron, Stefanie and Buck Murdo, Lea and Ricardo Folkins, Benjamin Rialto, the elderly man travelling alone, and Mamie and John Wilson who had taken it upon themselves to look after him. Mr Rialto did not look particularly pleased about this. Last came Caspar Dean in immaculate evening dress, his lofty manner and somewhat saturnine bearded features ensuring that the others offered no more than polite greetings.

'Which of you is responsible for security?' he asked Carrick and Hutch.

'I am,' Carrick replied.

'Kindly ensure that my room is closely monitored. It is most

88

irregular for there to be no locks on the doors. I have valuable camera equipment.'

'James!' said a voice behind Carrick when Dean had gone.

It was Kimberley Devlin. She was leaning on a stick and looked very pale but was otherwise magnificent: make-up, skilfully applied, concealing the bruising on her face. She was wearing a long, black, beaded skirt topped with a white satin blouse with a high mandarin collar.

As he had done once before, Carrick kissed her cheek.

'This is Patrick,' she said, drawing her bodyguard forward. 'It was one of the conditions of the police allowing me to leave Glasgow – that I hire a protector.'

The minder visibly thought about whether it was protocol to shake hands with castle servants but did so, then flicked some invisible dust off the cuffs of his evening jacket. His grey eyes met Carrick's without a trace of recognition.

Good, Carrick thought. *I'd rather play it like this.*

'I'm sure Lord Muirshire would be *quite* happy for Patrick to join us for dinner,' Kimberley said.

'Suppose you get rid of the stick and lean on me,' Gillard said with a gallant smile and offered an elbow.

'He has an answer for everything,' Kimberley said delightedly. Then, gazing at Hutch, the smile vanished. 'Don't ask me to sing. *Please.*'

'Not tonight,' he promised. And the pair went into the dining room, leaving Carrick clutching Kimberley's walking stick.

The arrangement was that 'senior helpers' would dine with Lord Muirshire after the guests had eaten on Friday and Sunday night, but would swell the numbers on Saturday when the medieval banquet was held. Some estate workers were invited to this too – the general feeling being that if the host had plenty of cooks and even more venison that night he might as well make a real party of it.

Carrick did his rounds, collecting Hamish Sanderson and Greg Logan from the kitchen were they had been having something to eat. He left the latter on watch at a strategic point on the staircase that led to the second floor, the marquess's private rooms, and then seated himself in a chair at one side of a long passageway where most of the guest rooms were situated. Hamish was sent on a roving patrol of the upper corridors.

'Phone call for you,' Andrew Kennedy said, arriving with his mobile.

It was Neil Macpherson.

'Just a quick word,' he said. 'Philip Graham. I went to see him and reluctantly gave him permission to travel up to Castle Stalker to give Miss Devlin the song he's written for her. I hope I haven't complicated things for you. Oh – Barr's dead. Someone knocked him out and then poured whisky and sleeping pills down his throat. It doesn't look as though there's a connection with the Devlin case. Following a tip-off, we've picked up the husband of the woman Barr indecently assaulted a while back, who's always threatened to stop him for good. When *he's* sobered up we might get a confession out of him.'

'So you no longer think Barr knocked Miss Devlin down?'

'I'm keeping an open mind. There was a confession – of sorts – written in the dust on top of a dressing table and a handwriting expert doesn't *think* it was Barr's. Och, James, it's a right muddle. I shall have to take early retirement. Either that, or lose my reason.' He laughed grimly.

'Miss Devlin's arrived safely. With her minder.'

'Good. It was her idea, you know – to get a heavy to look after her.'

'I rather thought it was yours.'

'No. You can't force an innocent person to stay in one place can you?'

'Will you do me a favour?'

'Say away.'

'Run the name Caspar Dean through your computer. He' probably international so probably won't be there. It's prob ably not his real name either.'

'Bit unlikely to get results then,' Macpherson said before he rang off.

'They're just about to start dessert,' Kennedy said, returning from a discreet distance.

Carrick handed him back the phone. 'I could eat a horse!'

'You might get one. Capelli's livid that Kimberley's minde

has been allowed in the dining room. The vibes are that he'll
let Luigi take his revenge when the guy's nice and mellow after
brandy and liqueurs.'

'You were in there? You've seen him drinking?'

'I just passed through. He was already a bit tight, I should
say – mind you, it's an excellent claret. It would tempt a
saint.'

'God help him,' Carrick muttered.

'My thoughts exactly.'

'Andrew, if you see Hutch . . .'

'I will do. Directly.'

'Tell him the bet's off.'

It would have been robbing the man.

The dining room, known as the Red Room and used only
when there were less than twenty for dinner, was furnished in
heavy dark crimson brocade. A much-repeated, but little
believed, story explained the choice; apparently, it had not
shown the bloodstains when the Marquess's ancestors
returned from battle. Hutch was relating this yarn to appropriate gasps when Carrick entered the room, having left Hamish
on guard.

Kimberley Devlin seemed relaxed and smiled broadly when
her escort whispered something in her ear. Her gaze went
across to Capelli who clearly had not believed a word of the
story either. He sat in a dark sulk, his fingers tapping the white
cloth before him.

Poochie – whose real name was Pauline but who forbade
anyone to call her that – leaned across the table to the bodyguard. 'You know, you really don't look like the kind of hunk
we have in the States to protect folk. They always look so
obvious, with their dark glasses and the gun under their jacket.
And the way they shout up their sleeves into a mike! I mean,
it's so ostentatious.'

Hutch grinned from the top of the table. 'The English way is
more Dixon of Dock Green than Arnold Schwarzanegger.'

'Now you betray your age,' Kimberley said, and there was
laughter from the Brits present.

'The powerful, talented woman protected by the sacrificial

91

lamb,' Caspar Dean said. 'It's quite a fantasy, isn't it?'

Gillard chuckled at this depiction of himself and the conversation moved on to the programme for the following day.

Carrick was prepared. Would there be a message that Gillard was wanted on the phone, a ploy to get him away from everyone else? An ambush in a dark passageway? Not if Carrick could help it.

'The lady harpist's in the lounge,' Hutch was announcing. 'Coffee will be served a little later.'

'I think I should like an early night,' Benjamin Rialto said in Carrick's ear. 'Would it matter, do you think? Will people be offended?' He was frowning anxiously, peering through his thick glasses.

'Not in the least,' Carrick said. 'Have a good night. Is there anything else you need?'

'No. Thank you.' He walked away, a little unsteadily, in the direction of the stairs.

Mrs MacTavish had been waiting, somewhat breathlessly, to speak to the steward. 'Is it true,' she said in what she mistakenly thought was a whisper, 'that Miss Devlin was deliberately hit by a car, so that's why Patrick's looking after her?'

'Nothing's been proved,' Carrick told her. 'It's just a precaution, that's all.'

'It's a dreadful world we live in,' she said sadly, shaking her head. 'Come, Bill, – we'll listen to the harp lady.'

The room was now almost empty. Moments later it contained just Kimberley and Carrick.

'Where's Patrick?' he asked.

'Andrew said he was wanted on the phone.'

'He had no business to leave you alone!' Carrick raged.

She grabbed him by the hand as he went by. 'You don't mean that. *We* should stay with *him*.'

'Yes, but looking after you is what he's *supposed* to be doing.'

'I'm coming as well,' she said, hanging on to him. 'I know what Capelli means to do.'

'All the more reason why you stay here,' Carrick told her grimly.

From somewhere in the rear of the castle there came a sound as of knights on horseback converging at the joust.

Carrick ran in the direction of the noise, dragging Kimberley – willingly, he trusted – along with him. The noise grew nearer and louder, the warriors having apparently dismounted, *fortissimo*, and commenced hacking one another to pieces with Lochaber axes.

The kitchen, a lofty beamed room complete with rows of gleaming copper pots on hooks and roasting spits set in huge open fireplaces, was crowded. Most of the spectators were crammed into an annexe where food was stored. All the catering staff, washers-up and waitresses, plus a few hangers-on, were watching the spectacle that was taking place before them of Agnes heavily basting Luigi with a cast iron ladle. Several pots and pans, some dented, were strewn over the floor around them.

'They're the ones she was going to give to the dustmen,' said Gillard's voice from somewhere above them. Carrick and Kimberley looked up to see him seated comfortably on a low beam.

Luigi, endeavouring to hide beneath a table, howled every time Agnes hit him.

'I think you should rescue him before she does him real harm,' Carrick said.

'Regretfully, I agree,' said Gillard and slid down to the floor via a supporting beam.

Even more regretfully Luigi resented being rescued and produced his flick knife. What followed could not be described as a fight. It was more along the lines of a ritual humiliation. Capelli arrived in time to find his unfortunate henchman trussed as for the oven on the kitchen table, a small Cox's Orange Pippin placed lovingly between his teeth. The audience were enthralled.

Gillard presented Capelli with the knife. 'It's probably safer in your hands – he might cut himself.'

'Take care,' Capelli hissed.

'If you send him in my direction again I shall break his neck,' came the stone-cold sober, whispered promise.

They left Agnes to reign gloriously in her kitchen.

'So it *was* a trap,' Carrick said as they went in the direction of the first-floor lounge.

'Indeed it was,' said Patrick wryly.

'It was quite something to watch,' said Kimberley. 'Now, do you think I could make use of your gallant services in another capacity?'

She looked rather pale and tired, and the two men suddenly realised that she could hardly keep up with them. Gravely, they made a seat with their clasped hands and, her arms round their shoulders, made a wild charge at the stairs bearing Kimberley aloft. All three arrived at the top breathless, laughing and exuberant to be confronted with Lord Muirshire, who was preparing to descend. With a pang, he realised that such levity had not occurred under his roof for as long as he could remember.

'My dear,' he said awkwardly, when she had been carefully set on her feet.

'Ross!' she exclaimed. 'I thought you would be away on business.'

'I – er – decided to stay put this time. To be honest I was rather – concerned about you.' His gaze went to Gillard. 'I understand that this is—'

'Oh, I'm sorry. This is Patrick. Patrick, Lord Muirshire.'

They shook hands.

'Have we met before?' the Marquess said. 'I've a good memory for faces, though I'm not so hot on names. A regimental dinner? I've a chum who is commanding officer of the Devon and Dorsets . . . Yes, I'm sure of it. We exchanged views on the wisdom of MI5 becoming involved with the fight against organised crime. You were all for it, if I remember correctly, and I got the impression that you yourself had a hand in – no? Am I right off the mark? If so, my apologies.'

Gillard sighed. 'I regret to say that you have a ferociously good memory. Is there somewhere we can talk briefly in private?'

Lord Muirshire looked anxiously at the man who had been speaking. 'I hope I haven't said the wrong thing.'

'Not in front of these people,' Gillard said. 'James is a good friend of mine.'

'Come into my study for a moment.'

They were ushered into a panelled room with bookshelves filling two walls from floor to ceiling. They seated themselves in easy chairs while their host wandered uneasily over to a magnificent partners' desk. He remained standing, however.

'Fire away,' he said.

'How long have you known Tony Capelli?' Gillard asked quietly.

'About eighteen months,' he was told.

Gillard turned to Kimberley. 'When I rang you in hospital and asked you to come to London to talk to me, you trusted me, didn't you?'

Alone in her private misery, she had heard that calm, reassuring voice and grasped at the offer as though it were a life-line. 'Yes,' she said.

'I told you my name and why I was interested in coming here this weekend.'

She nodded.

'Well, now I ask you to keep what you're about to hear in complete confidence. If you don't . . .'

'If I don't?'

'I might get a bullet in the head.'

'I see,' she said faintly.

'We're fairly sure that Capelli is involved in a racket that smuggles criminals into this country from overseas. Organised crime barons are willing to pay good money for the sort of people who aren't afraid to use firearms or even explosives. It's control we're talking about, control of streets, even whole cities.'

'No,' Kimberley whispered.

'Have you ever suspected that he might be involved in anything illegal?'

'No . . . Nothing like that. Tony has been very good to me.'

'James, you were asking about people who had left the tours for one reason or another,' Lord Muirshire said. 'Is that what was on your mind?'

'Yes,' Carrick said tersely.

'So we keep mum,' the Marquess said to Gillard.

'I'm just the minder,' Gillard said with a rakish smile.

'So what happened in the kitchen?' Kimberley asked.

'Not much,' Gillard said. 'A bloke called Andy took me

aside and said that he had an idea Luigi would try and catch me out. He told me a couple of other things too, so when I went to take the bogus phone call that I'd asked Andy to tell me about and saw Luigi skulking unawares outside the kitchen I arrested the miscreant and took him to Agnes. You see, Andy had spotted him spitting into the soup.'

'He's going!' Lord Muirshire said with an air of finality. 'I don't care if it means the end of the tours – I won't tolerate someone like that in my house.'

'If you could tolerate him a little longer,' Gillard said, 'it would help me. I don't think he'll step out of line after what happened to him just now.'

Carrick narrated the tale of Luigi's downfall to the Marquess, who uttered a satisfied chuckle.

Gillard got to his feet. 'I'm afraid I've kept you from dinner. Miss Devlin—'

'Kim,' she hastily corrected.

'Do you wish to listen to the harp, or am I right in thinking you would like an early night?'

'Definitely the latter,' she replied.

'Are you sleeping across her door?' Carrick enquired somewhat bullishly.

'In the dressing room,' Kimberley said primly. 'And I assure you that the key's on my side.'

'I'd be delighted to escort you to your room,' Lord Muirshire said.

Arm in arm, they left.

'She said she didn't want to sing,' Carrick mused.

'No, and that appears to be still the case.' Gillard had Carrick's full attention. 'I'm sorry, James, but she's in this right up to her neck,' he said softly.

'I don't believe it,' Carrick said, despising the hoarseness in his own voice.

'She makes contact with the men in line for being shipped over. The FBI have been watching her.'

The full implication of what he had been told hit Carrick. 'You've taken a hell of a risk!'

Gillard gazed at him calmly. 'She's very frightened. She probably thinks Capelli might have arranged what happened to her as a warning, in case she was thinking of stepping out

96

of line. It is a hell of a risk – but if she has the goods on who's going to do the disappearing act this time . . . Who knows? If she ends up feeling safer with us she might just . . .' He smiled. 'You made quite an impression on her. Why don't you capitalise on it?'

Chapter Nine

Joanna removed her apron and put it with a pile of others to be washed in the corner of the castle kitchen. Getting a job for the 'Live like a Lord' weekend had been ridiculously easy; she had merely presented herself at the tradesmen's entrance of the castle and asked to see the head cook. And yes, Agnes did need more helpers – how interesting that young Joanna had heard a couple discussing the weekends in the hotel bar! They must be getting quite famous! Caterers there might be, but Agnes preferred to keep her own flag flying and to have her domain left in its normal spick and span condition. So, with the Marquess's permission, she arranged to bring in additional helpers of her own to assist those organised by Kennedy and Hutch. In payment she could offer Joanna twenty pounds and a good meal each night of the weekend – she assured Joanna that she wouldn't go hungry.

Somehow, Joanna had managed to ensure that Carrick did not spot her loading the dishwasher in the corner of the kitchen annexe when he and Kimberley burst in upon the scene of Luigi's comeuppance. There had been no concealment from Patrick, however, who had given her a surreptitious wink as he unceremoniously bundled the hapless Luigi into the kitchen to face Agnes's wrath. But Joanna was not too alarmed; after all, he had given her free rein for the weekend, the only stipulation being that she keep him informed of her movements after the meals were over each night, courtesy of the mobile phones they were both secreting about their persons. She had been expecting him to speak to her this evening and she was not to

98

be disappointed. She was also amused to see that he was clearly the apple of Agnes's eye.

'*Mo ghaiol!*' she cried when she espied Gillard enter the kitchen, bustling forward, all buxom five feet nothing of her, her grey hair mercilessly skewered into a tight bun. 'Has that terrible Luigi gone home?'

'He's taken Capelli back to the hotel where they're staying in Inverness,' Gillard answered. He indicated a bench alongside the pine table that not so long ago Luigi had decorated with his presence. 'May I?'

'Sit yourself down and welcome,' Agnes said. 'Would you like some coffee – and perhaps a piece of apple tart?'

'Some coffee would be wonderful.'

Her face fell. 'Did you not like my tart?'

'It was the food of the gods,' she was earnestly informed. 'But if I eat any more I shall fall asleep, and then I won't be any good at my job.'

'Ah, yes. That poor child. I was forgetting.'

Joanna took a pot of freshly made coffee from an electric hotplate in the annexe through into the old kitchen, together with two mugs.

'I thought you'd gone back to your hotel, Joanna,' Agnes said. 'You're the last one here. Away with you now – you've been a great help.' She noticed the way the pair were looking at one another. 'Och, well, if you want to have some coffee with Patrick . . . But please be sure to put out the lights and lock up when you go.'

'I'll see to it,' Gillard said.

By the door Agnes paused. 'We're short of a couple of serving wenches for tomorrow night. Are you interested? You'll get paid extra for that and I ken the young people have a bit of fun.'

'Yes, please,' Joanna said.

'I'll tell Hutch. Goodnight.'

They both wished her goodnight and the door closed.

'Whereas this old man . . .' Gillard said, switching off the lascivious smile.

'You don't look a day over ninety,' Joanna said, helping them both to coffee. 'And I thought you were going to turn up as Shelvoke Dempster the Third? I was looking forward to that.'

Patrick sighed. 'Ah, yes, I would have enjoyed that. But it wouldn't have been – practical. By the way, does James often cut himself shaving?'

'No. Especially as he uses an electric shaver.'

'Ah! That would explain why he looked so delighted when I got Luigi ready for slow-roasting . . . Capelli's running a hoodlum import agency and, Joanna, some time this weekend one, or even two, of the visitors staying here is likely to leave, either because of illness or some kind of accident. Or family bereavement, perhaps. I said, "likely to leave" but in fact they won't, because I'm going to take their place. That's if it's a bloke. If it's a woman, that's down to you.'

'And if it's two blokes?'

'I'll let you know. I can't involve James – it might compromise his career if he gets caught up in this unofficially. After all, he is meant to be on holiday.'

'And Kimberley?' Joanna enquired, hoping that her inner turmoil was not apparent.

'James can look after her.'

'And won't Capelli notice that you've taken someone's place?' she asked sarcastically.

'It's immaterial what he notices. He'll be firmly under lock and key with his merchandise – plus Luigi, of course.'

'The police are being kept fully informed?'

'Of course.'

Joanna took a mouthful of coffee and almost drowned herself. When she had stopped spluttering she said, 'I'm sure you get annoyed when people keep asking questions, but—' She stopped talking. He had laughed aloud.

'I don't know any answers!' he said. 'I'm writing the script of this as I go along. All I know is what's gospel – info, I might add, that I managed to collate after we parted in London. And from one or two sources here it appears that after some kind of disaster strikes one of the visitors, Capelli – who always seems to be handy on such occasions – arranges transport to the airport or hospital or wherever. That tells me that associates of his are waiting in the wings, ready for the nod. Capelli doesn't go along. He stays here. What the police and I would like to know is who is on the receiving end of the deals. One big-time crook? Several?'

100

'Is Kimberley Devlin completely in the clear? I do wonder.'

'You're right to wonder. That's why I offered you a job. No, she isn't.'

'Does James know?'

'He does now. I've just told him.'

'Poor James!' Joanna murmured.

'I also told him he ought to work on her a bit in case she decides to confide in him. It's plain that the woman's scared stiff.'

'Patrick, that isn't *fair*!'

He smiled upon her gently. 'To James? Perhaps not. But he's only in love with a voice, you know. Not her. Really, she's quite ordinary.'

For a moment Joanna almost loved Gillard.

He finished his coffee and stood up.

'Does Kimberley Devlin know who you really are?'

'I told her my real name and that I'm involved with law enforcement. From what she's said since, I think she assumes I'm with the immigration authorities. That's OK by me.'

'She might inform Capelli.'

'That, I admit, is the stuff of my worst nightmares.'

'*You* work on her,' Joanna countered. 'James might seem sometimes to be carved from granite but he isn't. *You're* the professional interrogator, the one trained to get to the truth. Besides, you're in the woman's company almost all the time.'

'She was recently buried alive,' he pointed out gently. 'We can't be too tough on her.'

Joanna collected her bag. 'So everyone keeps reminding me. Perhaps I ought to offer my services to whatever's replaced the KGB.'

'Ouch,' Gillard whispered, the slam of the door ringing in his ears.

The following morning Buck Murdo slipped and fell on the stairs as he was coming down to breakfast. He made rather a lot of fuss about it, insisting that his wrist was broken. Carrick, 'on duty' since seven thirty, assessed the situation carefully. As Capelli was nowhere to be seen and the accident victim was in his seventies he decided there was no reason for a red alert and drove Murdo himself to the accident and emergency department of Inverness Hospital. There, a bad sprain was diagnosed and the wrist strapped up. On their return his only communication with Gillard was through mutually raised eyebrows and a quiet sigh of relief.

After this mishap, the day progressed as planned; following a guided tour of the castle the five couples elected to go with Carrick on a coach ride which took in a distillery, a bagpipe maker and a woollen mill, culminating in a late lunch at the best hotel in Braemar. Benjamin Rialto, still pleading weariness, had stayed in the library to read; Caspar Dean had gone clay pigeon shooting with Andrew Kennedy. Carrick made a point of asking Kennedy for a report on Mr Dean's proficiency.

When Carrick and his charges returned to Castle Stalker – the coach's boot crammed with shopping – Kennedy was in the main entrance hall, a one-man welcoming party.

'The man's a fine shot,' he said as Carrick paused on his way towards the staircase in order to rearrange an armful of parcels (all belonging to Poochie MacTavish).

'Is he?' Carrick said.

'I'm all agog as to why you wanted to know.'

'Thought we could hold a competition,' Carrick said lightly. 'Tomorrow morning, perhaps. No doubt Patrick's fairly handy with a shotgun.'

'Good idea.' Kennedy went to help with Mrs MacTavish's endless parcels.

The coach had had to be manoeuvred between the catering firm's vans, which were delivering provisions for the banquet. Somewhere behind the castle the piper was practising – no doubt due to Hutch's tactful suggestion that he might need 'rehearsal time'.

In the kitchen Agnes and her helpers produced sandwiches and cakes, Agnes's idea of 'a light tea' to keep everyone going until the evening.

Upstairs, Stefanie Murdo and her husband were putting their feet up. They were the eldest of the visitors, apart from Benjamin Rialto; of normally sedentary nature, they were finding the trip hard work. Buck's wrist was aching but he was feeling fairly sanguine about it; a large bottle of whisky sat on the dressing table, a gift from the Marquess as consolation for

102

his injury. Buck intended to thank the great man personally that night.

'How are your feet, Stef?' he asked.

She too had her fair share of aches and pains. 'Middlin' bad,' she answered. 'It's a strange sort of place, Scotland,' she added.

'How's that, honey?' he enquired sleepily.

'Well, back home, if you have servants, they *look* like servants. The folk helpin' out here look like gentry. That young, fair-headed one – he could be a dook any day of the week!'

'Perhaps he is,' Buck chuckled. 'Wrong side of the blanket, and all that.' And he dropped into a doze.

Next door, Lucy and Gene Cameron were writing postcards. Gene's grandfather, and his father before him, had been farmers in the area and that afternoon he had realised a life-long ambition and gazed across the small fertile glen where his ancestors had tilled the soil. It had been a sublime moment; even now he had to brush away a tear as he remembered it. *All of a sudden*, he thought, *I sort of belong here.*

'You're day-dreaming again,' his wife said to him gently.

'I guess I am,' he said gruffly, recommencing the postcard to his daughter.

'Would you like a little place in Scotland? So you could come back here, bring the family?'

'I wouldn't mind living at Castle Stalker, and that's a fact.'

'We'll buy a British lottery ticket,' she said decisively. 'Like they say, it could be us!'

Gene laughed loudly. 'Lucy, you were always the *most* practical woman.'

The Folkins had a room across the corridor. As usual, they were arguing. Lea, a small, shrewish woman, was seated at the dressing table glumly staring at her reflection. Her black hair needed tinting again; it was growing out grey at the roots. She had hoped it would last until she got back home; perhaps flying made it grow quicker. The dress she was going to wear that evening hung from the wardrobe and she dragged her gaze away from the mirror to look at it. It didn't raise her spirits either.

103

'I told you that pink was the wrong colour for a woman of your age,' her husband said waspishly.

'You've nothing to brag about, I can assure you,' she snapped, 'with that gut of yours hanging over your belt.'

'We're talking about the *dress*, not my belly. Wear your black one – even though it does make you look as if you're going to a wake.'

She swung round on her seat. 'One of these days I'm going to get that gun out of the closet and—'

'Fill me full of lead?' he chortled. 'You'd have had John Wayne in tears.' Expanding on the idea, he went on. 'There must be plenty of hardware in a place like this. Perhaps if you ask him nicely his lordship will show you how to load and fire a cannon.'

'Go to hell!' Lea shrieked as he flopped back on the bed, laughing helplessly.

Benjamin Rialto heard the sound and glowered in the direction of the room from which it had come. He had saved for a long time for this holiday and was desperately disappointed. Not with Scotland, or even Britain – except that some places seemed very grey and run-down, not greenly picturesque as he had been expecting. No, it was the company of his own countrymen that was the trouble. The insufferable Wilsons treated him as though he was in his dotage – and Dean behaved in a superior fashion to just about everyone, referring to him – him, Rialto, a retired professor of English! – as 'that silly old fool'. The Wilsons had told him that. He would rather not have known.

Caspar Dean himself was in the shower, carefully soaping his fit, well-muscled body. He too found the company very trying; but he felt no compunction to socialise. How could he have anything in common with such people? Although it mattered little to him, he had assumed that those able to afford such a trip would be people after his own heart: cultured, intelligent. How wrong he had been . . .

Mamie and John Wilson, never imagining that anyone could find them insufferable, were taking the air in the terraced garden. They were not enjoying themselves either; they had not realised that Scotland was so wild, so remote. John's great-great-grandmother had been born in Glasgow and had married a shipwright on one of the sailing ships bringing cotton from the States. She had travelled steerage to his home port of New Orleans and there she had prematurely ended her days after bearing thirteen children.

'I've never liked the wide-open spaces,' John said, staring with something approaching dismay at the hills.

'Relax,' said his partner sharply. 'This is the first holiday we've had in years. Remember the Queen stays near here in the summer.'

'Yes, but she can go straight back to London when she feels like it . . .'

Poochie and Bill MacTavish had chosen the lavish 'Duke's Suite', which comprised a large bedroom with a four-poster bed, a dressing room and a bathroom all giving magnificent views of the mountains. Right now, Poochie was gazing out of one of the bedroom windows, admiring the late afternoon sun shining on the calm waters of the loch.

'Such a drab-looking pair,' she commented. 'The Wilsons, that is. They don't look as though they're enjoying a single minute of it.'

'Nor the Folkins,' muttered her husband, glancing up from a newspaper. 'I don't know why folk come on such trips if they don't try to make the best of it.'

'And trust old Buck Murdo to fall down the stairs! Did you see the state of his slippers? Really down-at-heel. He was lucky not to break his neck.'

Bill chuckled. 'Rialto's not too happy with the way the Wilsons shepherd him around.'

'Why do they? He's perfectly capable of looking after himself. I wouldn't say that kind of thing came naturally to them. Perhaps they belong to one of those religious sects that force you to be kind to everyone, whether you want to or not.'

'You're an old cynic.'

Poochie laughed.

'So what do you think of Caspar Dean, Poochie?'

'He's an odd bird. I don't know *what* to think of him.'

'Come on! You're good at placing people.'

'*Placing* him? You didn't say anything about placing. Well, I wouldn't say his accent was from anywhere *I* know in the States. Perhaps he's lived in Canada for a while.'

'Right. So what does your delicate ear tell you about Kimberley Devlin's bodyguard?'

'You're only asking because you know I fancy him. Read your paper.'

Her bodyguard was the very last thing on Kimberley Devlin's mind. In an attempt to still the fears that now were never far away, she had switched on her transistor radio. But Mozart, it seemed, no longer had the power to beguile her. In fact, she was quickly coming to the conclusion that music would never again play a significant role in her life. The thought was unbearable, and meant that she greeted her visitor with brimming eyes.

'You're coming to the banquet tonight, I hope,' said Carrick, not sure how to react.

'I was wrong to come here at all,' Kimberley said quietly. 'I've no right to be here if I won't sing for my supper.' She switched off her radio.

'No one will expect you to sing at the moment, not after what you've been through. I think you'll find that—'

'Capelli was here just now,' she interrupted, her voice breaking. 'I told him how I felt. I told him that I just couldn't do it any more, stand up there with everyone looking at me, knowing that someone, somewhere, wants me dead. But he just smiled, said my confidence would come back gradually. He looked so smug. I was so angry about being treated like a child – and that he'd lied to me, about being in France – that I accused him. Said I thought *he* might have tried to kill me. And I'd *promised* Patrick I wouldn't say anything like that, nothing to make Tony angry or suspicious . . . The more I think about it, the more certain I am that Tony's mixed up in something illegal.' She flung herself on to the bed. 'It's as if everything I once took for granted, everything I trusted in, has been taken away from me.' She looked up. 'So why did you come to Castle Stalker?'

'Probably for something to keep me occupied. Joanna's left me.'

Kimberley looked horrified. 'Not because of what I said on TV! Really, I don't know what came over me. It must have been the drugs, or something.'

'So you didn't mean it?'

Kimberley's thoughts, trapped on a hurdy-gurdy of misery, broke free and something of her old spirit resurfaced. 'I never said I didn't *mean* it! I'm nothing if not truthful. But I do admit I shouldn't have said it. Not with all those cameras pointing at me, anyway.'

Carrick sat down on a chair next to the bed. 'Don't blame yourself. Joanna and I weren't on the best of terms even before I met you. Your TV appearance probably just hastened the inevitable.' He turned towards her. 'Tell me something – I've always been curious about how people who take part in the great classic tragedies – plays, opera – actually prepare for their roles. I mean, there you are as Tosca, about to leap to your death from the top of the prison walls, the entire audience carried away by the emotion of the moment. But what do you *feel*? What goes through your head?'

'That I get the timing right. That I don't trip and fall before the jump on to the mattresses behind the scenery.'

'So you're not really involved?'

'Not really. You can't be, or you'd have a nervous breakdown.'

'So personal suffering doesn't help you play the part with more conviction.'

'No. You have to empty your mind of *yourself*.'

'Can't you do that now?' he enquired gently.

She arranged herself more comfortably on the bed. She looked glorious in a dark blue velvet robe over a long cream silk petticoat, the folds of the robe at her neck revealing soft cream lace. Carrick was trying not to look at the soft swell of her breasts, endeavouring to keep his gaze instead on those wonderful eyes.

'Nothing so terrible has ever happened to me before,' Kimberley said. 'I can't stop brooding about it.'

'You promised me you'd sing for me one day.'

'I probably will. But not yet. Not here.'

107

'Are you sure there's nothing else that's frightening you?'

'Only worms,' she said harshly. 'And the thought of a grave. Of being just ma▓▓ts in a wooden box.'

There was a lo▓ silence. Then Carrick got to his feet. 'Please change your mind about this evening. It will do you good to be with people. And I promise you, no one will ask you to sing.'

'I'll think about it,' was all she would say.

When the door had closed behind him the tears flowed. Yes, she liked him. But he was a policeman . . . She leaned over to turn on the radio once more but there was another knock at the door.

'Just wondered if you were feeling up to a noisy evening,' said Gillard, putting his head round the door.

'James has just asked me that. I said no.'

He came in and sat down.

'James sat there too. Are you going to interrogate me as well?' She stared boldly at him as she spoke.

He smiled disarmingly. 'You wouldn't much like it if I did.'

'Tell me about yourself.'

'There's not much to tell. I'm forty-three years old, married to a novelist and we have two children, a horse and a cat. We live in Devon for most of the time, but as there's a nanny for the children we travel abroad sometimes, mostly so my wife can get ideas for her plots and undertake research. When she wants a *really* bad character – a serial killer or a hired assassin – she uses me.'

Kimberley laughed. Then she discovered that she had stopped laughing; it was something to do with the expression that had flickered across his face. A hint, no more, of something darker.

'You're my bodyguard,' she said. 'You promised.'

'Absolutely,' he replied, still looking at her in a fashion she found disturbing. 'And if Luigi, or persons unknown, come through that door with a view to doing you harm I shall do everything humanly possible to save you.'

Luigi . . . Luigi was part of the fear.

Gillard said, 'Caspar Dean was right when he said that the image of the powerful talented woman protected by the sacrificial lamb was a fantasy.'

Unaccountably, she shivered. 'I'm afraid I accused Tony of knocking me down. I didn't mean to! It was just that he made me angry.'

'But why should he do such a thing?'

'You said . . .'

'I said he was involved with criminals. But he's your *agent*!'

'But – you told me not to say anything that might make him suspicious! I thought that—'

'Yes. I asked you not to tell him that I'd contacted you and asked to accompany you here this weekend.'

'Oh, God,' she wailed, burying her head in the pillow. 'I wish that woman who found me had just left me in the hole in the ground. I'm stupid, stupid, stupid!'

Suddenly, unexpectedly, she was being lifted into a sitting position, a pillow carefully placed behind her back, her tears dried with a clean white handkerchief. Even more surprising, she was being offered a glass of champagne.

'Where did that come from?' she asked. How odd that she had ever found Gillard intimidating . . .

'In the fridge. A gift from the Marquess. I'm afraid I forgot to tell you about it.'

'I've never been very sensible,' she murmured.

'You mustn't think like that. You've had a terrible experience and you're also suffering from a guilty conscience.'

'You realise that I may not live very long if I tell you everything I know.' She half-emptied her glass in two swallows. 'Have some – it's wonderful.'

He glanced at the label. 'It should be. It's a *Grande Cuvée.*'

'Please join me. I shall be quite sloshed if I drink all that on my own.'

He needed no further urging. What a relief that he hadn't had to resort to *really* tough tactics!

'I shall go to prison for a long time,' Kimberley said. 'And then, when I'm released, Capelli will send someone to kill me.'

'How long have you known he's connected with the Mafia?' Gillard asked, ignoring this *cri de coeur*.

'No one's ever actually confirmed it. I guessed. He asked me to give messages to men who came to visit me backstage: times, places, that kind of thing. He said it was just in connection with contracts, with overseas artistes, but I knew better.

They were almost always Italians. And then, when the first few tourist trips here had apparently been successful and, I assume, several *Mafiosi* smuggled into this country under false names, he moved on to criminals of other nationalities.' She shrugged. 'What I do is simple – I'm the messenger.'

'In return for what?'

'My life. What else?'

'Kim, part of my job is finding out when people are lying. You are an appallingly bad liar and making this very easy for me.'

She held out her glass for a refill, her hand shaking. Gravely, he complied.

'For money,' she said dully.

'You don't seem to live a life of great luxury.'

'What it amounts to is that I can keep most of what I earn.'

'Do you mean that he only actually gives you your earnings if you comply with his instructions?'

She nodded. 'First of all I refused. He punished me by giving me only ten pounds a week – so I wouldn't actually starve. I have quite a large mortgage on my flat – my real home's in London, I only rent the one in Glasgow while I'm under contract to Scottish Opera – so I couldn't hold out for long.'

'Didn't you think of going to the police?'

'Yes. Several times. Have you met this friend of James's: Inspector Macpherson?'

'No.'

'He's so overworked he couldn't even stop Jimmy Barr from bothering me. What chance would he have to stop Capelli? You must believe me when I tell you that I gave it serious thought. But always there was Capelli – and Luigi. Luigi's a distant relation of his – too stupid to do anything but drive a car and beat people up. Capelli threatened to shut me in a room with him for an hour . . .'

Gillard took a reflective sip of his wine. 'I see.'

'Is that all you can say? What are you going to *do*?'

'With Luigi? If he comes within a mile of you, something not too pleasant.'

'No, I mean—'

'Who's the merchandise this time?' Gillard interrupted.

She agonised for fully thirty seconds and then told him. Afterwards, he briefed her very carefully, making sure that she knew what to expect.

'Trust me,' he added.

'I think I'm more scared of you than Capelli!'

For answer he leaned over and gave her a warm, passionless hug.

'I'm lying,' she whispered. 'He's like no agent I've ever met. I'm terrified of him. No one likes him, but people have him as their agent because he gets such wonderful deals. Most of them can't possibly know what he's really like . . . He grabs young musicians when they're just starting their careers, when they're poor and inexperienced. They depend on him because he gives them an allowance. Other agents don't do that, not if you aren't yet earning. And then they have no option but to stay with him – it's dreadfully difficult when you're an unknown. I know that other people have been threatened – friends of mine who wanted to leave him because they suspected he was a crook. But once he's got you, he won't let go.'

'So let's put him out of business,' Gillard said.

Chapter Ten

Inspector Neil Macpherson entered his office and sat down with a huge sigh. 'Buy an old man a coffee and a doughnut?' he wheedled when his assistant arrived.

'Did you have to miss lunch, sir?' Kerr enquired. He was not given to clucking around people in motherly fashion; nonetheless, he was increasingly worried about his boss's grey and haggard aspect.

'I thought I would be there until tomorrow,' Macpherson said. He had been attending a meeting at HQ in Pitt Street and, for once, had felt it relevant.

Kerr realised that he wouldn't get the full story until Macpherson had been refuelled. 'It's all right, sir,' he said, preparing to head back the way he had come and perceiving his boss to be digging in his pocket for change. 'This one's on me. You bought lunch yesterday.'

Left on his own, Macpherson rubbed his stinging eyes. *Yesterday*? Was it only yesterday when they had lunched on dry ham and limp lettuce between slices of bread that defied description? It seemed like a lifetime ago.

'I've volunteered you for a bit of action,' he told his sergeant on his return. 'Overtime, laddie. That's what you like, isn't it?'

Kerr, who was a mere five summers younger, nodded. Unlike Macpherson, he had five children and a wife with expensive tastes.

'Special Branch was out in force,' Macpherson said succinctly. 'All designer macs and dark glasses. But they're on to a good thing, it would appear. In a nutshell, it's this: the Mafia, no less, have a scam going bringing international gangsters into the UK, mostly for mobs in the cities who pay high prices for new talent. It would seem that Special Branch has a man on the inside who says the next delivery is for the MacCrudden gang – who, as I'm sure you know, hang out not a million miles from this nick.'

Kerr whistled. 'They've always wanted to rule the roost. Looks like they're expanding. Do we know any names?'

'Only that it's a man and a woman. And the drop's tomorrow morning. There's a premises being watched in London. It's where they reckon everything's organised from. It's a question of following every vehicle that leaves the place and making a move when the time's ripe.'

'There's some folk going to be doing a hell of a lot of driving.'

Macpherson took a large bite from his doughnut and spoke through a mouthful. 'Yes – you hate to put a damper on their enthusiasm, but it's going to finish up *here*.'

'I suppose one can always dream that the mob'll take their reinforcements and wipe out those other bastards, the Millikens,' Kerr said wistfully.

'And we'll discover that arms cache the snouts keep whispering about while they're at it? Dream on, laddie. The way they keep topping those who even hint it exists, it'll end up like a pharaoh's tomb. No one'll know where it is. But I've an ace up my sleeve as far as the MacCruddens are concerned. There's a snout with a grudge and the word from him is that the boss isn't a MacCrudden at all but someone altogether more reputable. I'm working on it.'

Neither of them felt like mentioning the fact that they had had to release the man they had arrested in connection with Jimmy Barr's murder. There had been the small matter of a cast-iron alibi. He had been at his daughter's wedding earlier on the day in question, in full view of a hundred people – plus, of course, a minister of God – and had then gone on to dance and drink the night away, again in the company of reliable witnesses. The thought of Jimmy Barr, he had insisted, had for once not even crossed his mind.

'I quite enjoy a bit of action,' Kerr was saying; he had once boxed for the police.

'You watch yourself!' the inspector said sharply. 'They're

armed, these people, and being useful in a fight is no defence against knives and bullets.' His phone rang and he snatched it up. 'Macpherson.' After listening for a few moments he said, 'Could you repeat that, sir?'

Kerr daydreamed, reliving past sporting glories.

Eventually Macpherson thanked the caller and rang off. 'That was the Grahams' son Jeremy,' he reported. 'He didn't tell me anything I didn't already know – but I'm concerned, nevertheless.'

'How so, sir?' Kerr asked, coming down to earth.

'His father's gone off, apparently to give Miss Devlin the song he's written for her. He took the train to Edinburgh, where he plans to spend the night before hiring a car and driving the rest of the way. Jeremy's worried. He thinks his father is close to some kind of breakdown.'

'You mean, he's worried he might top himself?'

'No, nothing like that. He heard Philip muttering something about how he'd "show her". Jeremy is sure that Philip gave her the first draft of the ballad when they had lunch together recently and Miss Devlin said it wasn't her sort of thing.'

'And he thinks . . .? Surely not, sir.'

'Young Jeremy took a look at it. Clearly Miss Devlin was being tactful. Jeremy said it's absolute rubbish. No singer would perform it in public if they valued their reputation.' Macpherson reached for the phone. 'I think I'd better have a word with James Carrick.'

Carrick was actually in the shower in his hotel room as Macpherson spoke. By the time the Inspector had been given the number of that establishment by Andrew Kennedy, who took the call at the castle, he was dressed.

'You ought to have a mobile,' were the inspector's first words.

'I do,' Carrick replied. 'But because I'm "on holiday" I left it at home.'

Macpherson told him what Jeremy had said.

'Kimberley might have mentioned it,' Carrick said slowly.

'Jeremy doesn't strike me as a lad keen on making mischief, but he might have got the whole story wrong.'

'*If* he showed her the song – she *did* mention having lunch

114

with Philip Graham two weeks ago – and she said she didn't like it, even if she chose her words carefully, he might have taken it very much to heart. What worries me is Jeremy thinking his father's near to breaking point. How did he seem to you?'

'Hen-pecked. That wife of his has him right under her thumb.'

'And he's coming here? Mrs Graham can't be too pleased about that.' Carrick looked at his watch. 'Look, I must go. Without any real idea of what's going on, we can't do a lot, can we? But I'll ask Miss Devlin what she really thinks about Graham and make sure her minder's in the know.' Something – instinctive caution, perhaps – stopped Carrick telling Macpherson the bodyguard's true identity.

'Is he any good?'

'Oh, the best. Without a doubt.'

Five minutes later, hurrying along an upstairs corridor, he cannoned into Joanna. In fact, he caught her in his arms; she was off-balance and in danger of pitching headlong down the stairwell.

'You smell nice,' she said accusingly after they had exchanged apologies on the one hand and thanks on the other. She held him at arms' length. 'My, you look good enough to be voted king of the ball!'

Joanna herself was dressed for the kitchen in jeans and a tee shirt with KEEP CUMBERNAULD TIDY written on the front. 'I once went out with a Scottish dustman,' she lied, seeing his gaze on it. In actual fact a friend had given it to her as a joke.

'That's how you know about dustcarts?'

'Yup.'

'Can I give you a lift?' he enquired politely.

'It's not far to walk to the castle.'

'It's raining.'

'How's MI5?' Carrick asked when they were in the car.

'Fine and dandy, thank you.'

He put the key in the ignition but did not start the engine, turning in his seat to survey her. Joanna had never seen him look so stony-faced.

'Patrick got the truth out of Miss Devlin,' she announced,

getting her revenge. 'Just a while ago, after you went to see her.'

All kinds of unbidden images went through Carrick's mind; they were not ones he relished. On the occasion when Gillard had rescued him from death the three hired thugs they had encountered had been bettered using fighting tactics that Carrick had never in his life witnessed before, not even when he was in the Met. Gillard fought dirty. Even in Carrick's state of *in extremis*, it had come as a shock. And it had been part of Gillard's job, hadn't it? – getting the truth out of people . . .

'He told you this himself?' Carrick enquired.

'Yes. I rang him just now to ask him what he wanted me to do.'

There was no point in asking her if Gillard had divulged anything further; he wouldn't have taken that risk, not over an open telephone line. That was assuming Joanna was inclined to share information. Somehow he doubted it. It seemed that the chasm between them was getting wider all the time.

The short drive to the castle was undertaken in silence. Neither spoke when Carrick stopped the car close to the back gate so Joanna could run through the rain to the tradesmen's entrance. His mind registered the slam of the car door as a kind of full stop to an episode of his life. The end. He parked in the usual place and went indoors.

The minder was not with his charge, nor in his own room next door. But walking back to the staircase he met Kimberley, extremely pale and a trifle unsteady on her feet.

'What's wrong?' Carrick shouted.

Her hand was wrapped in a towel. 'I was looking for Hutch,' she said. 'Do you know where there's a first aid box? I've—'

He bustled her back into her room and removed the towel.

'It's a bit of a mess,' she said simply. 'I drank too much champagne and—'

Again he interrupted. 'Did *he* do this?'

'*He*? Who? Who he?' she babbled.

'How did this happen?' Carrick asked slowly and clearly.

'I shut my fingers in the drawer. I told you, I drank too much champagne. You're not listening,' she said, and sat on the bed to drain the last dregs from the bottle into her glass.

116

Carrick had made a point of memorising all the important internal telephone numbers. He rang the kitchen extension. 'Agnes? This is James Carrick. Would you please ask Joanna to bring a first-box to Miss Devlin's room on the first floor? I happen to know she's trained in first aid.'

'Where are you going *now*?' Kimberley asked. There had been far too much coming and going for her liking – it was probably another effect of the champagne, but her head was spinning.

Carrick didn't answer.

Gillard was in the Great Hall, the eighteenth-century addition that was proving so useful in these modern, commercial times. He was one of many – estate workers and their wives were decorating the venue for the evening's entertainment. Some were up long ladders, hanging garlands of dried fruit and flowers; others placed large candles, deemed safer than the rush lights of the day, in cast-iron sconces, or laid the handsome long table with pewter plates and tankards. On a side table the local florist arranged flowers in distinctly twentieth-century table settings. Gillard, appropriately, was setting out four broadswords – part of the Marquess's collection, regarded as suitable for the occasion as the swords were blunted through heavy wear – on top of a carved oak chest. Young stalwarts would use them to provide a little light entertainment during the cheese course.

There had been times during Gillard's career when vigilance had more than proved its worth; it had become second nature to him. Running his hand appreciatively over the fine handiwork of one sword's basket hilt, he glanced up, just in time. These were Scottish claymores, and right now a Scot with a wild look in his eyes was heading in his direction. Casually, as though they were meeting for a little pre-arranged practice, he held out one of the weapons, hilt first. At that moment, words were unnecessary.

Carrick took the sword, advanced the point in his adversary's direction and had it smartly knocked aside as Gillard picked up a sword of his own.

'I warn you, I'm half-decent at this,' Gillard said casually. 'Believe it or not, I took lessons as a lad – I wanted to be a

117

stunt man. These days they only let me loose with a fly swatter.'

Claymores are heavy and are used two-handed, without the refinements of a dirk held in the other hand, or a shield to protect the vulnerable side of the body. Carrick, in no mood for charity, immediately took advantage of Gillard's weakness and drove him the length of the hall. And Gillard, who had endured dancing lessons to help overcome the disability of a right leg of man-made construction below the knee (a legacy of the Falklands War), let him. But at the end of the hall Carrick ran into a windmill armed with steel. Finally he stood helpless, his shoulder blades rammed against the wood panelling.

'Well, James,' said Gillard through his teeth, 'what the hell is all this about?'

Carrick swallowed hard. He had had the flat of the sword used on him a couple of times and, perhaps as a result, a lot of mental clarity seemed to be coming his way. 'I now realise,' he said, 'that Kimberley must have told you what you wanted to know of her own free will.'

'That's right,' Gillard said.

'And you had absolutely nothing to do with her shutting her fingers in a drawer and bleeding all over the carpet?'

'Did she? Hardly.'

Gillard, who had been keeping Carrick where he was by holding the sword horizontally across his chest, lowered it. Carrick stayed where he was, eyes closed, tears on his eyelashes.

'I've lost Joanna,' he whispered. 'Mostly because of my own stupidity.'

Gillard removed the sword from Carrick's limp fingers. He felt that, in the circumstances, he ought to be businesslike. 'It's going to happen tonight, James, but Kimberley doesn't know the exact details. All she knows is that it's a man and a woman. So, somehow, Joanna and I will take their places. I'm afraid that means you'll have to take over from me as far as minding Kimberley is concerned.'

They were both startled by a sudden burst of applause from their audience.

'That was fantastic!' Hutch said, calling down from the gallery above. 'Could you do it again tonight?'

118

'No,' Carrick and Gillard replied as one man.

'I'm sorry,' Carrick said as the swords were replaced on the carved chest.

'So am I,' said Gillard. 'Believe me.'

Sarah Graham hammered peremptorily on her son's bedroom door. 'Jeremy? Are you in there? Open the door.'

All was silent within and she was just about to go away when she heard the sound of the bolt being drawn and the door was opened.

'Where's your father?'

Jeremy had been asleep; although it was only seven thirty, he had sat in his chair and nodded off. 'You *know* where he is. He's gone to give the Devlin woman the song he wrote for her.'

Sarah groaned, eyes cast heavenwards. 'Oh, God! I never thought for a moment that he meant it! It had all the hall-marks of his usual stupid posturing.' She fixed her son with an unpleasant gaze. 'But his car's still outside.'

'It wouldn't start. Flat battery. He's gone by train to Edinburgh and he's going to hire a car in the morning.'

'Well, I suppose that makes it as expensive as possible, if nothing else.' She threw up her hands in a gesture of despair. 'If I hadn't had to go and see a client I might have been able to talk him out of it. Couldn't you?'

'I've been out too. Fyffe and I went to Vince's place – he's got a new computer.'

She started to walk away down the hall but called back. 'Have you eaten?'

'No, I was going to—'

'I'll fix you something.'

'Mum . . .'

She turned. 'What?'

'That night when you were out, and Dad went for a drive in the country . . .'

'Only he didn't. He ended up in the Nolan Hotel. He told me that after the police had gone.'

'He was in a hell of a state when he got back.'

Sarah came back a little way. 'Drunk, you mean?'

'No, not really. Well, he might have had a few. He was filthy dirty – his hands covered in mud. He said he'd tripped in the car park and fallen into a flower bed. But he seemed – upset.'

'It would have hurt his pride,' she pointed out.

'No. I think he might have . . .'

'What? Jeremy, don't stand there squirming like a five year old. What might he have done?'

'I think he'd knocked down Kimberley Devlin.'

'No,' Sarah said decidedly. 'He's not capable of anything like that.'

'She'd turned down the ballad he wrote for her.'

'Are you sure?' she asked after a silence.

'I heard him ranting and raving about it, the day they had lunch together. About two weeks ago. And, Mum . . . I phoned the police. I think he's gone after her. To kill her.'

She stared at him for a few moments and then said faintly, 'I need a drink.'

'There's more,' Jeremy said after his mother had provided herself with a gin and tonic. 'Apparently there was some nutter who used to follow the Devlin woman around – she got the police on to him. He's dead. At first the police thought he'd committed suicide, but in the paper this morning it said they now think it's murder. Someone filled him up with sleeping tablets and whisky.'

'What on earth has this to do with your father?'

'This Barr character was a suspect for what happened to Kimberley Devlin. It didn't say so in the paper, but it stands to reason that the police would have been straight round to where he lives after she was found. A clever person might have killed him to make it look as though he'd been overcome with guilt at what he'd done to her.'

Sarah put her drink to one side. 'And you think your father would do that? You think he's a *murderer*?'

'I think he's cracking up,' was Jeremy's calm response.

'How do you know about this Barr person?'

'Dad told me. *She* told him – how he used to hang around outside where she lived, phone her up all the time, pestering her.'

Sarah remembered her drink and took a large gulp.

'I think you should know that his bottle of sleeping tablets has gone from the bathroom cabinet.'

'Jeremy! Have you been snooping around?'

'No, Mum. I just noticed that they weren't there, when I was looking for some aspirin.'

'But your father might have finished them. Not bothered to ask the doctor for another prescription.'

Jeremy shrugged. 'There was a full bottle in there the last time I looked. And that was only a week or so ago.'

'I think we should go after him,' she said, trying to keep her voice steady. 'It would be sensible to talk to him – just to put our minds at rest.'

'You can count me out,' Jeremy said. 'Besides, you've been drinking and I'm not insured to drive your car.'

'You're not insured to drive *any* car, but that doesn't seem to stop you from borrowing Vince's when you want to,' his mother retorted. 'You're coming and I'll drive. One mouthful of gin won't put me over the limit. Sometimes a mother needs her son's support.'

Chapter Eleven

Flora MacDougal had dressed for the part of celebrity guest in a magnificent, if ghoulish, black gown and she crossed the threshold of the castle like a sequinned Angel of Death. Handing her cape to Hutch as though he were a bewigged lackey, she progressed into the Red Room.

'Where *is* everyone?' she demanded to know.

The head gardener's daughter-cum-Girl Friday, Carrie, came forward with a tray of drinks. 'I think they're still dressing. You're a little early. Sherry, Miss MacDougal?'

'I'd prefer something rather more – gutsy,' said the author, eyeing the tray with distaste. 'A gin and tonic for preference.' She gazed around. 'Ah! I'm not scorned, after all.'

Carrick, who had just come in, surveyed the woman shrewdly and deduced that she had already had several gins too many. But he did not have time to give his latent sense of mischief an airing as at that moment Gillard wandered in and Flora, unwisely perhaps, gave him her full attention.

'You're not authentic!' she told him. 'Even Sassenachs ought to wear a kilt on traditional occasions such as this. A dinner suit is not appropriate.'

Gillard gave her a leery wink. Looking at her impossibly *bouffant* hairstyle, he said, 'But unlike in the days when the Scottish nobility's head lice fell in the soup, we won't insist that you keep your hat on.'

'One has to accept the more unsavoury aspects of medieval life,' she argued. 'As a professional writer, I—'

He refused to let her get away with it. 'Madam, in medieval

122

times the female scribes would have been in the kitchen, skinning the dinner.'

Schooling his expression, Carrick made the introductions. Presented with her gin and tonic by Carrie, Flora flounced off to examine the paintings, simmering silently.

'Sherry is a highly under-rated drink,' Gillard said, accepting a glass. 'This is a Mariscal Amontillado, if I'm not very much mistaken.' In an undertone he added, 'Where the hell *are* they all?'

'Someone suggested – I think it was Mrs MacTavish – that there should be a grand entry. No doubt they're waiting for it. Has Kim really made up her mind to give tonight a miss?'

'Oh, no!' Flora exclaimed, having overheard. 'She must come. She can't disappoint everyone. I'll go up and see her.' She discovered that Gillard was blocking her route to the door. 'No? You don't think that would be a good idea? Very well.' And retreated, clearly sensing that she had met her match.

With an understandable but unfortunate wish to flatter her hosts, Poochie MacTavish had planned that the group from North America should form a procession down the grand staircase to the strains of 'Scotland the Brave'. Due to a muddle over the tape – Hutch was in a hurry and had forgotten to take his reading glasses with him – the music which actually blared forth from the Marquess's portable cassette player was an enthusiastic choral rendering of 'There'll Always be an England'.

Carrick, Gillard and Flora MacDougal had arrived to watch.

Gillard had a strained look on his face. 'If Murdo trips again and brings the whole lot down like a pack of cards, I shall be forced to take my mirth somewhere else,' he said in Carrick's ear.

Doubtless also amused by the spectacle, Lord Muirshire remained outwardly unperturbed, emerging through a doorway on the opposite side of the hall with Andrew Kennedy, who made the introductions. Mrs MacTavish, ablaze in a creation of crimson taffeta, curtsied.

Someone strangled the music. And Carrick watched, holding his breath, as Kimberley Devlin descended the stairs. No one else, seemingly, had noticed her; perhaps she did not want to be noticed. Wearing a long, silvery-grey dress with little in the way of decoration, she came painfully down, without her stick, holding on tightly to the ornate banister rail. Then she paused, her gaze searching the throng below. As though sensing her gaze on him, the one she sought looked up.

'My dear!' the Marquess of Muirshire exclaimed, hurrying forward. 'How delightful! You're going to join us after all.' He held out a hand and the singer took it to assist her to complete her descent. All eyes were on them and for a fleeting moment there was absolute silence.

'Ladies and gentlemen, please make your way to the Red Room,' Kennedy announced. 'The banquet might be authentic, but we always serve the alcoholic beverages of this century beforehand. You will, however, be able to sample mead and barley wine with your meal should you wish.'

'Talking of lice . . .' Patrick muttered in Carrick's ear as the group moved past them. And Tony Capelli briskly approached, smiling and relaxed. 'Good evening, gentlemen. Neither of you have attended one of my banquets before, I think? I assure you, it will be a night to remember.'

The Great Hall had been transformed. So comprehensive was the change that Carrick heard Patrick cursing under his breath. It was very dark. Too dark. The prolonged twilight of a Scottish summer evening had been shut out and almost all the curtains in the long, high room had been closed. The candles had been lit, as had log fires – for such a room is always chilly – in the stone fireplaces at each end. These – intentionally, perhaps – smoked. Further authenticity was provided by the Marquess's dogs, which wandered at will around the banqueting table.

Damn, Carrick thought. *We won't be able to see, or hear, once the piper and minstrels get going. Or be able to move quickly, not with these dogs everywhere.*

The seating plan was of no assistance either. Carrick had been placed at a top table positioned at a right angle to the longer one, Andrew Kennedy on his left, Kimberley on his right. Patrick was out of sight at the other end. Should he do something about it? Just then, a note arrived on his plate, brought by the quiet Carrie. It read: DO NOTHING. YET. P.

There were also far more people present than Carrick had anticipated: estate workers dressed as jongleurs and jesters, their ladies as serving wenches. There was a wizard with a tall pointed hat and a flowing wig, two huntsmen complete with flügel-horns, a fortune-teller and six 'acrobats', who looked more like members of the local football team. Probably they were.

Before the soup, Flora MacDougal was scheduled to read from her latest novel, thus explaining the alarmingly oversized handbag that she had been guarding so diligently since her arrival. There was a suitable hush: the only sound that of pots being clattered in the distant kitchen and the yelp of a dog as someone trod on its tail.

The lady writer donned spectacles and rose, clutching a sheaf of paper. She began 'Macdui the Red, son of Horne, son of Werric, was a credit to his race, being of great stature and a fine horseman. His horse, the stallion Ardic, was famed throughout the lands known as the Northern Kingdom of Frankish Scots as a beast that would come to the aid of its master in battle, with hooves and teeth. Many were the tales told of its valour and speed in time of war. Macdui, the chief, had obtained Ardic as a foal from the peoples of the plains to the south, and had paid a great price in gold for him.' Flora paused for effect. 'The gold of the Vikings!'

'I thought it was set in *Kilwinning*,' Kennedy breathed in Carrick's ear. 'That's what she told me. It's the wee place where you turn left for Ayr and right for Ardrossen. I don't remember seeing anything about a northern kingdom on the sign post. Perhaps it's behind B&Q.'

The acute hearing of the reader detected a mocker and she bent on him a withering gaze before resuming: 'In the year of the invasion by the Viking Torveld the Second, it came to pass that . . .'

Carrick blotted out the affected voice and turned to his right-hand neighbour. Kimberley was staring straight ahead, her eyes glazed. This was not unduly worrying, given the present circumstances. The Marquess was on her right; some sixth sense told Carrick that they were holding hands under the table. So that was the state of affairs, was it? Carrick had wondered earlier that evening, when Kimberley's hand had lingered just a little longer than was strictly necessary in that of the Marquess. Now his suspicions were confirmed.

Flora droned on. The assemblage fidgeted on the hard bench seats; stomachs rumbled audibly. Then, just as the authoress was really getting into her stride with an excruciatingly detailed account of Macdui's complicated ancestry, she was forced to pause for breath at the end of a paragraph. The Marquess seized the opportunity, jumped to his feet and thanked her profusely for a fascinating preview of her novel. After what had gone before, his brevity was much appreciated – though not by Flora, who sat down looking decidedly peeved.

'Thank God for that,' said Kennedy, as the audience relaxed into chatter and laughter. 'Did you ever hear such a load of havers in your life? Excuse me – I've got to find out why those fires are smoking. Everyone'll be kippered at this rate.'

Both fireplaces were indeed puffing out copious quantities of smoke and the scent of applewood was strong in the air. Hutch, Master of Ceremonies for the night, signalled to helpers to open a couple of doors; Carrick noticed that those unfortunate enough to be seated closed to the fireplaces were coughing and surreptitiously wiping their eyes. Together, Hutch and Kennedy moved the logs further back in the grate and the air in the room cleared sufficiently to make the consumption of the first course – vegetable soup with chunks of wild boar meat in it, taken with coarse brown bread torn from massive round loaves – a pleasure. The purists scorned the spoons provided for the socially timid and lifted the bowls to their mouths, mopping the remainder with more bread. As the meal progressed, and the mead and barley wine flowed, nearly everyone discovered the primitive joys of eating with the fingers.

'It's always like this,' Kennedy commented, a piece of venison speared upright on a knife before him. 'You revert to the noble savage. And in case you're wondering why I didn't fight you for that seat next to Kim, it's because Himself's here.' He gave Carrick a wry grin.

'They seem fond of one another,' Carrick said blandly.

'He treats her like the daughter he never had. It's hardly surprising – she's a dream.' His gaze focused on the girl bringing fresh trenchers of bread. 'She's not bad either.'

126

Carrick had already spotted Joanna and was desperately endeavouring to ignore her.

'I wonder where she's from?' Kennedy went on. 'I've never seen her before, although a red-haired girl was helping in the kitchen yesterday. I didn't have time to get a good look at her then.' Lowering his voice he said, 'I wonder how she'd react if my hand sort of brushed against her.'

'*I'd* react by pushing your teeth down your throat,' Carrick found himself saying. 'The mead must have dulled your wits. And there's gravy running down your chin.'

'No need to overreact,' Kennedy said, using his hand- kerchief to wipe the grease away.

'Over here, please,' Carrick said as the huge plates of bread came closer. A strange emotion had come over him, choking him with its intensity; the more he looked upon her, the stronger it became. Joanna looked wonderful. In the candle- light her hair was like a red-gold halo.

'Take a seat while I visit the john,' Kennedy said to her. 'Talk to James. He seems to have appointed himself your personal bodyguard.'

Joanna sat down and slapped half a yard of bread down in front of him. 'You've already got bread. Greedy pig.'

Carrick felt as though his tongue had stuck to the roof of his mouth. 'Marry me,' he managed to get out. 'When I asked you before, I made it sound like a business venture. I really mean it this time – I'm crazy about you.'

She peered closely at him. 'You're sober, too!'

'I've had hardly anything to drink. Jo . . .'

'Where's the wench with the bread?' someone roared. It was the Canadian, Ricardo Folkins; his shout was quite unneces- sary as he was seated a mere three places to the Marquess's right, at the top of the long table.

Absent-mindedly, Carrick frisbied his own in that direction. It found its target to a gust of laughter.

'I think he's asking her for a date,' Poochie MacTavish ventured.

'Male guests did sweet-talk the serving girls, of course,' Flora sniffed. 'It led to all kinds of debauchery.'

'That's what we need,' Buck Murdo yelled. 'More debauchery!'

'Would anyone like another helping of venison?' asked their host vaguely, emerging from a whispered conversation with Kimberley.

'Jo!'

'I can feel Patrick's eyes on us,' Joanna said. 'He'll say we're blowing the cover.'

'To hell with the cover. I'm asking you to marry me.'

The exact nature of her reply was lost to the room at large, much to their annoyance. Whatever Joanna whispered in the vicinity of Carrick's left ear would forever remain a secret. But the audience were not left disappointed for long as she shot to her feet and hit him over the head with a trencher. The onlookers sighed in commiseration; clearly his quest had failed.

'Takes a lot of guts to ask a girl for a date if you've never even spoken to her before,' Caspar Dean – rendered uncharacteristically convivial by the mead – commented to Gillard at the other end of the table. 'Guess he must be a little tipsy.'

'I think he was trying to chat her up beforehand, in the kitchen,' Gillard replied with a distinct lack of enthusiasm, and turned his attention with determination back to his plate. Dean abandoned his attempt at conversation and turned to Mamie Wilson on his other side. The Wilsons were unfortunately separated by the head gamekeeper: a cheerful soul, all too ready to make small talk, but possessed of such a broad Scots accent that they could not understand a word he said.

'This is quite something, isn't it?' Dean said, indicating the gathering.

'He must be loaded,' Mamie said, nodding her head in the direction of the Marquess.

'Not according to *my* definition of the term,' he told her grandiloquently. 'Oh, sure, there are the family paintings, the antique furniture. But that's all inherited. The accumulated clutter of other people's lifetimes. And these estates cost a mint to run. The prestige, the title – those are the real benefits of being a marquess.'

Cheese made from ewe's milk was served, piped in as the cheesemaker, a local man, was present. For the main course

128

the piper had also given his all: a lament of uncertain ancestry, fitting perhaps for the demise of an unknown stag.

'I'll fill his drones with superglue,' Andrew Kennedy avowed. 'Hello, here are the lads with the broadswords! Perhaps they'll lop his head off for us.'

It was at this point that the joking definitely stopped.

By the cunning persuasion of young minds together with the chance of financial reward, the display of 'swordsmanship' had been converted into something much more dangerous before the contestants even entered the Great Hall. Of all those present, Patrick Gillard was probably the first to guess that all was not well. He rose immediately, and with difficulty, a minstrel standing right behind him apparently intent on serenading him alone in as close proximity as possible. A small country dance display was in progress to one side of the hall and he struggled to force his way between the bouncing couples, his eyes watering from the woodsmoke.

On the other side of the hall blades rattled and clanged fiercely in the hands of the profoundly inexperienced as the Americans innocently cheered them on. Mamie Wilson produced a camera and got up from her seat to take photographs, oblivious to the risk of possible dismemberment.

'Excuse me,' said Gillard to the wizard, who was blocking his way. In reply the wizard produced a small aerosol from his magic box of tricks and sprayed it in Gillard's face.

The substance it contained was banned in most countries and Gillard was unconscious before he hit the floor. Because of the smoke and lack of light, as well as more obvious distractions, no one but the wizard saw the real reason for the fall.

At that moment one of the swordsmen hooked the point of his weapon inside the basket handguard of his opponent's and wrenched it from his grasp, the sword spiralling in an arc to land with a crash among the platters on the table. Mamie took a flash photo.

'I hope there aren't any fingers adrift,' Carrick remarked dryly to Kennedy.

The estate manager frowned. 'They seem to have left their senses and their manners outside. It's supposed to be a display, but it won't be the first time a little betting's gone on. I'll have a word with them before limbs start flying through the air.' He stood up and saw consternation instead of dancing. 'What's happened?' he called.

The reply was lost in the general hubbub. But Kennedy managed to understand and waved at the speaker in comprehension.

'Everything all right?' Carrick asked.

'Someone's fainted. I'm not surprised, in this bloody fog. I think it's time to call a halt to all this.' He went off purposefully towards the remaining pair of duellists, but before he arrived the wizard ran up, false hair streaming, snatched the sword that had fallen on the table and commenced to play the fool. Posing in mock-heroic style, he attacked the two estate boys with gusto.

'Attaboy!' Buck Murdo yelled. 'Ten bucks on the magic man!'

Benjamin Rialto was quite enjoying himself. 'From what I've read of the times, this kind of entertainment – duels to the death – took place quite frequently.'

'They didn't have nylon wigs though,' Flora commented acidly. 'It was my understanding that the Marquess would aim for more authenticity.'

'Hell, we don't care what his wig's made of,' Poochie declared. 'We're not nitpicking folk.'

'They had witches in those days too,' her husband said in an undertone, gazing at Flora with some fascination.

The Marquess was anxiously watching the swordplay. 'It's getting a bit out of hand,' he said to Carrick. 'Would you mind giving Andy a little support? They must have been drinking – it's unlike them to be so irresponsible.'

Carrick had been about to offer his assistance in any case. He stood up. Patrick was nowhere to be seen – Carrick prayed he was monitoring events somewhere nearby.

Kennedy was having no success in forcing the contestants to desist; they appeared to regard his presence as all part of the fun, all three running away down the room. Seconds later the wizard collided with Mamie Wilson, who had been closing for an action shot, and the quartet fell in a heap with a sound like an ironmongery stall overturning.

'Mrs Wilson? Are you all right?' Kennedy was asking when Carrick arrived.

'Where's that wizard?' Carrick demanded to know.

'Gone to fetch Capelli.'

Mamie Wilson had been lying quite still but now her eyes fluttered open. 'Is my camera OK?' she enquired faintly. 'I got some great shots.'

Her husband had appeared and was telling the two young men what he thought of them. 'You should have taken charge of this!' he shouted at Carrick. 'It's a shambles. Like a damn beargarden.' He threw himself down at his wife's side. 'Mamie, are you hurt bad?'

'It's my leg,' she whimpered. 'I guess I need a doctor.'

'We'll get you to another room,' Carrick said to them both. In an aside to Kennedy he whispered: 'Get Gillard! Now!' He couldn't believe that Patrick would desert him. What was he thinking of?

The news was not brought until the Wilsons had been transferred to an adjacent room. Capelli had appeared and smoothly taken charge; Luigi had been posted at the door to keep away the inquisitive.

'He's *what*?' Carrick exclaimed.

'They've taken him upstairs. Out like a light,' Kennedy reported. 'Perhaps the heat got to him. It doesn't seem to be too serious – I felt his pulse and I'd say it was normal. Perhaps the doc ought to see him too.'

Carrick went up the stairs two at a time.

Chapter Twelve

Joanna was alone with Gillard. He had been laid down in the recovery position on the camp bed in Kimberley's dressing room and was still insensible.

'Have you any official back-up?' Carrick asked frantically.

'If we have he didn't tell me.'

'You realise that we've a roomful of international criminals down there and can't do anything about it?'

'Yes.'

'What was he going to do?'

'Patrick has been about as forthcoming as a clam. I should imagine he intended to shepherd them down into the dungeons at gunpoint. All I know for sure is that he and I were going to take the imported crooks' places.'

'You and I *can* take their places.'

'James, you're not thinking straight. You're a detective chief inspector! You can't just—'

'Yes, I can. Thanks for reminding me. I can go down and arrest the bloody lot on suspicion.'

'He *meant* it!' Joanna gasped as the door slammed. 'James! Wait!'

The door opened again. 'Leave Patrick a note. Tell him that Philip Graham is on his way here.'

It was second nature to Carrick to have his warrant card with him at all times. When he produced it and held it under Luigi's nose the result was utterly gratifying. Inside the room the four were taken entirely by surprise: Mamie Wilson standing by the window, her full weight on her supposedly broken leg; her husband in animated conversation with the man in

132

wizard's costume; Tony Capelli by the fireplace tapping his fingers impatiently on the mantelpiece.

'Boss . . .' Luigi began.

'You're all under arrest,' Carrick said. He just had time to finish the caution before the wizard headed towards him, one hand reaching into his pocket. Carrick kicked the hand when it emerged and the little canister clattered into a corner; Luigi made a dive for it.

If he had been asked to describe what happened next, Carrick would have been unable to do so. It all took place too quickly. Life became eccentric, if not to say bizarre. He knew that they were hitting him and that he hit back; he had a clear memory of sending Luigi into oblivion right across the room. But the canister still ended up in Capelli's possession. Carrick slithered through the hands that were trying to hold him; then their feet found him instead. His sight began to blur. And he was dimly aware of the wizard, looming over him, the canister held high.

Unaccountably, the wig flew through the air in one direction while its erstwhile owner went in another. A foot came from nowhere, slammed the magic man face down on the floor and stood on him. Then a hand – possibly, Carrick was beginning to realise, part of the same human being as the foot – got a grip on Carrick's collar and yanked him upright. Carrick, understandably, began to choke. When he could breathe properly again the room had gone strangely quiet.

It looked like a massacre. Six prone bodies.

Then one of them stirred, crawled to the nearest chair and pulled himself into it.

Carrick made his way, also on his knees, to the chair. He wasn't feeling too good. 'I could do with you more often,' he said. 'For arrests and similar occasions.'

Gillard was taking deep, uneven breaths. 'They've all . . . had a dose.'

Carrick then saw that Joanna was also in the room, holding the canister. She looked rather dazed, as though she might have taken a whiff accidentally; this surmise proved to be correct when her knees suddenly buckled.

'Open the effing window,' Gillard said faintly.

Carrick and Joanna somehow managed it between them, on

their knees, using both hands and all their diminished strength to shove open one of the large lower windows. Warm, pine-scented summer night air wafted in. After a few minutes Joanna felt well enough to soak her handkerchief in the water in a nearby flower vase and wipe it over her face and neck.

Where the hell is *everyone?* Carrick thought.

'I've had this stuff used on me before,' Gillard said. 'I'm afraid I shall be a write-off for anything up to twenty-four hours. It affects balance and co-ordination and makes you feel as sick as a dog. And when my co-ordination's affected I can't walk. We'll have to abort the swap.'

'I'll take your place,' Carrick offered.

'You're not cleared to do anything dangerous.'

Carrick made for the door. 'I'll get their cases – it would look odd if we went without them.' He looked back. 'Don't try to kid me that you haven't the authority to get clearance.'

'Aren't we rather forgetting that none of us looks like the Wilsons?' Joanna said.

'I don't think disguise was ever an option,' Gillard said. 'We simply didn't know in advance who it was. On previous occasions it would appear that Capelli has whisked people away so we must assume that it was he who actually gave the OK by handing them over personally. If we go ahead with this we shall have to take a chance by telling whoever does the collecting that he's otherwise engaged – say, smoothing over the other Americans, some of whom reckoned their evening had been spoilt.'

'If photos of the Wilsons have been issued . . .' Joanna began.

'That's when it might get interesting,' her prospective boss told her.

Carrick encountered hardly anyone on his journey upstairs. No one would have questioned his activities in any case; the rumour had already gone about that Mrs Wilson was to be taken to Inverness Hospital with a suspected broken leg. Naturally, her husband would accompany her. And, as Carrick had guessed, their cases were packed and ready to go.

There was also the problem of what to do with five unconscious suspects.

'Leave it with me,' Gillard said. 'No, don't argue. I'll use my mobile to report in. You station Andy outside the door. Tell him what's happened – we have to trust someone. Do you want me to contact anyone in particular?'

'You might give Neil Macpherson a ring and brief him on what's been going on,' Carrick replied. 'Strictly speaking, this lot ought to be put into custody as soon as possible.' He gave Gillard the number.

'There *is* a surveillance operation, in case you were wondering,' Gillard said. 'But it's nothing to do with me. All I know is that it's in place, so you'll be watched every inch of the way.'

After they had gone, collected by a private ambulance of some kind, Joanna in a wheelchair, Gillard felt ill and very useless. He had failed in his duty. He wished desperately that he had been in a state to be more helpful: to brief Carrick properly, to advise what to do if the subterfuge was discovered. But his sole pathetic contribution had been to remind Carrick to change his clothes, something Carrick had already worked out for himself.

Later again, when the castle was quiet and he and Andrew Kennedy waited for the police to arrive, the five still comatose on the floor, he was able, although still nauseated by the effects of the chemical, to track down Neil Macpherson and speak to him. After this the police came and went; by this time he felt so ill that he had no choice but to leave the explaining to Kennedy. Then he was left alone and must have slept, for when he next opened his eyes it was dawn, the first silvery light on the dew on the lawns. It was two thirty. One tended to forget how early the sun rose in these northern climes.

Immediately, his anxiety returned. He went through the events again in his mind, forcing his still sluggish brain to concentrate. Capelli, Luigi, the Wilsons and the anonymous wizard had been taken into custody; Special Branch were tailing the ambulance; and he had briefed a certain police inspector friend of James's who was involved with the Glasgow end of the operation.

His main worry was that he himself had been taken out, removed with maximum efficiency before he could do anything. Had he been targeted simply because he had made the first move to prevent the swordplay getting out of hand? Or had Capelli been warned? By Kimberley?

Gillard struggled to his feet, almost overcome by nausea. Perhaps he would feel better if he could actually *be* sick. He managed to reach the main hall where he stood for a while, taking deep breaths. Slowly, he began to feel better. He was wondering whether it would be possible, or even advisable, to attempt the stairs with a view to going to bed, when there was a thunderous knocking on the front door. With the Marquess and, no doubt, all his staff in bed, he had no choice but to open the door himself. Finally, after a struggle with seemingly endless bolts and catches, he stood face to face with three men, one of whom waved a small card at him.

Gillard grabbed the hand before the card could be stowed away again, removed it from the man's grasp and examined it more closely.

'Well, Inspector, what can I do for you?' he asked, handing the ID back and ushering the three indoors.

'I have orders to take into custody five people who I believe are being held here.'

'They've been collected already. Ages ago. Perhaps you'd better check . . . I've a nasty feeling about all this.'

One of the men swiftly grabbed his radio and conducted frantic enquiries. At the end he turned to Gillard, his face grave. 'They must have been bogus police officers. Even worse news is that we've lost track of the ambulance. The surveillance car had to follow at a safe distance to prevent the driver of the ambulance spotting that he was being tailed and suddenly, on the outskirts of Inverness, it put a spurt on, jumped all the red lights and disappeared in side streets. By the time they caught up with it at the hospital the vehicle had been abandoned with no trace of the occupants.'

'It's just as well I put a homing device in the Wilsons' luggage then,' Gillard said.

As a sergeant in the Met's Vice Squad, Carrick had often worked undercover. This had sometimes involved adopting a highly unsavoury persona, a ploy not only necessary but often life-saving. With this in mind, he stretched out on the back seat of the car, giving Joanna very little room, and pretended to doze with what he hoped was a thuggish smirk on his face.

The ambulance had come to a skidding halt in a narrow side

street in Inverness and he and Joanna had been bundled out and into a waiting Mercedes. A few quiet words were exchanged by the men in both vehicles and then the ambulance had been driven away.

'Where *was* Capelli?' the man in the front passenger seat asked. 'I was told that he didn't personally deliver the goods this time.'

'Soothing down the old man – his lordship,' Carrick answered. 'He was upset by our little accident.'

'I'm with you. He's not in the know, is he?'

'You tell me,' Carrick retorted.

'You've got a split lip.'

'I fell over, didn't I? How was I to know that people would be arseing around with real swords?'

This seemed to answer the man's concerns. For several miles there was complete silence but for the drone of the tyres on the road. The man said, 'This might be the last drop for a while. The boss is getting nervous. I hope you're worth all the bother.' After a short silence he added, 'You don't seem to have a Yank accent.'

Carrick grabbed him by the hair and hauled his head back. 'You seem to have a big mouth, though. If you must know, I haven't much of an American accent because I've spent most of my life in goddamned Scotland. Wilson, right? It's a Scottish name.'

Air whistled down the other's throat. 'OK! Take it easy.' Carrick released him. 'You have quite a reputation – you and her. She's quite something, eh?'

'She has ears, too,' Joanna snapped. 'Shut your trap and concentrate on navigating.'

The driver spoke for the first time. 'So you're not wanted here for anything?'

'No. I served my time in Barlinnie and decided to emigrate. But I'm prepared to come back to the old country if someone makes it worth my while.' Carrick flung himself back in his seat and pretended to doze again.

They had come about fifty miles by this time and were at present approaching Pitlochry. Carrick guessed that their final destination was south of the border; neither of their escorts had Scottish accents. Unless, of course they were merely delivery boys, covering the entire British Isles.

It might be a long journey.

They stopped near Perth, where the man who had spoken first left the car to use his mobile phone, presumably for privacy.

'He's not answerin',' was all he said when he returned.

He wouldn't be, Carrick mused, not if it was Capelli with whom they were trying to speak. He glanced across to Joanna; her eyes were closed but it was impossible to tell whether she was asleep or not. Perhaps he too ought to rest. He might need all the energy he could muster.

The car stopped again when they were still well north of Glasgow; again the man with the phone got out and walked away for a short distance.

'I could do with the loo,' Joanna muttered.

'You'll have to make do with the bushes over there,' said the driver. 'I'm not stopping in built-up areas until we get to where we're going.'

Joanna and Carrick took it in turns to visit the shrubbery at the side of the lay-by. Carrick, the last to do so, almost bumped into the man with the mobile phone on his way back to the car; he could not help but notice that the man's expression was grim. Clearly, this second attempt to make contact had not been successful either. It *had* to be Capelli that he was trying to talk to.

The car drove off at speed and soon they were in the outskirts of Glasgow. At this point they got hopelessly lost; this particular journey was obviously not one the driver was accustomed to. After going through the Clyde Tunnel three times in different directions they drew into the car park of Harry Ramsden's Fish Restaurant. Dawn was just breaking.

'We'll have fish and chips twice,' Carrick said.

'If we don't make the meeting-place, you just might be winging your way back across the pond,' said the man in the front seat. His phone beeped and he wrenched open the door and got out. 'That was our customer. Head towards the airport,' he said when he got back. 'Horrel Street.'

'Where the hell's the airport?' asked the driver.

'I know where it is – I've been there before. Just drive and I'll direct you.'

On a Sunday morning at this early hour the streets were

utterly deserted, the long straight roads canyons of stone, the only colour the occasional set of traffic lights. On a low-arched railway embankment a lone diesel engine progressed at stately speed towards a row of red Post Office wagons.

'This place is a dump,' said the driver.

Carrick made no comment. He had not expected their destination to be Glasgow. In London he would have felt reasonably at home, sure of finding his way around as far as topography was concerned, confident of plotting an escape route if necessary. He took a deep breath. *Stay calm. No need to worry. Nothing will go wrong.*

For half an hour Patrick Gillard had fumed in impotent wretchedness. Help came, oddly due to oversight; the doctor that Andrew Kennedy had forgotten to cancel arriving on the doorstep. By a quirk of fate he had done an overseas attachment and worked in a country where the chemical that had been used on Gillard was not banned. The patient was given oxygen, an injection and told to rest.

'There's a snag there,' the medical man was told. 'I can't.'

'You have that look about you,' the doctor retorted dourly.

'Can I drive safely?'

'I don't recommend it.'

'Am I a danger to *others*?'

'No, your brain's probably OK as far as that's concerned. But you might fall over and break your leg in fifteen places getting out of the car. Your physical mobility's going to be a mess for around twenty-four hours.'

'You haven't a magic pill for that, I suppose?'

'Are you trying to get me struck off?' was the stern response.

'They certainly won't ever penalise you for optimism,' said Gillard, who usually had to have the last word.

The electronic tagging device that he had placed in John Wilson's suitcase should have been monitored from Gillard's own car. He had had no choice but to order the monitor to be removed and refitted to a police vehicle. He had the Special Branch inspector's word that he would be kept closely informed of the suitcase's – and therefore Joanna and Carrick's – whereabouts. But he had no intention of sitting idly waiting for messages. It wasn't in his nature.

First of all, though, there was the matter of an informer to be dealt with.

When the doctor had taken his leave Patrick said to Kennedy, who was still hanging around looking helpful, 'Would you be so kind as to go and fetch Kimberley?'

'It's only three fifty,' the estate manager pointed out.

'I'm aware of that.'

'You can't just rake a lady out of bed in the wee small hours and—'

'Just *get* her,' Patrick interrupted quietly. He waited until the door had closed and then hauled himself out of the chair. A couple of experimental turns around the room later, he had not actually gone headlong and felt a lot happier.

'You wanted me?' said Kim from the doorway.

'No, stay,' Gillard said to Kennedy, who had accompanied her and was now preparing to depart. He took from the top pocket of his evening jacket the note that had been put into it. 'I found this earlier – a memo from James. Saying, keep an eye open for one Philip Graham.'

Kimberley pulled her long silk dressing gown around her protectively. 'He's coming *here*? What on earth for?'

'You tell me. Who is he?'

'Just a friend. He's writing some music for me, a ballad. To be honest I was doing him a bit of a favour – his career's in a mess, after he was hurt in an accident, and—'

'Please sit down by the fire if you're cold. Presumably James knows all about this but didn't have the time to tell me before all hell broke loose. So why should Philip Graham be a threat to you?'

'Is that what James said?' Kimberley said, taking the arm-chair that Patrick had been sitting in.

'Yes. Tell me about it.'

'There's nothing to tell. James knows it all – how I had a short affair with Phil, and his wife found out . . . *She's* the one to be careful of, not him.'

Patrick drew up a wooden stool and sat opposite her. 'Look, Kim, James Carrick is no fool. If he writes me a note warning me about something, it's to be taken seriously. I'll ask you again: why could this man be a threat to you?'

She sighed. 'You say he's coming here?'

140

'So it would appear.'

'He did say he might do some more work on it – the song, I mean. He showed me a rough draft and I told him it wasn't my sort of thing.'

'Is that all?'

'Actually, it was terrible.'

'And he took it badly?'

'He was upset. I wished I'd been more tactful afterwards – I hadn't realised how much it meant to him. But it's certainly possible that he wants me to look at it again. When he's got the bit between his teeth he doesn't give up easily.'

'Could it conceivably have been Philip who knocked you down?'

Her eyes flooded with tears. 'We were *friends*,' she choked.

'And did you phone someone tonight and tell them that Capelli's plans had gone badly wrong?' Patrick asked in a deadly whisper.

Her face went blank with shock. 'No! I didn't even know that they had. How could I have done? I thought the Wilsons had left the premises as planned.'

'Someone might have told you.'

'No! Why would—'

'Andrew here, for example.'

She stared at him, her mouth open, the tears running down her face.

'Of course I didn't,' Kennedy said furiously. 'Leave her alone!'

'I *wouldn't*,' Kimberley stressed. 'Not after the talk we had. Even though I'm so scared I could . . .' She broke off, biting her knuckles.

'That leaves you,' Patrick said to Kennedy. 'I know nothing whatsoever about *you*, only that you were the only person who knew what was going on earlier. I had no choice but to trust you.'

'I've done nothing wrong,' Kennedy said roughly. 'Anyway, you're not a cop. What gives you the right to interrogate us?'

Patrick stood up and carefully got his balance. 'As far as you're concerned I'm worse than a cop. And I'm running out of time and patience. I'm not feeling too good either – as you can see. Because I've had a dose of dope, not to mention the

141

business of the tin leg, I'm by no means a hundred per cent physically. That means there won't be any – finesse.'

'*Finesse*? What do you mean by that?'

'It means that normally I'd be happy to stay here – for the rest of the night, if necessary – until I'd satisfied myself that you were telling the truth. At the end of that time you might be feeling a bit hot and bothered, but you'd be otherwise unharmed.'

Kennedy took a step back, his face wary. 'Are you threatening me?'

'I think I probably am. Put it this way – if you don't co-operate I shall be forced to take measures.'

Kennedy, fit, mobile and younger by some eight years uttered a crow of derision and made for the door. But he never reached it. He was beaten to it by a small, heavy knife which thudded into the frame on the same side as the handle but at head height, missing him by no more than two inches. Shock effected a fatal pause, then a hand like a gin trap closed over his right wrist. He swung wildly with his left hand, fist balled; that also was swiftly captured. To his utter shock, Kennedy discovered that he was soon unable to move at all.

'You can learn a lot from spiders,' said the voice he hated most. 'They're very scientific creatures – know precisely how to handle prey far larger and stronger than themselves.'

'You're a bastard,' Kennedy said, surprised that he could still talk.

'Oh, I can be a *real* bastard when I want to be. Right then. You have the choice of being a good boy and telling all, in which case we can do this in civilised fashion or I can prise the words from you one at a time – which you might find a little painful. The choice is yours.'

As the last word was spoken something so exquisitely agonising happened to Kennedy's wrist that he almost fainted. Sweating, he said nothing. But when it happened again and his vision dimmed he shouted: 'And if a woman and child's lives are at stake? What then? Do I have to have two deaths on my conscience as well?'

He was released from torment, and spun round to face Gillard, all in one smooth movement.

'Who?'

142

'My ex-wife and our daughter Cara.'

'There is such a thing as police protection.'

'Do you have the authority to arrange it?'

'Yes. Shall we talk?'

'I – I've never done it before,' Kennedy stammered. 'But nothing's ever gone wrong before—'

'Sit down.'

'*Capelli*,' Kimberley said in disgust. 'It's Capelli. Everyone's terrified of him. He can make you do anything.'

Kennedy sat down, rubbing his wrist. 'It was down to me to ring a certain number if there was ever a hitch. If I failed to do so Susan and Cara would have some kind of accident . . . God, I don't know if the filthy bastard even knows there they live! It's *not* knowing with these people. It gets to you in the end. You start convincing yourself that they can see through walls, read your mind.

'It was inevitable that he had someone on the inside,' Patrick murmured. 'So who's the wizard?'

'He's like Luigi – only with a few more brain cells. I've only seen him once before, on an occasion when Luigi couldn't be here for some reason. I don't know his name and I didn't ask. He persuaded the boys to carry out their swordplay for real – said someone wanted to place a heavy bet on the outcome and there'd be something in it for them. Don't blame them – they're good lads. But he plied them with beer from the moment they arrived.' Kennedy closed his eyes in anguish. 'Help me. Please. I couldn't bear it if any harm came to— You must believe me when I tell you that I was relieved when Carrick arrived. Although he told me was on leave, not on official business, I was praying that this scam would get busted wide open. I really tried, I even told him Capelli wasn't to be trusted . . . When he arrested the whole lot of them I nearly didn't make the phone call. But then I thought of that ape Luigi, how there were plenty more just like him waiting in the wings ready to—' He broke down and sobbed, his hands covering his face. Gillard was just able to catch the words: 'I did help you! I thought if I did that . . .'

'Better give me your ex-wife's name and address,' Gillard said gently.

*

143

A little later, following a phone call from his contact in Special Branch, Gillard drove away from Castle Stalker. The sun had risen and looked quite beautiful: a blood-red ball in a sky fading from dark mauve to palest azure. But he did not want to think of blood just then.

The tagging device had failed.

Chapter Thirteen

Sarah Graham was normally a good driver. But this particular journey was taking all her powers of concentration. By contrast, Jeremy seemed oddly calm; he sat day-dreaming, the road map spread across his knees.

'It might not be the one from the kitchen,' he said, breaking what had been a long silence. 'It might not be ours, I mean. Someone else might have put it there.'

'I'm sure it is,' Sarah fretted. 'I'm certain there were three in the cupboard under the sink and now there are only two.'

Jeremy had noticed a bundle on a shelf when they were getting the car out. It had proved to be a hand towel – one of the blue ones from the downstairs cloakroom – wrapped around an empty pill bottle, a half-full bottle of whisky – and a funnel.

'But why are these here?' Sarah had asked, as they stared at the discovery.

'Perhaps he didn't have time to get rid of them,' Jeremy had suggested. 'Wipe the prints off them – whatever.'

'But a *funnel!*'

'Whoever killed that Barr character must have got the whisky and pills down his throat somehow.'

It was grisly, abominable, downright ghastly. Sarah shuddered as she thought about it. But it had to be faced. 'I really wish you had discussed all this with me before you informed the police,' she said.

'You weren't around. I panicked. Perhaps it's just as well I did, seeing what we've found.'

Sarah could not imagine Philip capable of murder. She

145

simply didn't think he had it in him – although he had been behaving very strangely lately . . .

She knew exactly where in Scotland Philip was headed. He had told her, on more than one occasion, about the song recitals at the castle. It appealed to his innate pride, she supposed: the beautiful soprano – who had, all willing, taken him into her bed – trilling under the chandeliers, one dainty hand resting on the grand piano beside her . . . Oh yes, Philip must have really thought he was going places when he started screwing that bitch.

'You realise that the police will almost certainly get there before us,' Sarah said. 'It might be a trifle awkward.' She had a sudden thought. 'We should have brought those things with us – they're evidence!'

'We have. I put them in the boot.'

'The important thing is to stop him doing anything else.' She glanced sideways at her son. 'This must be terrible for you, Jeremy. That your own father's—'

'He's not a bad person. That crash affected his mind.'

'Poor Philip. I'm afraid it couldn't look much worse for him.'

The disused warehouse in Horrel Street, not far from the sewage works, had been set ablaze the previous year by vandals and was now a gutted, blackened ruin. The centre of the roof of the main building had collapsed on the night of the fire and the rest had been slowly following suit as wind and rain dislodged slates and rotting roof timbers. At the northern end a two-storey structure survived more or less intact, but with every window broken. This had been used variously as an office, staff accommodation and originally, when the building had started life as a rope factory, engine house. On this particular morning it was being put to the purpose of meeting place.

The car had been driven right up to the door of the warehouse, crunching over splinters of wood and broken glass. The driver got out and carefully looked around before walking towards the entrance. When he was still several feet from it, another man appeared from the doorway of the old engine house farther along. At a sign from him the driver approached and went inside. Moments later he came back into view and beckoned towards the vehicle.

'That means me,' said the man in the front seat. 'You stay here until you're called. I want the dosh before you're handed over.'

'Would it be too much to hope for police marksmen on nearby rooftops?' Carrick wondered aloud when he and Joanna were alone. 'I didn't dare keep turning round to see if we were being tailed but one does anticipate . . . I don't really rate our chances of fighting our way out if there are any setbacks.'

'Patrick didn't offer you a gun.'

'I don't think he carries one.'

'I'm afraid I left my mobile phone behind. What with all the excitement and being half-gassed. It's in my bag in the castle kitchen.'

'It's probably just as well. If they'd spotted you with it they might have become suspicious.' He gazed at her soberly. 'Take care, Jo. I've no idea what they expect from you. It's anyone's guess why the Wilsons are in demand – but when a woman is involved in this kind of violent crime she's usually had to work at it far harder than a man.'

'That applies to the right side of the law too!' she countered acerbically.

'Oi! You Yanks deaf?'

The individual who had bellowed to Carrick and Joanna from the doorway of the building dodged inside again when it became apparent when his words had not received a warm welcome. There was no escape, however, and he found himself picked up bodily by the fair-haired man – far taller and stronger than he had appeared when seated in the car – and taking a short airborne journey that ended in a painful forced landing on the remains of a set of shelves.

There was a huge guffaw of laughter.

'Anyone else want to say hello?' Carrick said, emphatically not amused as he surveyed the motley collection of men: five of them, not counting the two who had brought them. Scathingly he went on, 'What the hell are we doing in this craphole? I'm used to doing business in hotel rooms.'

Why such a large reception committee? he wondered to himself. *To impress us? Or are they expecting trouble of some kind?*

No other greetings seemed to be forthcoming.

They were in the first of what was apparently two rooms; an open doorway led into an area at the rear where an old-fashioned sink with a single tap over it could be glimpsed among piles of rubbish. Air tainted with what smelt like diesel fuel fanned through the open window and into the room where they were standing, which was rectangular and measured approximately twenty feet by twelve.

Carrick noticed these details automatically, in the same way and for the same reasons that Patrick Gillard would have done. They represented the set and props that he would use to assist him in any defensive action he had to take.

'OK?' asked the driver, breaking the silence.

A fat envelope was tossed in his direction and he and his partner left without uttering another word. Soon there came the sound of a car driving away.

'Where are you going?' one of the remaining men said to Carrick.

'I'm not staying in this shithouse a moment longer,' Carrick replied, halfway to the door.

'There's a motor round the back.' A gap-toothed grin was aimed at the man who was still busy extricating himself from the splintered shelving. 'Hey, Jamie! You'd better try your hand with the lassie now, before she leaves.'

To his amused disbelief – he knew what the outcome would be – Carrick realised that the said unfortunate, clearly not very bright, had every intention of complying with the suggestion. So after Jamie had been resoundingly cartwheeled back into his previous place of rest – his colleagues holding one another up, crying with laughter – they all left.

The vehicle, a van painted with the faded legend FANNY'S FRESH FLOWERS, was parked in a large puddle. Carrick insisted that it be moved forward a few yards so he and Joanna could get in dry-shod. The seven of them squeezed in, much encumbered by the Wilsons' luggage, which their original escorts had thrown unceremoniously into the back of the van. Carrick and Joanna swayed from side to side, jammed knee to knee on the makeshift bench seating. There were no windows in the rear; what little light there was filtered through the metal grille that separated them from the driver's cab. There was no air either; just a smell of fuel oil and, oddly, fish.

'Not like me to get travel-sick,' Joanna said through clenched jaws.

'If you throw up on me I may well retract the offer I made you last night,' Carrick said in a fashion that made Joanna suspect that he wasn't joking.

Mercifully they did not have far to go and were unloaded at the foot of a modern tower block some ten minutes later. There was a lift but it was out of order, so there was no choice but to climb the stairs. Naturally, no one offered to help Carrick and Joanna with the cases. There was graffiti in lieu of paint on the walls and enough litter in the stairwell to start your very own infill site.

They arrived at the eleventh floor and one of the men rang the bell of a flat with a red front door, well-protected by a security cage and several large padlocks.

'The land of my fathers,' Carrick muttered.

'It's to keep the police oot.'

'While everyone inside jumps out of the windows?' Carrick enquired, eyebrows raised.

Keys grated in locks and the door was opened. They lugged the cases into a long narrow hall and left them there, suddenly alone as their escorts departed, the sound of their feet endlessly clumping down the concrete stairs audible almost all the way to the bottom.

'Come in,' called a man's voice from a room at the far end of the passage.

Not what Carrick had expected – this building society branch manager in light grey suit, quiet tie and polished black shoes. But Carrick had been in the police long enough not to be surprised by anything. 'We appreciated the travelling companions you selected for us,' he said. 'They traipsed all the way up here, and now they've gone right back down again. So what was the point of all that? Did they think we might change our minds?'

The man laughed softly. 'I'm afraid they aren't very clever, Mr Wilson. Men like that can drive a car and provide a little muscle when it's needed, but that's all. I prefer to do their thinking for them.'

'But that's getting a little wearisome, so you've imported a couple of brains to do your donkey-work instead? No, thanks.

I didn't come all this way to be your errand boy.' Carrick had decided to continue acting tough. Polite affability cut no ice with the criminal underworld.

'I think you ought to sit down and hear what I have to say before you get on your high horse. And I haven't introduced myself to you and your companion. My name's MacCrudden.'

'I can't say I've heard the name before,' Carrick told him, dropping into a chair. 'Meanwhile, Mamie and I would appreciate some hospitality.'

'Certainly. A colleague of mine will be here at any minute and we can all have breakfast together. What can I get you to drink? Coffee, tea? Something stronger?'

'Coffee would be fine for both of us. Black, no sugar. And I'd be very surprised if your real name's MacCrudden,' Carrick added in the same breath.

The man, halfway out of his chair, sat down again. 'What made you say that?' he asked guardedly.

'I have a suspicion that the men who brought us here are the MacCruddens. They all look pretty much alike – I'm guessing that they're brothers, or cousins maybe. Even if you were the cuckoo in the nest you didn't go to the same school. You don't look anything like them and you obviously don't think like them either.'

The other leaned back in his chair and subjected Carrick to a hard stare. 'Capelli said you were good. But I'd rather you didn't ask questions.'

'Fair enough,' Carrick said calmly. 'Just idle curiosity. So is there a specific job you have in mind for us?'

'Just one. Today. After that, you go south.'

'Capelli said nothing about that!'

'Just the one job,' the man calling himself MacCrudden repeated. 'You'll get one hundred and fifty thousand dollars.'

'Pounds. We're living in the UK now.' Carrick smiled in a way that made Joanna shiver. *I'm glad he's a cop and not a crook,* she found herself thinking. *He's taken to this deception like a duck to water.*

'OK. Pounds.' MacCrudden's voice had a distinct edge to it. A woman put her head round the door. 'You want coffee?'

'Yes,' said the man.

'Harry's here. He's just parking his car.'

Carrick looked at his watch: a quarter past five.

Harry was admitted a few minutes later, out of breath from climbing the stairs. 'Harry Milliken,' he said, offering a hand when he saw the visitors. 'I hope we can do business together.'

'It's just the one job, I understand,' Carrick said.

'Is that right, John?' Harry asked the first man.

'Capelli's calling the tune,' he replied sourly. 'And now the little rat seems to have spies everywhere you can't argue with him.'

Carrick scrutinised the pair. 'Now, *you* two look more like brothers. And being as John here is not a MacCrudden, I take it, Harry, that *you* aren't a Milliken.'

Harry looked at John in some anxiety. 'What have you been telling him?'

'Nothing. He's just playing silly games.'

'I just like to know who I'm really working for,' Carrick said. 'And frankly, so far I'm not impressed. You'll have to be straight with me, or the job's off. Capelli might run your lives, but he doesn't run mine.'

'You're asking questions when one hundred and fifty thousand bucks are on the table?' Harry asked, amazed.

'Pounds,' John corrected. 'I told you, he'd want pounds not dollars.'

'I have my reputation to think of,' Carrick said smugly. 'I'm not in the paying peanuts, getting monkeys, circus. So how do you operate?'

'Right,' Harry said, shooting a desperate glance at John. 'After the war, when everyone came home and unemployment was the name of the game, families and blokes who'd fought together formed themselves into gangs. We're talking about folk you wouldn't want to meet on a dark night. You must have heard of the knife gangs in Glasgow in the fifties? The MacCruddens were one, the Millikens another. They've always been rivals. John and I came up from the south. We had something that they wanted – guns. It wasn't too difficult to take them over: old man MacCrudden had had his throat cut the week before we arrived and the Milliken lot was being run by a woman – the police had her husband in the slammer for murder. As far as the cops are concerned the gangs are still

151

rivals, but – well – they aren't. Look on it as a merger. John and I want to take over the whole of Glasgow eventually. It's just a question of picking off the right people and going in when the others are at their weakest.' He grinned.

'But then there was a grasser,' John muttered. 'Someone who didn't know which side his bread was buttered.'

'Someone we'd promoted, who got too big for his boots,' Harry continued. 'He didn't take kindly to being slapped down and went and told a policeman. We had no choice but to – remove him from his post.'

'You want me to take him right out.'

'No, *we* did that. Last night.'

'He was surprisingly stubborn, in the circumstances,' John said. 'But we went to work on him and found out what we needed to know. A deathbed confession, it was – very dramatic. Apparently he'd made initial contact with the copper weeks ago, but only spilled the beans just before we grabbed him. They'd had a cosy little *tête-à-tête* in this copper's local – how clichéd can you get? But this snout couldn't take the sort of pressure we were exerting. Told us everything – the copper's name, where he lived . . . A regular mine of information, he was. Anyway, that's who we want you to take out.'

'The *copper*?'

'That's right. Before he gets the chance to act on information received.'

'You're not thinking! He'll have recorded it – the information, I mean. Killing him won't achieve anything.'

'We're taking a bit of a gamble there,' said Harry. 'It's his weekend off, you see. He's not due back at the nick until Monday morning.'

'There was another job we were going to get you to do,' John said. 'But then this came up, and it takes priority. This needs a real professional – and one who won't hang around to be Scotland's Most Wanted.'

'His name's Macpherson,' Harry said. 'Detective Inspector Neil Macpherson.'

Carrick laughed. From shock as much as anything.

'What's so funny?'

'I don't get it. This Macpherson'll be a sitting target. Why do you need to call in an expert?'

'We don't want anyone – *anyone* – looking in our direction over this. We don't want to take any chances. Once that copper goes to work on Monday morning, we're finished.'

Carrick got up from his seat and went over to the window, hands in pockets. He hoped he was giving the impression that he was mulling it over.

Behind him there was the muted clatter of crockery, as the woman brought in coffee on a tray. 'Weapon?' he asked when the door had been closed again.

Harry had been carrying a small briefcase when he came in and now took from it a pistol that Carrick recognised as a 9mm AT84. He tossed it towards Carrick, who caught it automatically.

'You get the ammo when you're closer to the target.'

'Don't you trust me?'

'We don't trust *anyone*,' said John bluntly. 'For the same reason, the woman stays with us. You get her back, plus the money, afterwards. Not here, though. There'll be a rendezvous that you'll be told about later.'

'This is like a B-movie,' Carrick observed, picking up the gun.

'Will it do?' Harry enquired, ignoring the remark.

'It's Swiss. They're always good.'

'We'll brief you properly after you've had breakfast.'

'I could do with a couple of hours sleep, too.'

Harry glanced at the clock on the wall. 'We've timed the hit for nine thirty. What you do between now and then is your business.'

But Carrick knew he would not dare go to sleep. He could not afford to drop his defences to that extent. Instead he cultivated a monumental sulk: ate his breakfast in a surly fashion and spoke in monosyllables only when he was spoken to. Inside his sullen exterior, however, his mind was racing. How the hell was he going to get out of this one? Where was the back-up he'd assumed would be forthcoming when he needed it? Had he said too much earlier, asked too many awkward questions? Had he – God forbid – behaved like a *policeman*?

The makeshift meal over, Carrick and Joanna retired to the small bedroom allotted to them for their personal use. The doors and walls were flimsy, insubstantial, and Carrick knew

153

he and Joanna could not risk a conversation being overheard. So they sat on the bed together, lost in their own thoughts. Carrick, despite his better instincts, silently cursed Fate for getting him into this situation. Joanna, meanwhile, stared out of the window, memorising every detail of the unrelentingly dreary view. She had a sudden, unexpected hankering for a thatched cottage, a pretty garden, and a kitchen with a dark green Aga.

Chapter Fourteen

At ten minutes past nine Carrick stood in the hallway of the tower-block flat, ready to leave. Brodie MacCrudden, who had driven Carrick and Joanna there, would be arriving any minute to escort Carrick to a suitable surveillance point close to Macpherson's house. Brodie would check out the premises surreptitiously and then give the signal for Carrick to go in. When Carrick had completed the mission Brodie would enter the house by the back door and check that everything had gone as planned. Brodie would then appear at Macpherson's living-room window at the front of the house and give the nod to observers in another vehicle, parked opposite the house. They, in turn, would use their car phone to call John and Harry, who would give permission for Carrick to be taken to the rendezvous where, hopefully, Joanna would be waiting for him.

To Carrick, it all sounded unnecessarily complicated. But he wasn't in a position to point out the flaws in their plan. He was also fully aware that, if Brodie failed to give the all-clear at the scene, Joanna would not be taken to the rendezvous. Useless, then, to beat Brodie into submission and make his own getaway. Somehow, Carrick had to be at that rendezvous with an apparently successful mission behind him. In the car, being driven south, when he and Joanna were no longer seen as a problem: that was when they would bail out. That was when Carrick would have a gun, with plenty of ammunition.

So where, in the name of everything holy, were Strathclyde Police?

*

Five miles into his drive Patrick Gillard relaxed. The dose of chemicals he had received the night before clearly wasn't going to impede his driving ability. He put on speed, the needle of the speedometer moving into the interesting, illegal part of the dial. Being stopped by the police did not worry him; his MI5 ID card would extricate him from any difficulties in that direction.

He had contacted Neil Macpherson with the latest news; the failure of Special Branch to maintain a tail on Carrick and Joanna and the subsequent disappearance of the signal from the tagging device. Macpherson had been concerned, to put it mildly.

'Could you come down? I don't really want to talk about this over an open line, for obvious reasons,' he had said. 'I'm at home right now – there's no point in my going to the nick this weekend. Nothing to do with this can of worms is happening there yet – and it'd only be farther for you to drive.'

'I'm supposed to be looking after the fair soprano,' Gillard had reminded him.

'To be honest, I don't personally think Philip Graham's that dangerous. But I'll send someone from the Inverness nick to keep an eye on her.'

'Not a probationer,' Gillard had insisted. 'Someone who knows the ropes. Do you really need my presence?'

Macpherson had sighed gustily. 'Probably not. But I have this feeling in my weary bones ... Let's just say that I'd appreciate having you along. As an *observer*. I ken you're the one who got James out of his predicament in the north Midlands.'

'There was a fair bit of luck involved in that one. OK, I'll be with you as soon as I can.'

Obviously relieved, Macpherson had given him his address.

'You didn't waste any time,' Macpherson said when he opened the door: his back door. Gillard had parked a couple of streets away and made his way along a lane that provided access to the garages at the bottoms of the gardens. He did not necessarily want to advertise his arrival.

'Are you alone?' Gillard asked.

'My wife's at church. Then she's going off to a friend's

house for coffee. That's her regular Sunday routine. Can I get you a drink?'

'Anything, as long as it'll keep me awake.'

'This isn't really my case,' Macpherson said from the kitchen. 'At least, it *wasn't*. Special Branch were doing all the organising – all I was supposed to be doing was providing personnel. What's the range of the bug thing that went off the air?'

'About a hundred miles,' Gillard answered, going to stand in the kitchen doorway.

'It packed up in the Perth area, I've since been told. But we already knew that this little game was going to finish up in Glasgow, so try not to worry. James and Joanna can't be too far away.'

'No doubt. But dead or alive?'

Macpherson shook his head. 'The Wilsons were booked for a job. We know that. It presumably hasn't taken place yet, so I'm not too concerned.'

'You're forgetting. Capelli and Co. escaped.'

'Ah, yes, the bogus policemen. How long does that knockout spray last?'

'You're out cold for twenty minutes or so. But I'm afraid Capelli will be in a position to issue orders by now.'

'Capelli might want to lie low for a while. He won't want the gang here to know he's screwed up on this one.' He handed Gillard a mug of strong coffee. 'Sorry it's instant. Biscuit?'

'No, thanks.' There was still the threat of sickness at the back of Gillard's throat. 'Do you know what this job was?'

'To take out a rival drug pusher in the east end of Glasgow. The MacCrudden gang are out for total control. They and the Millikens have put most of the other gangs out of business – this other guy was more or less a one-man band.' He took a biscuit and dunked it in his coffee. 'I don't know what we can do right now but wait. Why don't you lie down? You look all-in.'

'So why do they need to import a hit-man from the States to take out a rival?' Patrick enquired when he had wearily stretched his aching body on Macpherson's sofa.

'This one's special. He's a one-off, the sort of murderous

157

bastard who only comes along once in a generation. Born with a sub-machine gun in his hand. He's fairly new on the scene – only in his early twenties – but he makes it his business to know every villain for miles around. He's got eyes in the back of his head, that one – believe me, if anyone went after him, he'd know about it before they did. Everyone's terrified of him, so there's always someone who'll tip him the wink to get on his good side. They wouldn't want to take the chance – so it makes sense for them to bring in a stranger.'

'And *you* can't touch him?'

'You'd need to do my job for a few months to answer that question.'

'And this is the guy James is going after?'

'Well, he won't do what he's told, not if he has any sense. I'm hoping he's simply going to bolt for freedom at a convenient moment. Don't forget, he's not a prisoner.'

'If they keep hold of Joanna as an insurance policy . . .'

'Lieutenant-Colonel, Special Branch might have screwed up their side of this operation, but I haven't – not yet. Since you first contacted me I've had watches put on every premises that the MacCrudden gang has been known to frequent. And since last night I know exactly who controls them. Better still – the snout hinted that the same men are now controlling the Millikens as well.'

'Did the snout tell you when they'd planned to dispose of this rival drugs pusher?'

'He said it was to happen in the early hours, when he was in his bed. But you can't rely on what snouts say.'

As Gillard slowly sipped his coffee, Macpherson's pager bleeped.

'They *know* I'm here,' he fumed, grabbing his mobile phone.

Gillard half-closed his eyes, trying to guess the inaudible side of a telephone conversation.

'*Where*? . . . Cause of death? . . . Is the pathologist really *sure* about that . . . So, you've seen the body yourself and there's no doubt in your mind . . . Thanks. No, I'll let you know if I want you.' He rammed the aerial back into the phone. 'That was my sergeant. A body's been fished out of the Clyde. My snout. And he'd been tortured before he died.'

'Yes,' Patrick said. 'And the MacCruddens – may the Lord

have mercy on their souls – probably know that you know . . .' He broke off and went over to the window, moving the net curtain slightly to one side in order to look out, being careful to keep himself out of sight. 'That means there might have been a change of plan. Tell me, Inspector, that old armchair – is it valuable?'

'That?' Macpherson said, baffled. 'No, not at all. We were going to throw it out, as a matter of fact. But why—' He stopped speaking. Gillard had moved the chair into a corner where there was no other furniture.

'Is your front door locked?' Gillard asked calmly.

'Yes. I've learned to be careful.'

Gillard went into the hall to inspect it for himself. 'I'm assuming that this snout knew where you lived.'

'Yes. Funnily enough, he had a flat in the next road. Not sure exactly where – I only ever knew him as Archie. I'm not in the phone book and I try to keep a low profile, but it's no secret where I live. Everyone in this area knows – I've been here for years. He wouldn't have had to look far.' Macpherson swallowed. 'Are you thinking what I'm thinking?'

'There's a car outside that wasn't there when I arrived and there are two men sitting in it trying not to look as though they're watching the house. Therefore, with your permission I shall unlock the front door and jam a credit card in the lower door catch – the one that doesn't lock – so it will fly open dramatically if kicked from the outside, but with no damage done to either the door or the kicker.'

'You've lost me,' Macpherson admitted.

'Well, neither of the men outside is James and my instincts tell me that they're waiting for something to happen. I think that something might be the Wilson job.'

The inspector was lost for words.

'The important thing is not to panic,' Gillard went on, returning to the window in the front living room after his small adjustment to the door.

'I'm sure I have no reason to,' Macpherson said hoarsely.

'Is James a good shot?'

'He's done the usual firearms training.'

'That's something. I shall watch from here. When I give the go-ahead, I want you to go in the kitchen and lie on the floor. I

159

should warn you – he'll be hyped up to the skies when he comes through that door.'

'But he won't really shoot me!'

'*He* won't. But he might not be alone. I'm only taking precautions.'

Another eight minutes ticked leadenly by.

'It's not going to happen,' said Macpherson, at the end of his tether.

'The men are still there.'

'Are you armed?'

Gillard tut-tutted placidly. 'Only with a grown-up skene-dhu.'

Macpherson did not looked reassured. He was not to know that Gillard with a knife was more dangerous than most men armed with a firearm.

It was three minutes to nine thirty.

'There's the back way,' Gillard recalled. 'The way I came.'

'But it would be difficult for James to know which house it was from the rear – they all look the same.'

'Not at all. I worked it out easily. Yours is the one next to the house with the big bunch of aerials on the roof. Radio hams, are they?'

'Yes,' said Macpherson meekly.

'And you must be able to see the top of that monkey-puzzle tree that's in the front garden of the house on the other side from the rear – it's massive.' He left the room and went into the kitchen. 'I'm losing my grip – anyone with any savvy would come in the back!'

Right on cue the door detonated towards him and smashed back against a cupboard, breaking the glass. Gillard did not bother to issue any instructions to Macpherson; he had already dived for cover. But such caution was unnecessary. The man coming towards him looked as dangerously hyped-up as a glacier.

'Brodie's watching,' said Carrick, not about to waste words on greetings.

'Then go and put two shots into the small armchair standing on its own in a corner of the front room,' Gillard said. 'Is Joanna with you?'

'No.' Carrick crossed into the other room, and two shots cracked loudly into the stillness.

'What now?' Gillard called.

'I signal to Brodie, who comes in the back, checks the body for signs of life and then goes to the window, where he gives the thumbs-up to the two over the road in the red Volvo. They scram and phone in on the way to say that all's well. Then Brodie drives me to the rendezvous. Where Joanna – please God – will be waiting.'

Gillard came after the assassin. 'Do you know where that is?'

'Not a clue.'

'OK. Wave to Brodie and I'll organise the rack and hot pincers.'

'Where's Neil?'

'Here,' said Macpherson, emerging from the hall cupboard.

'Slump in the chair! Play dead,' Gillard instructed. 'We've no time for silly things like tomato ketchup.' He stepped into the cupboard. 'When he's done his thumbs-up, I'll pop out and make his acquaintance.'

Carrick was on his way back into the kitchen. 'He's as tough as nails. You won't get him to talk easily.'

'I'll just use a bigger hammer,' Gillard said cold-bloodedly, pulling the door to.

'*I'll* talk to him,' Macpherson announced. 'I know the politics of this lot.'

'As you wish,' said the cupboard politely.

Brodie, a bulky man always slightly out of breath, could be heard wheezing up the garden path. In his fifties, he clearly was not relishing his role, for he gave Macpherson no more than a cursory glance before going to the window and making his signal. When he turned to retrace his steps, he came face to face with one man risen from the dead and another who appeared seemingly from nowhere and held a knife to his throat. Brodie went a ghastly shade of grey.

'Brodie MacCrudden, you're under arrest,' Macpherson said. 'But I might listen to reason if you tell me where you were about to take this man.'

Brodie had his back to the wall and commenced to slide down it slowly. His mouth moved but no sound emerged. The

161

interrogators had no choice but to bend their knees and follow him down. Outside, tyres squealed as the car roared off.

'Just think,' Macpherson said, 'if I turn a blind eye to this morning's little escapade, you might be able to make a clean break while there's still time. Go and help that crook of a son of yours run that second-hand car business in Forfar. Or, of course, turning Queen's Evidence might be—'

'He's having a heart attack,' Carrick interrupted.

'God! So he is!' Macpherson exclaimed, and reached for his mobile.

Brodie was stretched out on the floor by now, ashen-faced. He seemed surprised to find himself with a cushion under his head, covered by a blanket.

'Pray he doesn't lose consciousness so we have to give him the kiss of life,' the inspector muttered as he arranged for an ambulance.

Suddenly, Carrick, the nearest to Brodie, found himself grabbed and hauled close to the gasping mouth. There was a breathy explosion of sound in his left ear. 'Glen – what?' he said. Another gale of bad breath later, he was none the wiser.

'Well?' Macpherson said.

'It sounded like Glenifa-braze. That means absolutely nothing to me.'

'You're not a Glaswegian. Gleniffer Braes – a pile of hills back of Paisley with electricity pylons instead of trees on them. Is it a building on the braes, Brodie?'

Brodie nodded and directed his next burst of near-incomprehensible information at Macpherson.

'A barn,' he translated. 'Near the dam. I'll alert all units.' He looked almost happy. 'That'll teach Special Branch to tell us how to catch criminals! And where are you off to?'

'To find Joanna,' Carrick said, having located the keys to the van in Brodie's pocket.

'There might be complications,' Gillard said, following him to the back door. 'Capelli and the others were collected by bogus cops while I was out for the count.'

'James! If you mess this up I'll have you!' Macpherson bellowed after them. 'Start a war up there, and you'll end up in the slammer!'

When they reached the van, parked in a road at the end of

Carrick took a deep breath. 'OK.'

'Unless my eyesight's failing, there is in fact a small window, almost overgrown with ivy, on the end wall nearest to us. There might even be one to match on the other end. No doubt the noble inspector has the place surrounded. But if he hasn't . . .'

'While everyone's attention is on the front . . .'

'Quite.'

They went down the hill.

Chapter Fifteen

It was lack of sleep, Carrick supposed, that was to blame for the emotions raging through him. Either that, or a mid-life crisis, he told himself savagely. First of all he had made a fool of himself over Kimberley Devlin; now he was so much in love with Joanna that words could not do it justice. In truth he was embarrassed by the way he felt; it was unprofessional, downright childish. Fortunately Gillard didn't seem to think he was too much of a fool, and for that he was profoundly thankful.

Walking down a hillside, in unfamiliar terrain, into what was potentially a very dangerous situation, was not unduly alarming Patrick Gillard. He'd been there before. When you'd lived in the wilds of the moors for a week, clad only in a thin tracksuit and armed with a small pocket knife, knowing that if you survived you'd face inquisition, torture – anything else seemed easy as long as you kept your wits about you. And that had just been the army Special Operations training course. Still, that was all in the past. But the memory would stay with him for ever and it certainly helped to focus the mind at times like these.

Gillard could sense that Carrick was utterly exhausted. The man was even stumbling as he walked. But he knew Carrick well enough to be sure that there was plenty of native stamina in the younger man yet. Gillard felt desperately sorry for him. The girl he loved was in the hands of violent thugs – how was any man expected to react? But, of course, Carrick wasn't just any man. He wasn't a civilian and he had to behave accordingly. If things got really difficult, Gillard would watch him

ke a hawk. No room for headstrong bravado where this
peration was concerned.

They reached the boundary of the pasture and negotiated
barbed wire fence that spanned a gap in the hedge. By this
ime they were a matter of only twenty yards from the rear of
he barn, the bulk of the building preventing the police from
potting them.

'I reckon they've done a recce and discounted that little
vindow behind the ivy,' Gillard whispered as they paused to
urvey the area of tussocky grass that lay before them; there
vas a rusting tractor, some rolls of wire with weeds growing
hrough them, and little else. 'OK – go for it.'

The helicopter was still hovering over the reservoir, a little
loser than it had been before. The partly obscured window
vas, fortunately, no more than an unglazed opening in the
tonework.

Inside, stacked right up against it, were bales of hay. In
ilence Carrick signalled that he would check what lay at the
ther end of the barn and was back a minute later, shaking his
ead. This was the only window.

They pulled the ivy to one side. With his knife, Gillard cut
he strings on the nearest bale. Together, Carrick and Gillard
nanoeuvred a section of hay towards them and put it on the
round at their feet. Soon, most of the bale had been removed
nd another bale had been revealed, stacked end on.

'This lot might be sixty bales thick,' Carrick breathed.

'I think we decide when we see what's on the other side of
his one. Take care that the whole lot doesn't collapse when I
aul it out – and be ready for instant boarding if they hear us
nside.'

The bale came out like a cork out of a bottle. Immediately,
bove the sound of the helicopter, they heard Joanna's voice.

'You do realise,' she said loudly, 'that half of Strathclyde
²olice are out there? Just five of you against one hell of a lot of
hem.'

Carrick glanced towards Gillard and raised his eyebrows.
²atrick's reaction was unexpected, to say the least – he
aunched himself into the hole they had made and disappeared
rom sight. The sharp reports of several shots came almost
nstantaneously, followed by a man's scream.

Carrick heard two more shots when, with broader shoulder than Gillard, he was wriggling through the gap in the bales. When he tumbled out the other side and fell on to an earth floor he instinctively rolled over and dived for the cover o some sacks of cattle feed. All was dim, dark. Silent, but fo someone's rasping breath.

Then a shadow fell across Carrick where he crouched. H peeped round the sacks to see a man backing towards him, th barrel of a sub-machine gun just visible at the side of his body He suddenly swung it round to the right and fired.

The weapon was still firing when Carrick tackled him from behind; this was no time for ethics. When he was down Carrick punched him in the face, hard enough to ensure tha he stayed down.

'Got him?' came Gillard's voice.

'Yes. Are you OK?'

For answer he walked into view, his right leg dragging a little. When Carrick rose and went into the light he saw th blood trickling down Gillard's cheek.

'It's nothing,' he said, wiping it away. 'A splinter from th stone wall, that's all. And a slug that hit my stainless stee ankle and knocked me over. That's merely a damned nuis ance.' He smiled. 'Don't worry – Joanna's over there. She' fine.'

When the shooting started, Joanna had hurled hersel beneath a pile of heavy black plastic sheeting, which, havin previously been used to cover a silage pit, proved to be hom to all kinds of things she preferred not to think about. Now sh wriggled out – quite unharmed but for a bruised shin wher one of the heavy-booted MacCruddens had vented his wratl on her, but liberally smeared with dark, evil-smelling slime an the creatures that lived therein. Carrick kissed her cheek on a clean bit, quite unable to put his relief into words.

Gillard pushed open one of the barn doors. 'You can com in now,' he called.

Neil Macpherson had only just arrived. His gaze wen straight to the three dead bodies and the scattered weapons John and Harry were sprawled together; both had been armec with hand guns. One of the MacCruddens had fallen forwarc across some straw bales, behind which he had been hiding to ake a shot at Gillard. He had not been given the chance to fire a second time.

The barn was suddenly full of people. Macpherson called for medics to attend to another man who, having had a sawn-off shotgun smashed from his grasp, was nursing an injured hand. Carrick also directed them to the prone sub-machine gun bearer.

'Who were they really?' Carrick asked Macpherson, gesturing to the bodies of John and Harry.

'Their real name was Smith,' said Macpherson soberly. 'That's all my late snout knew of their personal details, other than that they originally came from London. And, of course, I haven't been in the know long enough to have had time to investigate properly. That's the next job.'

'This is highly irregular,' said the Special Branch inspector, belatedly on the scene. 'No one is to leave this building until they've made statements.'

Gillard had been leaning on the wall and now stood upright. 'So you want statements. In that case, I'll have one from you. Explaining why you managed to screw this up to such an extent that a member of the armed services had to intervene to save the lives of your men.' Limping with considerable dignity, he walked out.

'The man means it,' said Macpherson with a tight smile in his colleague's direction; a fact that clearly had not escaped the Special Branch inspector, who did not pursue the matter. So Carrick and Joanna went out into the fresh air.

'I think they smelt a rat,' Joanna said. 'They all armed themselves to the teeth before we set off to drive here.'

He took her in his arms and for a very long moment it was as if no one else existed in the world.

'Are you heading back north?' Macpherson shouted to them from the barn doorway.

'Are we?' Joanna whispered.

'Perhaps we can persuade someone to marry us in Inverness,' Carrick said. 'I saw a ring in a shop and –' he grinned at her provocatively – 'bought it.'

'An engagement ring?'

'No. A wedding ring.'

'One usually gets both,' she pointed out, also grinning. 'Still, I suppose I'll just have to make do.'

169

'It's two rings intertwined, really – one plain gold, the other with diamonds.'

'Perhaps I love you after all.'

He looked away from her and up at the hills, thanking God with a fierce joy almost more than he could bear, and at that moment she went limp in his arms. The sound of the shot seemed an afterthought. As if in a dream he was kneeling on the ground, still holding her, another shot buzzing angrily off a wall nearby. Then he had left her and was running back towards the barn. The sniper's rifle held by a member of the Tactical Firearms Unit was somehow in his own grasp, although he had no awareness of having snatched it. He ran effortlessly up the lane, flying past Joanna, lying on the ground.

The figure he had seen by the hedge bordering the road was running too, back towards a car. Between man and car there was a gap in the hedge where posts and netting had been erected. *Ten yards wide*, thought Carrick: *ten strides. Ten strides when he'll be unprotected.* And Gillard's gun did not have the range.

The annihilating blow between the shoulder blades slammed him face down into the mud of the lane, his weapon lost from nerveless fingers. Numbed, yet in agony, he writhed. He did not care now that he was dying too; he knew that you never hear the shot that kills you. He found that he was crying.

The rifle cracked. Afterwards there was an endless silence. No, not quite. Up on the road there had been the smallest sound: a falling.

No sound of a car driving away.

'Luigi,' Patrick said. 'How the hell did he get here?'

Carrick was pulled to his feet. He staggered; again hands were laid upon him, this time to comfort, to steady.

'I told you I wouldn't let you do it.'

But Carrick shook off the assistance and went back, an odd ringing sound in his ears. Joanna was being laid on a stretcher when he reached her side. Her eyes were closed.

They took her away.

Macpherson arranged transport; he wanted to make a few

170

enquiries of his own at Castle Stalker. He made sure that one of the best drivers in the division was at the wheel of one of the fastest cars. A phone call to the castle, and a man who called himself Hutch had volunteered the information that the Marquess was still at the hunting lodge where he had taken Kimberley Devlin for safety – at James Carrick's request. The lodge, although on the estate, was ten miles away, halfway up Ben Duinne, and accessible only by a rough track.

'Ask them to return,' Macpherson had requested.

'James gave strict instructions that I ignore everyone's orders apart from his,' Hutch had said cheerfully. 'I'm not in a position to check your warrant card, am I?'

'Has a man called Philip Graham arrived asking to see Miss Devlin?'

'No, but his wife and son are here. They seem to think he's a madman . . . Is someone going to tell me what's going on?'

'I'll get Carrick to ring you,' Macpherson had said lamely.

This might be difficult, however; Carrick and Gillard were at the hospital and Macpherson was fairly sure that Carrick would not regard the opera singer as a priority at the moment. In truth, the man was too distressed and exhausted to think of anything other than Joanna. Macpherson was glad that the army officer was with him and had an idea that he might spirit the two lovers back south, if and when Joanna was well enough to travel.

The 'if' was very much a reality right now. The bullet had penetrated Joanna's chest. She had been in the operating theatre by the time Macpherson left the barn and he had been more than content to leave the routine work to the Special Branch inspector – he still did not know the man's name and didn't really want to. He didn't anticipate forming a lasting friendship.

Macpherson had said to this individual that, in his own view, Carrick had been acting under instructions from the man from MI5 when he grabbed the rifle from the Tactical Fire-arms Officer. Gillard had, after all, been the only person with an unimpeded view of Luigi and his rifle. He would have been aware that the handgun he was himself carrying did not have the range. But Macpherson didn't hold out a great deal of hope that Carrick would be absolved from responsibility when it came to the official inquiry. One look at the Scot's face when he snatched the rifle would have told any onlooker all he needed to know of Carrick's intentions. Luckily the shrubs and trees bordering the lane had screened Carrick from public scrutiny. In fact, hardly anyone had known what had happened until Gillard suddenly appeared on the top of a grassy bank, holding the rifle, and fired the shot that had ended Luigi's criminal career.

It had to be faced, though, that Carrick had out-ranked every policeman present. He had taken the rifle and therefore responsibility for his actions.

That Luigi's bullet had been intended for Carrick was obvious. The car Luigi had been driving was now being examined by Forensic, and ports and airports were under surveillance for Tony Capelli, the people calling themselves the Wilsons and the wizard, whose identity was not known. Macpherson had an idea they could be heading for London, where Capelli was based and the Metropolitan Police had been informed.

It was a little after three thirty when Macpherson arrived at Castle Stalker. He was met at the door by Hutch.

'May I have your full name, sir?' Macpherson said.

'Cuthbert Hutchinson,' said Hutch, with a grimace. 'And I'd appreciate it if you didn't tell anyone – I'd never live it down. James rang me so I assume you got a message to him. I had no idea the girl had been shot. He seemed to take a shine to her when she was waitressing that evening – but quite how she got mixed up in this I don't really—'

'Ah, no,' Macpherson said. 'There's more to it than that. She's his fiancée.'

Hutch looked bemused. 'His *fiancée*? But – no, I won't ask. Actually, I think I'm confused enough at the moment without asking more questions. Shall I take you to the Marquess? I think he'd appreciate a full explanation even more than me. This is his house, after all. He hates to think he's been harbouring criminals under his roof.'

'I'll see him right away. Put his mind at rest.'

'Oh, you might like to know why the fires smoked that evening – someone had stuffed a load of sacks up the chimneys.' When Macpherson looked baffled Hutch added, 'Quite literally, a smokescreen. It made it difficult to see what was going on. I think they were really worried about James and Patrick putting a stop to it all.' He paused in his stride as they crossed the entrance hall. 'The American party is still here, you understand. We're trying to play this down.'

'Of course,' Macpherson said. 'But I'm actually more interested in talking to Mr Philip Graham, if and when he arrives. The other business isn't my case.'

'Oh, I see,' said Hutch, not sounding as though he did. 'The wife and son have gone into Inverness to see if he's staying at an hotel there – one they've been to before, apparently. He doesn't seem to have checked into the one down the road.'

After banishing any lingering traces of self-condemnation from the Marquess's mind, Macpherson requested an interview with Kimberley Devlin. She was resting, he was told, the journey back from the lodge over an unmade road not having hastened her recovery from existing bumps and bruises. But she would see him in her room. He found her in the frame of mind most women would be in after such a journey – tired and slightly irritable.

'You know this man Graham,' he began, not in the mood for polite preamble. 'He doesn't appear to be in the district, yet we think he's on his way, apparently to give you this song he's been working on. When do you think he'll do it?'

Kimberley, wrapped in a fluffy blanket, her feet up on the bed, was nursing a bandaged hand. 'Knowing Phil, he'll go for a dramatic entry. If he's still annoyed with me he'll turn up this evening, *just* at the time when I was scheduled to sing. Only – I won't be.'

'No?' Macpherson said gently.

'You were asking me about Philip, so let's talk about him instead. I have an idea that you think he's some kind of dangerous fool. He isn't. But neither is he the man he was. Sarah is destroying him. When I first met him, Philip Graham was a good-looking, witty and appealing man. The plane crash did a lot in prematurely ageing him, but Sarah has done the rest. She's sapped what confidence he had left. His only hope is to leave her.'

'My impression of him was of a man under severe stress.'

'As I said: Sarah.'

173

Macpherson kept his reservations to himself. 'It's nothing to do with me really, but I'm disappointed that you're not going to sing tonight. Everyone will be disappointed – some of the visitors have spent a considerable amount of money on this trip. Is that fair?'

Tears brimmed in Kimberley's eyes. 'No,' she choked. 'And what happened to me isn't fair either! It's a different woman who was unearthed from that grave – someone who isn't Kimberley Devlin. Someone who can't sing. I tried, you know. I tried to sing in the shower. But I can't. Not properly. I sounded like any woman. I know now how Philip felt after that plane crash . . . Please go away. My hand hurts terribly.'

Macpherson went. It had been his shortest interview ever.

Chapter Sixteen

Surprisingly, it is not too difficult to find a technician in a large hospital who is prepared to undertake an emergency repair on a stainless steel ankle joint on a Sunday, if you are prepared to exercise patience and charm. It has to be said that Patrick Gillard was in short supply of both these qualities on that particular day, but finally the job was done.

He went straight back to the intensive care unit. Joanna had returned from theatre two hours previously; her condition was stable. The bullet, fortunately near the end of its range, had lodged in her left lung and though removing it had not been easy, medical opinion declared that she should make a complete recovery – providing there were no complications.

Only one visitor was permitted at a time so Gillard asked a nurse to tell Carrick he wanted to speak to him. When he emerged it was plain that the matter of forgiveness for a clout between the shoulder blades was still pending.

'You've had it fixed?' Carrick asked coolly.

'Yes. James, are you going to stay here?'

'Yes, but there's no need for you to do so. As you know, Macpherson's on his way to the castle and I asked Hutch to tell the Marquess what's happened. I can't do any more.'

'Has Macpherson gone alone?'

'With a driver.'

'Do you think that's enough?'

'If you want to go, then go,' Carrick said after a short pause. 'You're the wretched woman's bodyguard.'

'You need rest,' Patrick observed. 'Man, you're almost out on your feet!'

'I can sleep here. I asked.'

'Fine.' He turned to leave.

'Actually, I'd feel better if I knew you were keeping an eye on her.' Carrick's gaze went to the clock on the wall. 'But I don't know how you're going to get there this side of midnight. And your car's miles from here.'

Gillard smiled. 'Probably farther by now. I gave the keys to a cop and asked him to put it somewhere safe for me, otherwise there might not have been much left when I went to collect it. D'you know, I might just call me up a chopper.' And with a wave of his hand he departed.

Slowly, Carrick went back into the unit. 'Oh, God,' he muttered, leaning on the wall to ease the ache in his back.

'She's waking up!' a nurse called.

Half-fearful, he went over to the bed. It did not seem to be Joanna lying there but a puffy-faced stranger with tubes up her nose and down her throat and another into a vein in her neck.

But she was looking at him.

'Can she hear?' he asked.

'Oh, yes,' the nurse replied. 'But obviously she'll be under sedation for a while, so she will keep dropping off to sleep.'

He took the hand that did not have any drip attachments in it. 'You're going to be fine. Soon we'll go away and get married and I'll take you on the most fantastic honeymoon.' He hoped he wasn't babbling. 'But first you're going to get better. I'll stay with you. I promise.'

Her eyes wandered away from him and around the room.

'Who do you want?' he asked, then, realising that she could not answer, added, 'Patrick? He's all right. He's gone back to Castle Stalker.'

Joanna shook her head almost imperceptibly from side to side.

'Jo, I couldn't stop him.' He pulled himself up short: that was a lie. Shockingly, tears pricked his eyelids. 'He wanted to go,' he managed to say. 'And I wanted him to, so I can stay with you. Kimberley Devlin isn't my responsibility now.'

Again she shook her head.

'What do you mean?' he implored.

She removed her hand from his and made writing motions on the blanket. It took a few moments to arrange paper and

176

pen, as the nursing staff were not in full agreement, but Joanna only wrote two words and they were large and angry ones, both in capital letters.

PATRICK IS.

'You want me to go after him?'

She nodded as vigorously as she was able.

He leaned over and kissed her eyes and cheeks. Dropping the pen, she stroked his face gently. When she touched his lips he caught the hand and kissed that too. As he stood up his ears roared and he thought he was going to faint from sheer exhaustion, but he made for the door and went through it and did not look back.

Outside, in the fresh air, he could not hear any helicopters. *Idiot*, he berated himself – *such things can't be had at the wave of a magic wand*. If only he and Joanna had stayed at home instead of coming to Glasgow . . .

'No. If I'd stayed at home we wouldn't have sorted things out,' he said out loud. A man pushing a wheeled container full of laundry looked at him suspiciously.

'Have you seen a chap with a limp?' Carrick asked him.

'Hundreds of 'em in my time,' was the sour response as the porter went on his way.

A taxi that had just picked up a passenger and moved off stopped again and the rear door was opened. The passenger beckoned. Carrick got in and sank on to the seat with a sigh. Seconds later he was asleep.

'To the airport,' Gillard told the driver.

Late afternoon on that endless day, as the sun dipped towards the peak of Ben Duinne, the drone of an aircraft caused Agnes to look up from rolling out dough for wheaten biscuits – to her, the bought variety simply didn't pass muster. It was rare for there to be air traffic in this glen and she went to the window to have a look. A military helicopter surged importantly into view, crossed her field of vision and swung round towards the front of the castle. She dumped down her rolling pin and strode quickly down the long corridors into the main entrance hall. Opening the front door she was just in time, to her undying joy, to see it land on the huge expanse of lawn. In the time it took her to step outside on to the gravel, it seemed

177

that every window overlooking that part of the garden had been flung wide open.

'Ah,' said Agnes to herself, seeing two men emerging from the helicopter, 'I thought there was more to the pair of them than met the eye.'

The helicopter roared away again in a gust of exhaust and grass-scented air, leaving its former passengers windblown and dishevelled.

'My!' Poochie MacTavish's voice said, floating down from above. 'I didn't even realise that you guys had been away! But you sure have come back in style.'

'There's a policeman here,' Hutch called, joining Agnes on the doorstep.

'I know,' Carrick said. 'We've already met.'

'Tea?' Agnes enquired. 'Lots of it, with hot buttered bannocks and home-made strawberry jam?' Moments later she was returning to the kitchen, beaming, her cheeks glowing where two kisses had been planted on them.

The much-needed refreshment was being enjoyed when the Marquess came into the kitchen.

'Please don't let me interrupt you,' he hastened to say. 'I was out with the dogs when you made your dramatic arrival – Hutch told me it caused great excitement.' He sat down at the kitchen table. 'Is there a spare cup, Agnes? I'm parched.'

While he drank his tea, Gillard brought him up to date.

'And now you've got to keep a look-out for this Graham character?' said Lord Muirshire. 'As though you haven't had enough to concern you! Well, I'll tell you something. When I was out just now I went up to the old duck decoy, near the northern boundary of the estate, where the road runs past the oak wood. There was a car parked up there, to the side of the road. It was red – a Ford Escort, I think. A man was sitting in it behind the wheel. I wonder if it's him?'

'Did you get the number of the car?' Carrick asked.

'Yes, I wrote it down. Always keep a pen and bit of paper in my pocket. I had a funny feeling he wouldn't be there at all unless he was up to no good.' He handed over a sheet torn from a small pad. 'I couldn't really describe the man clearly – I wasn't that close, and there were trees in the way. But I'd say he was fair-haired. With glasses.'

'Is Inspector Macpherson still here?'

'I think he's determined to stay for as long as it takes. I said he was more than welcome if it protects Kim from harm. He sent his driver away through – probably thought *you'd* offer him a lift back.'

Carrick took the piece of paper. 'I'll go and give this to him. He can get on to his office, run a vehicle check.'

'He's got a room on the second floor. Turn left at the top of the stairs – it's the one with the Dürer drawing outside.' After the door had closed he rose to clarify the instructions but Gillard detained him.

'It's all right. I'm sure James knows a bit about art. He'll find it.'

Macpherson was sound asleep, stretched out on the top cover of the bed, with his shoes off. But he awoke instantly at Carrick's knock: a long career of broken nights saw to that.

'The son told me Graham's hired a car,' he said when Carrick had explained the reason for disturbing him. 'But it's worth checking. I'll go and find a phone.' He paused. 'I know it's my case – but I wouldn't have been offended if you'd gone into this yourself.'

'Ah, but I don't have a room here,' Carrick said, taking Macpherson's place on the bed. 'Although I do have my evening rig in Patrick's. I don't suppose he'd mind if I . . .' His voice trailed into silence.

'The fastest sleeper in the West,' Macpherson said softly.

On this, the last night of the Americans' trip, the Red Room was again used as a dining room. As befitted the Sabbath, the flowers and decorations were subdued. But the room still looked quite magnificent: the table laid with damask, glittering silver and sparking crystal, red and white carnations arranged with fern in Caithness glass vases.

Carrick had had two hours sleep before Macpherson pummelled him awake. He had then gone away to have a shower, finishing with the water stone-cold. This had had the effect of walking him fully and he then visited upon Gillard the same rousing treatment as had been meted out to him by Macpherson. He got thoroughly sworn at for his trouble.

'I rang,' Carrick said, ignoring the tirade. 'They think she'll be all right!'

Gillard uttered a few more choice expletives, this time addressing the ceiling, but his heart was no longer in it and he broke off, smiling. 'Thank God for that,' he said fervently. 'Do I take it the lady now intends to marry you?'

'Yes.'

'I'll be most put out if you don't ask me to be best man.'

'I'll be most put out if you refuse.'

'How are the shoulders?'

Carrick turned his chilly blue gaze on Gillard. 'I'd have *given* you the bloody thing if you'd asked for it.'

'Not in the frame of mind you were in. And not in the time available.'

Carrick smiled ruefully. 'I might get a hell of a carpeting, you know.'

'Has this Graham bloke arrived?'

'No. I was talking to Neil. Apparently, Kimberley reckons he'll make a grand entry at the time the song recital's due to start.'

Gillard jerked his head in the direction of the interconnecting door. 'I hope she's making a public appearance again tonight.'

'The Marquess has talked her into it. But she's pretty depressed, according to him. At this rate she'll need to talk to a psychiatrist.'

'A striking-looking woman,' Patrick said musingly, 'but when you talk to her it's hard to grasp her international status.'

'Are we being fair? Most celebrities are ordinary folk when they're out of the public eye.'

'So you fell in love with her voice?'

'I've *never* been in love with her! I just sympathised with what had happened to her. I knew what she was going through – call it fellow-feeling. I'd been there too, remember. I wanted to talk to her because I had this fear . . .' Carrick shrugged. 'Yes, I *was* in love with her voice. I was really fearful that she'd never have the confidence to sing again. And it looks as though I was right.'

The overseas visitors were in complete ignorance of the real events of the previous evening. They knew only that Mamie

180

Wilson had been taken to hospital with a suspected broken leg and that her husband had left with her. People voiced sympathy but privately there was relief; the couple had been bad company. And, as Poochie MacTavish put it, 'we can all spread ourselves out a little.'

No doubt Mrs MacTavish felt that she had plenty of space to spread herself out in the Red Room – it was about the size of a tennis court. She had certainly dressed to be noticed, despite the subdued lighting; she was arrayed in a long flowing gown in a sickly mauve that did dreadful things to the nerves of those beholding her.

Kennedy had taken Gillard aside just before dinner. Gillard knew what was on his mind.

'Don't worry,' Gillard had told him. 'A watch has been put on your ex-wife's home, but no one suspicious has been anywhere near her. Capelli's too involved with saving his own skin at the moment to think about settling scores.'

'Will I be arrested?'

'Well, obviously, someone's going to come here asking questions. I had to give a reason for the request for protection. Come clean. Tell the truth. You aren't the first person to cave in under such threats and you won't be the last. But I must tell you, due to your actions several highly dangerous criminals are at large.'

'I wish to God I'd told Carrick!'

'We all do.'

Inspector Macpherson had voiced a preference not to dine with the guests – partly because he did not have suitable clothes with him, partly because he did not wish to excite gossip amongst the tour party about the meaning of his presence at the castle. With luck they would think he was a member of staff. He hoped to interview Philip Graham when he arrived and, if necessary, arrest him. From the Marquess he had learned that Mrs Graham and her son, if they failed to run Philip to earth in Inverness, would return to the castle at eight thirty. Meanwhile, Macpherson tucked in to smoked salmon sandwiches and a glass of beer in a cosy nook of a room referred to as the Snug. The staff were instructed to inform him as soon as there were any visitors. So he waited, in warmth and contentment, idly flipping through a *Country Life* magazine. He felt he had the best part of the bargain.

The message, when it came, was brought by the tall, quiet girl with whom, earlier, he had had a lengthy conversation about motorbikes, Carrie being attired at the time in leathers and about to mount what she described as a cracker of a machine. Now, wearing a long blue skirt and white blouse, she reminded Macpherson of his daughter.

'Mrs Graham's here,' she said. 'And Jeremy. They want to talk to a policeman if one is on the premises.'

Macpherson glanced at his watch. Eight twenty. So be it.

'The Marquess thought you might like to use the music room.'

'Most suitable. If the husband turns up, perhaps you'd let me know. But don't show him in until I give the word.'

She smiled.

'Thank you, my dear,' Macpherson said as he went out. Why did his daughter have to go and get married to a sheep farmer and then emigrate to Australia?

In the company of his escort Macpherson went into the entrance hall. From the direction of the Red Room the muted clink of cutlery and a murmur of conversation could be heard, as the guests consumed crown of lamb and summer vegetables accompanied by a claret of fine vintage. But just then the inspector would not have changed places with them for all the wine in the world.

Mother and son looked tense and weary.

'I didn't expect to see you here,' said Sarah.

'Policemen travel great distances to solve crimes, Mrs Graham,' Macpherson said. 'This young lady will show us where we can talk in private.'

The music room, situated at one end of the L-shaped library, housed a grand piano, an eighteenth-century harpsichord and several sets of historic bagpipes, the latter in a large glass case together with hunting horns and a regimental drum. Macpherson checked that there was no one in the library end of the room and asked the Grahams to be seated.

'I brought you these,' Jeremy said, indicating a plastic carrier bag. 'I found them in the garage at home.'

Macpherson collected the bag and peered within.

'I picked them up with a cloth,' Jeremy continued. 'I thought you'd want that, because of fingerprints.'

Sarah cleared her throat. 'The bottle contained sleeping tablets prescribed to my husband. The funnel, I *think*, is one that normally is kept in the kitchen. The whisky speaks for itself. They were all on the shelf in the garage. I – that is, we – are worried that they might somehow be connected with that man who was murdered. Jimmy Barr.'

'I see,' Macpherson said dubiously. 'Thank you.'

'And there's something else I remembered,' Jeremy said. 'On the night that the Devlin woman was knocked down, Dad came home covered in mud. He said he'd fallen over, but he seemed really upset.'

'He told me he went to a pub for a bit of supper, if I remember correctly,' the inspector remarked.

'According to Dad he was a bit pissed, tripped and took a header into a flower bed.'

'His hands and knees were muddy?'

'Yes. And he looked as though he'd been crying.'

'My husband has not been himself for quite some time,' Sarah said. 'If that – *singer* turned down the music he wrote for her, it would have had a devastating effect on his morale. On his whole character.'

'And now it looks as though he's going to present her with a revised version . . . Is it possible that he could have got hold of a weapon of some kind?'

'*Weapon?*' Sarah echoed.

'No old army revolvers hidden away at home?'

'Oh, no. Nothing like that.'

'No knives, shotguns? Antique duelling pistols?'

'No.'

'Yes!' Jeremy cried. 'There's that old sword. You know, the one given to Dad's great-great-somebody-or-other by that rajah.'

'It's a cutlass, Jeremy. It was presented to one of your father's forebears and it had been taken from a captured British seaman a long time before that. I hardly think it would fit in an overnight bag.'

'Where is it kept?' Macpherson asked. You never knew . . .

'In the loft somewhere, in one of the old trunks. The last time I saw it, it was very rusty. I hardly think my husband would even consider . . .' She shook her head. 'But who knows what he's been driven to?'

'No matter,' Macpherson said. 'I shall ask Miss Devlin's bodyguard to search him, if and when he arrives.'

'I feel very awkward, barging in to a private house like this,' Sarah said. 'If only my husband had accepted that his composing days are over! Life would have been so much simpler.'

'Are there any other musicians in the family?'

'Apparently,' she answered grudgingly. 'In the male line there have been various pianists, writers of madrigals, things like that. Philip's uncle was conductor of a provincial orchestra until he retired last year at the age of eighty-two.' She smiled at her son. 'Jeremy, too. He's studying music at college and has already started to compose.'

'There's music in the blood, then,' Macpherson said.

There was a tap at the door; it was the girl who looked like his daughter. She did not have to speak for him to know that Philip Graham had arrived.

Chapter Seventeen

Unusually, the Marquess had decided to dine with his guests on the last evening of the weekend, instead of just making an appearance beforehand to chat to them over pre-dinner drinks. In truth, in spite of what had occurred, he was finding the experience a pleasant one; especially as he was sitting by Kimberley in an effort to boost her confidence. Her body-guard, keeping surveillance from a position facing her, appeared to be in a watchful world of his own; the Marquess felt his spine tingle every time a door opened or someone made a sudden movement, the wintry grey eyes opposite him immediately alert, wary, pitiless.

Carrick had been told that Philip Graham had arrived and was being interviewed by Neil Macpherson. Upon hearing this he had nodded slightly to Gillard, the signal a pre-arranged one. When everyone had finished the cheese course, he turned to Kimberley.

'Would you rather see Philip in private? Or would you be happier if a few people were present?'

'Is he here?' There was no apprehension in her reaction.

'Yes.'

'Perhaps he could have coffee with us.' She smiled. 'Why not? He loves to be the centre of attention.'

'Do you think it matters if his wife and son are present as well?'

Kimberley grimaced. 'I suppose there's not a lot I can do about her being here, is there? Just as long as you don't let her anywhere near me . . .' She looked at Gillard, who gave her a reassuring smile.

The permission of Lord Muirshire had already been sought for such an arrangement and, following his invitation, everyone moved through to the music room in an animated buzz of conversation. When they had been provided with coffee – including Sarah and Jeremy Graham, who looked surprised at the sudden influx of people – Patrick Gillard left the room.

Macpherson and Philip Graham had been closeted in an office off the gun room for twenty minutes, during which time the inspector had subjected the composer to a diligent grilling. But neither showed any sign of what had taken place when Gillard knocked and entered. Graham had exhibited more strength of spirit than Macpherson had expected.

'I've explained to Mr Graham that you're Miss Devlin's bodyguard, and that because of the attack on her you're going to search him. He has no objection.'

Philip's immediate thought was that here was a very up-market minder. But the man was pleasant enough and made the business of frisking him, and searching the contents of the document case he had brought with him, inoffensive and speedy.

Gillard, trained to assess, mentally wrote a short paragraph on the man at his side in the time that it took to reach the door to the music room. He listed pride, excitement, anxiety and shyness, and thought that that was a sufficiently heady mixture to be going along with. Graham had dressed with care: the black velvet jacket was striking with the cream shirt and trousers, his deep blue silk cravat tied with dashing elegance.

Most of the Americans were clustered around the glass case containing the bagpipes when the three men entered, Macpherson bringing up the rear. The Marquess came forward and introductions were made.

'My apologies, sir, for invading your privacy,' Graham said, inclining his head in salute. 'Doubly so, as I undertook a little research and have discovered that, at the battle of Killiecrankie in sixteen-eighty-nine one of my forebears took prisoner the brother of the then chief of your clan.'

'My dear Mr Graham,' the Marquess chortled. 'A large proportion of the male population of Scotland was either killed or taken prisoner on that unhappy occasion. I take it we're talking about the Grahams who sundered from Viscount Dundee and went over to the other side?'

'That's correct, Lord Muirshire.'

'Terrible times, Mr Graham. Some families changed sides more often than they had hot dinners – it was how they survived. But from what I can remember, the feud was caused by Dundee himself.'

'Murder,' Graham said quietly. 'He regarded one of the younger members of the family as a threat to his own position.'

'It's all in the past now, thank God. I understand that you have something for Miss Devlin? She's over there talking to Mrs MacTavish – I'm sure she'd like to be rescued.'

'May I borrow the piano?'

'I'd be delighted.'

Macpherson had sidled away to stand by Carrick. 'I hope we're doing the right thing,' he whispered.

Carrick made no comment. He found he was actually holding his breath.

The Marquess too found himself a little tense. No one had played the Steinway, his late wife's piano, since her death and he was not at all sure that he wanted a stranger to lay hands on that which she had loved and cherished.

The conversation lulled as Graham seated himself. He sat up very straight, and stared ahead for a few moments, motionless. Then his hands descended to execute a thunderous bass roll.

Upon hearing the first few bars of the National Anthem, played loud enough for a concert hall, the room leapt mentally – and in Gillard's case, physically – to attention. Even the Americans, in a clatter of dropped coffee spoons and *petit fours*, stood ramrod-straight; the Murdos, culturally confused, placed their hands upon their hearts.

The last note echoed brassily into silence. And the pianist sat there, grinning like a goblin.

'Philip!' Kimberley Devlin exclaimed. 'I might have known.'

'It's finished,' he said, and rummaged in the document case that he had placed on the piano. 'Here. See what you think of this.'

Hesitantly, she came forward and took the sheets of music manuscript paper from him. '"St. Margaret, Queen of Scots?"' she said, reading what was written at the top.

'BBC Scotland are planning a six-part children's serial,' Graham replied. 'The producer rang me several days ago. This will be the title music.'

'There are no words.'

'It's a song without words. It's music from the past: the wind in the trees, water in the rivers, the moan of the oldest hills in the world.'

Her eyes went down the page. 'This isn't what you showed me before.'

'Of course not.'

She held it out. 'Play it.'

He played. It was a stark, haunting melody; one could indeed imagine the wind in the trees and mountain streams, time itself moaning in the hills. When he had finished there was a burst of applause. But Kimberley frowned.

'There's something missing,' she said.

'I know,' Philip muttered.

'It should be in the key of A minor. And at the end of the last stanza, in the repeat theme, the E should be E flat and the G, G flat.'

Beguilingly, his fingers drifted over the keys and what had been merely beautiful was powerfully brilliant. He continued to play.

And Kimberley sang. For what was really missing was St Margaret, Queen of Scots. It was a song without words because no words were necessary – a song from the mists of the past. It made all who listened yearn to be at that magic place from whence the music came.

Carrick discovered that his cheek was damp and rubbed at it surreptitiously, hoping no one had noticed. No one had; some were smoothing away tears of their own. Too soon the music ceased; for a full five seconds, there was utter silence. Then came a storm of clapping.

Kimberley looked startled for a moment, as if emerging from a dream. In the next she had flung herself into the Marquess's arms. No one really noticed the young man until he stepped forward and went to Philip Graham's side.

'That is *my* music!' he shouted. 'Mine! How dare you try and make it your own? I've heard of plagiarism – but I'm your *son*, for God's sake ... Shall I tell all these people

188

what a bastard I've got for my father?'

Jeremy Graham's face was white, strained; the audience stood still, embarrassed, as he went on, 'I'll tell them the truth about this particular musical genius, shall I? How you ran Kimberley Devlin down with your car and left her for dead because she'd dared to criticise your pathetic attempts at songwriting? How you murdered Jimmy Barr, an innocent man, to try and pin the blame on him? Now you steal my music and try and pass it off as your own – is there nothing you won't stoop to?'

Jeremy was shaking with anger as the accusations spilled from his mouth. But Philip, by contrast, was oddly calm. He had donned half-moon spectacles to read the music and he now removed them and gazed steadily at his son. 'And what does your mother have to say about all this?'

'I have no wish to make a scene,' Sarah said. 'Jeremy, we can pursue this later—'

'We found the stuff you left in the garage,' Jeremy went on, ignoring her. 'The whisky and the sleeping pills and the funnel that you used to get them down that poor bastard's throat. Did you really think you'd get away with this? You aren't even very good at murder, are you?'

With hands that were now trembling, Philip handed his son the manuscript paper. 'Read what it says at the top.'

'We all know what it says!'

'*After* the title.'

In a low voice Jeremy read, ' "Adapted by Philip Graham from original music – *Landscape with Clouds* – by Jeremy Graham" . . . You said it wasn't any good!'

'I deny that utterly. I said it was thin. Instead of doing more work on it, you went away and sulked like a three year old. You're still behaving like a three-year-old. Worse, you're ruining these good people's evening.' He brightened and played three bold major chords. 'Or perhaps not. For after all, isn't it quite the thing nowadays to hold murder mystery weekends at country houses? Assembled here tonight we already have a victim, most of the suspects and, indeed, the officer in charge of the case. Ladies and gentlemen, may I introduce Detective Inspector Neil Macpherson of Strathclyde Police?'

Macpherson got what amounted to a standing ovation, went pink, opened and closed his mouth a couple of times and, finally, said nothing.

'Supporting players,' Philip continued, 'must include our host, the Marquess; members of his staff; Kim's minder – who looks as though he's 007 in his spare time – and the gentleman with fair hair who is either another policeman or the Marquess's minder. No matter. The tale will begin to unfold. To set the scene and put us in the right mood, Miss Devlin will sing for us again. I suggest Dido's great lament from *Dido and Aeneas* by Henry Purcell. I'm afraid we'll have to make do without the orchestra.'

'No,' Carrick whispered as Kim gave the speaker a beseeching look. 'It's too cruel.' But there was no stopping Graham.

'Ready, Kimberley? Right, ladies and gentlemen: "When I am laid in Earth".'

And again, after a faltering start, Kimberley sang. It was a harrowing spectacle and this time, when she had finished, the audience did not applaud.

'And then,' Philip said into the silence, 'our heroine, who had been knocked down by a car and buried in leaves, was found. She could remember nothing of what had happened to her but thought that the car that hit her might have been light in colour. Police suspicion immediately fell upon one Jimmy Barr, an unfortunate individual who had developed a fixation about our heroine – understandably, perhaps – and who drove a light grey three-wheeler. Miss Devlin had made public her worries about this man, but there was nothing the police could do unless he actually broke the law. When he began to phone her and generally make a nuisance of himself he received several warnings. And then Mr Barr was found dead. It appeared, at first, that he had committed suicide.' And Graham played a few ironic bars of Chopin's *Dead March*.

Sarah leapt to her feet. 'What the hell are you trying to prove?' she shouted. 'This stupid charade won't make it any easier for you!'

'As most of you will have gathered by now, this lady is my wife,' Graham said grimly. 'And you might say that our marriage is not a happy one. Sarah is not a forgiving woman. She's never forgiven me for making a mess of my career and, above

190

all, she's never forgiven me for going elsewhere to find the affection and support she isn't capable of giving. Ladies and gentlemen, to set the record straight, I would like you to know that Miss Devlin and I enjoyed a brief affair. I realise that a gentleman should not discuss such things in public and I hope that all of you – and Miss Devlin – will excuse my impertinence. But it's important for the facts to be known.'

He paused. Carrick noticed that Kimberley's face was suffused with a deep blush – but, to his surprise, all he could read in her expression was kindness and compassion.

'We digress. On the night that Miss Devlin was attacked and left for dead in a shallow grave, I borrowed my wife's car – a white one – because mine was almost out of petrol. I went – alone – to an hotel for a drink and a meal. As you may guess, my own home is not the most comfortable of places. After my meal, as I went back in the dark to where I had parked my car, I tripped and fell headlong into a flower bed. It's possible that I may have had one glass of wine too many – I also couldn't properly see where I was going. One of the sins I will admit to is vanity: I am too vain to wear my glasses where others can see me, having no wish to look like a geriatric owl. My son saw me return that night with mud all over my hands and knees. My wife has poisoned his mind against me – what could be more natural, in the circumstances, than that he should suspect me of attempting to murder my former mistress?

'I mentioned the hapless Mr Barr, the most likely suspect in The Case of the Buried Opera Singer. When Mr Barr's body was discovered, so was what appeared to be a confession: the words "I did it" scrawled in the dust on top of a dressing table. Case closed, one might assume. But then forensic tests proved without a doubt that Barr had been murdered. And the scrawl on the dressing table didn't match Barr's writing. A man was arrested – am I correct so far, Inspector Macpherson? – following a tip-off to the police – some months previously Barr had indecently assaulted the man's wife. But this suspect proved to have a cast-iron alibi. The plot thickens.'

Carrick couldn't help but be impressed by the man's forcefulness. For the first time he could understand why Kimberley Devlin had been attracted by this man. And clearly

Macpherson had some involvement in this *denouement* – why else would he have given Graham classified information into the circumstances of Barr's death?

'What is all this nonsense?' Sarah enquired coldly. 'Really, Philip, you're wasting the inspector's valuable time. You forget one thing – we have evidence against you. We found the stuff you'd used to kill Barr hidden in our garage. If we're to play games, at least let us not lose sight of the facts.'

Macpherson cleared his throat. 'Last night a man gave himself up in connection with Barr's murder. He is a friend of the man we arrested previously and has made a statement to the effect that he agreed, for five-hundred pound, to slip away from the wedding and – I quote – "give that bastard Barr a fright he wouldn't forget". Unfortunately he'd been drinking heavily and the whole thing got way out of hand. Barr wasn't a strong man and he'd already made his way through the best part of a bottle of whisky. With sleeping tablets on top, forced down his throat – he choked to death pretty quickly. Our wedding guest chummie didn't really take it in. Thought he was in a late-night movie, and wrote "I did it" in the dust in a moment of stupid bravado. When he got home and sobered up, he realised what he'd done. And, finally, his wife persuaded him to come to us. And, Mrs Graham, there's no forensic evidence to suggest that a funnel was used. Barr was virtually comatose – it wouldn't have been necessary. And the whisky in Barr's stomach was a much cheaper, rougher blend than the whisky in the bottle you've given to me tonight.'

Everyone turned to Sarah.

'This is nothing whatsoever to do with me!' she cried. 'Jeremy was the one who found the things! Besides, he still tried to kill that bitch! Nothing you say will make me believe otherwise!'

Philip Graham crashed out a short excerpt from Dvořàk's *The Noonday Witch*, cutting Sarah off in mid-shriek. Having silenced her, he lifted his hands from the keys. 'Well?' he asked his son, swivelling on the piano stool to face him.

'I've nothing to say to you,' Jeremy replied sullenly.

Graham closed his eyes as if in pain. 'So that's the verdict of my family. Guilty until proven innocent.'

'I could have you arrested for attempting to pervert the

course of justice,' Macpherson said to Jeremy. There followed a long silence.

'I despise him,' Jeremy said eventually. 'He made my life a misery. All he and my mother ever do is row, row, row. It drives me mad. Every time I come home they're yelling abuse at each other. All I ever wanted was a normal family, like it used to be. But he ruined all that. Yes – I threw those pills down the toilet and then hid the bottle in the garage with some whisky from the drinks cabinet. I was stupid about the funnels though, wasn't I? I just wanted to make him suffer.' He buried his face in his hands. 'And the last straw is that he's stolen my music.'

'Oh, doesn't he break your heart?' said Sarah venomously. 'Let me tell you one thing – I've suffered more than either of you. My life has been nothing but hell since Philip had his accident!'

'And you wanted to punish him too!' Jeremy sobbed.

'Perhaps it isn't quite that simple,' Macpherson said slowly. 'You see, we've now examined the car belonging to your mother's – er, gentleman friend, Simon Adams.'

'Don't bring Simon into this!' Sarah cried. 'He knows nothing about that bitch.' And she cast a contemptuous look in Kimberley's direction.

'No, but you do. You've threatened her in the past. You'll be interested to know that Mr Adams is rather vague at the moment about the details of what happened that evening. He'd got back from a business trip to the States that morning and was feeling very tired. I suspect his memory will improve, given time and a little gentle persuasion. But he's quite sure of one thing: *you* were driving. He was feeling very sleepy and you offered to drive. You wanted to talk to him about leaving your husband, so you drove to a quiet place where you wouldn't be disturbed. Before he knew what was happening you had driven straight at a woman and she was lying in the road. That is when his memory seems to desert him.'

'No!' said Sarah. 'He's lying!'

'But the dent in his car isn't a lie. Nor are the fragments of beech leaf and peaty soil ground into the carpet on both the driver's and the passenger's side of the car.'

193

And Philip Graham struck up triumphantly with a musical flourish. *The Arrival of the Queen of Sheba.*

'Bastard!' Sarah screamed at him. But her words were lost in the sheer joy of the music.

'It must have seemed too good a chance for her to miss,' Macpherson said later. He was on the point of leaving, transport for him and Sarah Graham, now duly cautioned and arrested, having been provided by the local police. 'She and Adams had gone somewhere to talk. Then, suddenly, there was the woman she hated most in the world. She must have thought it was a real piece of luck when her son began to point the finger of blame at her husband. No doubt I'll get to the bottom of it when I question her tomorrow.'

Carrick thought he probably would. Now that Adams had talked there was hardly any point in Sarah remaining silent. He watched his friend and the woman he had arrested drive away and was returning indoors when Philip Graham and Jeremy approached from within, the latter pale and subdued.

'We're staying in Inverness overnight, and then I'm taking Jeremy home,' Philip said. He smiled sadly. 'This whole affair has shaken both of us up, as you can imagine.'

'Thank you for coming,' Carrick said, meaning it. 'You were the only person who could have helped Kim to sing again.'

'She's in fine voice. The rest obviously did it good.'

And they walked towards Philip's hired car like soldiers leaving the field of battle.

Kimberley and the Marquess were crossing the entrance hall, arm in arm.

'Poor Philip,' Kimberley said when they reached Carrick. 'He's not got much to look forward to, has he? Watching his wife stand trial for murder . . . He's a good man at heart, you know – just has a fragile ego. I owe him a lot. It was the music. It was so beautiful that I *had* to sing it.'

'Yes, I think on the whole he deserves to be happy,' Carrick said. 'My guess is that he'll take his leave of Sarah and make a fresh start with Jeremy.'

Kimberley frowned. 'I wonder why he didn't tell Jeremy that he'd adapted his music?'

'I imagine he genuinely wanted to surprise the boy. He felt

guilty, knew he'd been a bit of a let-down as a father. We all know he likes to make dramatic gestures – presenting Jeremy with a finished piece of music was just the sort of thing to appeal to him, especially if *you'd* put your seal of approval on it. Of course, he didn't know Jeremy would be there tonight – and his son immediately seized the wrong end of the stick.'

'I hope you're staying the night,' Lord Muirshire said.

'I have a hotel room to go to,' Carrick replied.

'Nonsense! I'll ask Hutch to give Jim a ring. We can sort it all out in the morning. Go in the Snug and I'll organise some supper – I'm sure you ate very little at dinner. I'll join you in a short while.'

Patrick was already comfortably ensconced in the Snug, half-asleep, stretched out in front of the log fire. One hand rose lazily to waggle his mobile phone in the air.

'They've got the so-called Wilsons,' he reported. 'They were trying to board a flight for New York at Heathrow. I gather there are a lot of faxes flying around, trying to find out who they really are.'

Carrick dropped into a chair. 'It's vital that Capelli and his sidekick are taken too.'

'I agree, if only for our own peace of mind. These gangsters do love revenge – they're old-fashioned like that – and it must be said that you busted Capelli's little import business wide open.'

'With quite a bit of help,' Carrick commented sleepily. 'May I borrow that thing to find out how Joanna is?'

The phone was passed over. 'I rang too, about ten minutes ago. She's fast asleep. They're moving her out of intensive care when a bed becomes available in a ward later on.'

But Carrick rang anyway, just to be sure.

Chapter Eighteen

Much to his surprise, Carrick heard no more about his adventure with a sniper's rifle. He had been asked to write a detailed report and did so; the others present had, he knew, also been asked for their version of events. He decided it would be diplomatic not to pursue the matter with the person at the centre of the inquiry and it was not until several months later, three days before Christmas, that he was again in that person's company, the Gillards having invited Carrick and Joanna to spend the holiday with them.

'Am I allowed to kiss the bride?' Patrick wanted to know as he greeted them on the doorstep.

'With all due propriety,' Carrick told him.

This accomplished, Gillard said, 'Ingrid's just fetching Justin from the play group. Come in to the living room – it's warmer in there.'

'You know, I just can't imagine you with babies,' Joanna said, going straight to where the youngest child, Victoria Louise, lay surrounded by fluffy toys on a blanket on the carpet.

'Well, we've given the nanny Christmas off,' he said, picking up his daughter and sitting her on his knee. 'I'll let you know how I feel about multiple parenthood in a few days' time.' He surveyed the pair of them. 'Marriage suits you.'

'We're buying a house in the country,' Joanna said. 'We're selling my flat, James's flat and my business and I'm going to vegetate for a while in domestic bliss. Then I'm going back to university to get another degree. *Then* I'm going to decide whether I want a career.'

'That's if I accept your resignation,' Gillard said.

'You never formally took me on in the first place,' she countered, uttering a peal of laughter.

'Seriously,' he said, 'Ingrid's decided to stick to writing. She's had enough excitement for one lifetime.

'So have I!'

'She's going to run a consultancy and charge me for advice,' Carrick said contentedly. 'What's it *like* to hold a baby?'

'Damp,' said Gillard, handing her over. 'Keep a good hold or they turn turtle, and then it's hellish noisy as well.'

Victoria beamed gummily at her new friend.

'Now don't you start getting all broody,' Joanna scolded. 'I have no desire for broken nights and a handbag full of nappies and rusks – not yet, anyway.'

Later, when they had dined and the women were up in Ingrid's study talking about the foibles of husbands, Carrick subtly broached the subject he had wanted to discuss ever since he arrived.

'So – any news of Capelli and his sidekick?'

'Nothing of the wizard – he's sitting pretty in Rio de Janeiro, no doubt. As for Capelli – there's an unconfirmed report that he went home to Italy forgetting that he'd left in a hurry because of a family feud. Someone cut his throat for him.'

'I can't say that I'm devastated by grief.'

Carrick took a deep breath. 'By the way, what happened about the shooting of Luigi?'

'I took responsibility, of course. Only right and proper, as it was me who shot him. And I'll be eternally grateful to that passing policeman who kindly handed me his rifle.'

'That wasn't quite how I put it in my report.'

Gillard smiled. 'James, whatever your intentions may have been, I took aim and pulled the trigger. So let's consider the matter closed. Actually, I think the powers-that-be were more interested in the ineptitude of that Special Branch inspector. If he'd set up proper road blocks Luigi wouldn't have been able to get to us in the first place . . . Is Joanna fully recovered?'

'Just about. She still gets very tired. Moving out of Bath into the country will do her good. By the way, I had a letter from Kimberley. She and the Marquess were married last month. A quiet wedding.'

From upstairs came the wail of a baby.

'Care to have a crash course in nappy-changing?' Patrick asked.

'It can't be worse than breaking into that barn.'

'Want a bet?'

Laughing, they went up.